# THE ASSASSIN'S CHASE

## Also by Cap Daniels

**The Chase Fulton Novels Series**

Book One: *The Opening Chase*
Book Two: *The Broken Chase*
Book Three: *The Stronger Chase*
Book Four: *The Unending Chase*
Book Five: *The Distant Chase*
Book Six: *The Entangled Chase*
Book Seven: *The Devil's Chase*
Book Eight: *The Angel's Chase*
Book Nine: *The Forgotten Chase*
Book Ten: *The Emerald Chase*
Book Eleven: *The Polar Chase*
Book Twelve: *The Burning Chase*
Book Thirteen: *The Poison Chase*
Book Fourteen: *The Bitter Chase*
Book Fifteen: *The Blind Chase*
Book Sixteen: *The Smuggler's Chase*
Book Seventeen: *The Hollow Chase*
Book Eighteen: *The Sunken Chase*
Book Nineteen: *The Darker Chase*
Book Twenty: *The Abandoned Chase*
Book Twenty-One: *The Gambler's Chase*
Book Twenty-Two: *The Arctic Chase*
Book Twenty-Three: *The Diamond Chase*
Book Twenty-Four: *The Phantom Chase*
Book Twenty-Five: *The Crimson Chase*
Book Twenty-Six: *The Silent Chase*
Book Twenty-Seven: *The Shepherd's Chase*
Book Twenty-Eight: *The Scorpion's Chase*
Book Twenty-Nine: *The Creole Chase*
Book Thirty: *The Calling Chase*
Book Thirty-One: *The Capitol Chase*
Book Thirty-Two: *The Stolen Chase*

Book Thirty-Three: *The Widow's Chase*
Book Thirty-Four: *The Sacred Chase*
Book Thirty-Five: *The Assassin's Chase*
Book Thirty-Six: *The Reckoning Chase*

**The Avenging Angel – Seven Deadly Sins Series**
Book One: *The Russian's Pride*
Book Two: *The Russian's Greed*
Book Three: *The Russian's Gluttony*
Book Four: *The Russian's Lust*
Book Five: *The Russian's Sloth*
Book Six: *The Russian's Envy*
Book Seven: *The Russian's Wrath*

**Stand-Alone Novels**
*We Were Brave*
*Singer – Memoir of a Christian Sniper*

**Novellas**
*The Chase is On*
*I Am Gypsy*

# THE ASSASSIN'S CHASE

**CHASE FULTON NOVEL #35**

CAP DANIELS

The Assassin's Chase
Chase Fulton Novel #35
Cap Daniels

This is a work of fiction. Names, characters, places, historical events, and incidents are the product of the author's imagination or have been used fictitiously. Although many locations such as marinas, airports, hotels, restaurants, etc. used in this work actually exist, they are used fictitiously and may have been relocated, exaggerated, or otherwise modified by creative license for the purpose of this work. Although many characters are based on personalities, physical attributes, skills, or intellect of actual individuals, all the characters in this work are products of the author's imagination.

Published by:

** USA **



13 Digit ISBN: 978-1-951021-79-5
Library of Congress Control Number: 2026937652


Cover Design: German Creative

Printed in the United States of America

*The Assassin's Chase*

**CAP DANIELS**

# Chapter 1
## *Four Score and Earlier Today*

Spring 2019 – Gettysburg, PA

"It would've been July third, eighteen sixty-three," I said. "And this is Pickett's Charge."

Pogonya Fulton, my seventeen-year-old daughter, sat on the blanket in front of me. It was a perfect day beneath a cloudless sky—so unlike what the same patch of earth had seen during the heat of the Civil War as it drank in the seemingly endless flow of American blood, while brother fired on brother and America toiled in earnest to tear itself apart.

"It's terrible, Father. Everything about it is terrible."

"I couldn't agree more," I said as we watched reenactors play out the climactic assault of the bloodiest battle in the American Civil War, a battle in which our divided nation lost over fifty thousand of its sons.

Pogonya leaned back against me. "Why do they do this?"

I considered the timeless question that even the greatest minds had difficulty fully answering. "Because it's what their country asked of them."

Pogonya twisted to look up at me over her shoulder. "No, I mean, why do these people play it out again and again?"

I was uncertain if that question was any easier to answer than what I'd believed was her original query. "War is the worst thing humanity does," I said.

She frowned. "And yet, it's what you and Mama have chosen to do for most of your lives."

"I'm not sure that's true. Some people choose war, but I believe it chose us."

She took a sip from her water bottle. "You're starting to sound like some battlefield Aristotle. Are you vying for a seat among the great philosophers, Dr. Chase Fulton?"

I chuckled. "Philosophy ain't my bag, baby."

Anya Burinkova, former Russian SVR assassin and Pogonya's mother, laid her head on my shoulder. "Is maybe not so good time for jokes, Chasechka."

"There they go," I said. "Those are Confederate Generals Garnett and Armistead leading the second and third brigades of General Pickett's division against the Union center on Cemetery Ridge."

The artillery loaded only with black powder on that day roared as the Confederates fought their way forward in their doomed charge across the open field toward a few scattered clumps of trees where the superior Union forces returned massive volleys of musket and artillery fire. Blue and Gray fell in wave after wave, replaying the battle from a century and a half before.

Pogonya pointed to a third group of men clad in the gray of the Confederate Army. "Why aren't they moving?"

"They will," I said. "That's General Kemper's first brigade. He was the last to get the order from General Pickett to advance. See the hole in the line between the other two brigades?"

She nodded, and I said, "Kemper's men will fill that gap and charge the hill."

Just as I'd predicted, based on what little I'd learned in high school American history, Kemper's brigade did indeed fill the break. The massive gray line fought beneath billowing musket smoke and waving battle flags of crossed stars and bars as history repeated itself in dramatic pretense.

As impressive as the display before us was, I couldn't shake Pogonya's question from my head.

*Why, indeed, do they do this?*

The charge continued, and men pretending to be soldiers fell by the dozens, just as thousands of Americans had fallen on that fateful day in one of the most horrific moments of our nation's history.

The difference, however, was when the smoke cleared on that morbid afternoon in 1863, over 6,000 Confederates and 1,500 Union soldiers lay on the bloody ground, never to draw another mortal breath, while the day's reenactors would all go home to their families, hang their authentic-looking uniforms back in their closets, and continue their lives as if the day had never happened.

The cloudless sky grew barely visible as smoke from the simulated musket and cannon fire rose into the air, absent of even a breath of wind, and the battle raged on. After less than an hour of fighting to take the Union center, the Confederates finally succumbed to the massive Union force that had continued to rain fire from atop the ridge and close on the Southerners' flanks.

The man dressed as General Robert E. Lee ordered the buglers to blow retreat, and the surviving Confederates obeyed, even if reluctantly, just as they had in 1863, leaving their fallen brothers behind as remnants of a war that should've never been fought and sacrifices that should've never been made.

Pogonya said, "Look at that horse, Father! He looks just like Richter."

I held a special kind of hatred for equines of any breed, but my daughter had gifted me a gorgeous black Arabian gelding out of some apparent combination of cruelty and self-amusement. Richter was the only living exception to my distaste for the beasts. I loved him simply because the daughter I adored gave him to me and named him after her grandfather and my mentor, Dr. Robert "Rocket" Richter.

"He does," I said. "Please tell me you didn't give my horse away to the Army of Northern Virginia."

She gave me a shove. "Stop it. Where's his rider, though?"

The remnants of my American history class rattled inside my skull, and I said, "It could be General Kemper's horse. If the smoke would clear, we could see if they play it out as it really happened."

As if God Himself granted my wish, a breeze blew the hanging white smoke from the battlefield and revealed the scene just as I remember Mrs. Hamilton describing it in tenth grade.

I pointed. "I was right. There they are. Watch. See those four men carrying that guy up the hill?"

Pogonya nodded, and I said, "Keep watching. They won't carry him far."

I was so thankful I'd paid attention that day in class as the lesson came to life in front of us. The four men carrying the general fell under fire from three Grays firing muskets across the body of their fallen general. With the Blues on the ground, the Confederates reclaimed their commander and hurried him back down the hill.

"What just happened?" Pogonya asked.

"General Kemper was shot from his horse, and apparently, a Union officer ordered a handful of soldiers to retrieve him and take him to one of their surgeons."

"If that's what was happening, why would the Confederates kill them?"

"They couldn't let their general fall into the hands of the enemy."

"But they were trying to save him."

"That's what we assume from letters and first-hand accounts of the day, but the good news is that General Kemper survived. The Confederate surgeons removed the musket balls from his abdomen and thigh, and he went on to become the governor of Virgina ten years after this battle here at Gettysburg."

"I guess that's a pretty good outcome," Pogonya said, obviously still uncertain about the meaning of any of the American history she'd never learned in the boarding school in Switzerland before I knew she existed.

"Yes, it's definitely a good outcome, especially since Kemper was one of the first post-war Confederate generals to officially advocate for the civil rights of former slaves. It didn't necessarily make him popular among some of his former supporters, but he was living proof that hearts and minds aren't made of stone."

She smiled. "I think you may be a philosopher after all, Father."

"No, sweetheart. I'm just a guy who knows a lot about being wrong."

We packed up our blanket, and each of the two most important women in my life took an arm.

"Thank you for bringing me here, but if it's all the same to you, I don't think I want to see any more reenactments."

"I understand," I said. "Your mother and I have seen far too many of these days in real life, so we both know how it feels to never want to see it again."

* * *

Dinner was a magnificent affair. All three of us got to dress up and pretend to be adults at Minibar on E St. NW, one of the two Washington, D.C. restaurants to have earned two Michelin stars.

After three courses of food that I could neither adequately describe nor identify, we came to dessert, a course I understood well. It was the first fried ice cream donut of my life, but I vowed that it would not be the last.

Pogonya said, "That was unbelievable. Maybe I want to be a chef."

I rubbed my belly. "If you can recreate those donuts, I'm absolutely on board with that plan. You should consider doing the summer with Maebelle in Miami. You know she owns one of the hottest restaurants on South Beach."

Her eyes lit up, and a mischievous grin appeared. "Hmm. Summer on South Beach for an eighteen-year-old girl who looks like her Russian supermodel mother. What could possibly go wrong?"

"On second thought," I said, "maybe you'll be summering with the nuns at Our Lady of Anything Other than South Beach."

Pogo giggled. "I thought you might say something like that."

In the cab back to our hotel, Anya flinched and straightened. "Please turn up volume on radio."

The driver glanced up at the mirror and twisted the knob.

The voice said, "We have just learned that Congressman Parker Kemper of Virginia's First Congressional District has died following an incident during a reenactment of Pickett's Charge at Gettysburg earlier today. The first-term congressman was reportedly taking part in the reenactment and playing the role of his great-great-grandfather, Confederate Brigadier General James Lawson Kemper, who was wounded but survived the battle in eighteen sixty-three. Details are limited at this hour, but we will keep you informed as more information becomes available overnight."

## Chapter 2

## *Not That Kind of Doctor*

Pogonya sipped her coffee across the breakfast table without a word, and that was rare for her.

"Is everything all right?" I asked.

"No. We came here to see the cherry blossoms and visit the monuments and museums, but instead, we watched a congressman die while playing a silly game."

Everything inside me wanted to protect her from the realities of humanity and let her revel in the innocence of childhood, but I suppose that's every father's wish for their little girls. And just like every other father, even I couldn't stop the hands of time and shield my daughter from what inevitably lay ahead.

I folded *The Washington Post* open to the story and tossed it across the table.

She didn't reach for it, but her eyes couldn't resist. Finally, she slid the paper closer and read the first several lines. "Oh, my gosh. He was murdered."

I stuck a bite of French toast into my mouth. "It would appear so."

"So, what are you going to do about it?"

"About what?"

She raised both eyebrows as if I'd missed the beginning of World War Three. "The murder. You and Mama have to do something."

Anya scooped a wedge of grapefruit from its peel. "This is not what we do. We are not police officers."

"You were," she said.

"Yes, but only for short time. I am now . . ." The Russian paused as if frozen in time.

Pogonya and I stared at her in amused anticipation until she said, "I do not know what we are, but is not police officers."

"You're my parents, and you're just as weird as everybody else's parents, but most of them don't carry fighting knives and automatic weapons."

I finished breakfast and leaned back to enjoy my coffee. "What do you want us to do?"

Pogo wiped her mouth. "I don't know, but people can't just go around killing congressmen. What if it's a terrorist or something?"

Anya tasted her juice and made a sour expression. "Terrorists claim responsibility for things they do. No one has done that, have they?"

Our daughter tapped the paper. "They don't say anything about it in the article, but why would somebody just kill him for no reason?"

"I'm sure there's a reason," I said. "It's probably not reasonable, but there's always some crazy rationale in the heads of people who do stuff like that. I don't know anything about Parker Kemper. Do either of you?"

They both shook their heads, and Pogonya said, "Not yet, but I will soon. I'm going to read everything I can find on him."

I wadded my napkin into a ball and tossed it at her. "Then maybe you can solve the case while your mother and I hit the Smithsonian."

She returned fire by adding her napkin to the ammunition load and returned the volley across the table at me. "Oh, no you don't. I'm not missing that, but I still think you should do something about the murder."

* * *

It would take a reasonable person a month or more to see the entirety of the Smithsonian, but we crammed what we could into one very long day before finding ourselves back at the hotel, exhausted and starving.

"We can have service inside room tonight, yes? I am too tired to dress and go to restaurant for dinner."

Pogonya rolled her eyes. "Mama! You know it's called room service. Can we do pizza?"

I jumped in. "Don't screw up your mother's accent. You know how much I love it."

Pogo shook her head. "You two. Sometimes, you're too much."

"We're always too much," I said. "You're just too focused on everything else to always notice."

"Oh, I notice. I just keep it to myself because I know you're never going to stop. Can I tell you something, though?"

"Sure," I said.

She seemed to blush for an instant. "I hope that I find what you two have someday. You've known each other for twenty years, and you still flirt like teenagers. It's weird for old people, but I think it would be kinda nice."

Anya took my hand. "Is very nice, but I hope you do not have to wait half of lifetime to have this."

The moment was turning into something out of a Hollywood rom-com, and I was getting nauseous. "Pizza sounds great. Here's my card. Order whatever sounds good to you. And we're *not* old!"

The pizza arrived, and I approved. "Nice call on the extra mushrooms."

Pogonya speared one with her fork and held it up. "Is for only you, Chasechka."

I laughed. "Close, but you'll never top your mother's abuse of English. You just don't have it, but you're cute, so maybe there's still hope for you to land a decent man."

She said, "You're going to terrorize any boy I bring home, aren't you?"

I palmed my chest. "Who, me? Never. Now, your mother on the other hand. I can't stop her from threatening to gut him like pig."

She tried not to laugh. "I'm vacationing by myself next year."

Anya pulled a slice from the box. "Good. This means your father and I do not have to wear clothes next year on holiday."

"Mother! Please!"

The chirp of my phone saved me, and I welcomed the distraction. "Hello, this is Chase."

"Hey, it's Skipper."

Elizabeth Woodley was the daughter of my college baseball coach and practically my little sister, but in real life, she was the best covert intelligence analyst in the business, and I trusted her with everything. She earned the moniker of Skipper as a teenager because of the way she danced and skipped every step instead of walking. That frolicking ended, but the nickname stuck, and she became the nerve center of my operation.

"What's up?" I asked. "We were just having pizza and talking about being naked."

"What? Isn't Pogonya with you?"

"Yeah, she's the one who started it, and I'm doing everything I can to make her regret it."

"Speaking of regrets," Skipper said, "I'm afraid you'll have to cut your vacation short. Somebody took a shot at Dominic."

"What? Is he hurt?"

"He's alive, but the shooter got him in the right shoulder. They stabilized him on the island, and he's in the air and on his way to Miami now."

"Do we know who did it?" I asked.

"Not yet, but it's going to be our case. The cops on Bimini don't have the resources to figure it out."

I said, "We'll be in Miami by lunchtime. Get to work on collecting intel."

She sighed. "Thanks for telling me how to do my job."

"Sorry. I didn't mean to—"

"I know. I'm on it."

I ended the call and looked at the faces of the two beautiful women holding their breath.

"It's Dominic," I said. "Somebody shot him in the shoulder, but he's alive and on his way to Miami. I have to go, but you two are welcome to stay here."

In unison, they said, "No, we're coming, too."

Anya's Cessna Citation wasn't the fastest jet in the air, but it was comfortable, easy to fly, and small enough to land where the airliners couldn't. It would never be a tactical tool, but for the three of us, we couldn't ask for a better time machine.

My favorite Russian pilot touched down as if the ground were made of silk, and we taxied to the FBO, where a driver waited beside a black SUV with the rear door held open. If Skipper weren't an analyst, she'd be the world's best travel agent.

The driver dropped us at the hospital, and we found Clark Johnson in the surgical waiting room. He wasn't only my oldest friend in the covert ops business, and my handler, but also Dominic Fontana's only surviving son.

"How's your dad?"

Clark shook his head. "Not good. If I'm right, it was a large-caliber round from a long way away. It was an assassination attempt, Chase. It couldn't be anything else."

"Is he going to be okay?"

He shrugged. "Who knows? He lost a lot of blood. I pinned one of the surgical nurses to the wall and made him tell me the truth. He said the bullet got part of his lung, three ribs, and a lot of soft tissue, but it missed most of the major blood vessels."

"Any theories on the shooter?"

He groaned. "I haven't gotten that far yet, but I need you on it."

"I'm here, brother. Let's get your dad through this, and then we'll . . ." It was suddenly my turn to be pinned to the wall.

He said, "Unless you plan to scrub in and march your tail into that operating room, there's nothing you can do here."

"I'm not that kind of doctor," I said. "So, I guess that means it's time to go to work."

Clark glared into my eyes. "Find this guy, Chase. Find him and drag his bloody butt in front me. Don't you kill him, though. This bastard is mine."

I took a breath and said, "I know this one is personal, but is the Triad sanctioning it?"

He tapped a thumb against his phone. "I just got off the line with General Michaels and General McFarland right before you showed up, and they signed a blank check. Go get this guy, College Boy. I'll be in your back pocket as soon as Dad gets out of surgery."

"Stay here," I said. "Dominic needs to know you're with him. I'll take care of everything else. Have you called your mom?"

He swallowed hard. "Yeah. She's trying to get here, but she's in Aspen, and there's still a lot of snow up there."

Anya stepped beside me. "I will go for her. Do not worry."

Clark nodded. "I appreciate that. God only knows how many island girls are gonna show up here worried about Papi, but it'll be Mom's face he wants to see when he wakes up."

Clark's parents had been divorced for decades, but sometimes, years and miles have very little effect on old bonds.

* * *

Anya dropped Pogonya and me at Bonaventure—the former pecan, cotton, and tobacco plantation that had been in my family since before America was born. After I inherited the property from my great-uncle, Judge Bernard Henry Huntsinger, it quickly morphed into the tactical operation and training center for my team of covert operators who thrived on saving the world, one catastrophe at a time. However, the team was far more than just a collection of gun-toting knuckle-draggers. We were a family, and Dominic Fontana was just as important to every one of us as he was to his own son. Part of that devotion to the man who served as one third of the Triad that directed our operation was based on the loss of a brother, Dominic's other son, Tony, who lost his life to a wound nearly identical to the one the surgeons in Miami were repairing at that very minute.

Skipper had the team assembled and waiting when I stepped through the door to our state-of-the-art op center that occupied the entire third floor of my house.

I took my seat, pulled out my notepad, and said, "This one is family, but we're running it by the numbers. We can't let emotion screw it up for us, so let's hear what you've got, Skipper."

## Chapter 3
## *When and Where?*

Skipper struck a few keys. "What little I have is now on your tablets, but since none of you neanderthals read your tablets, I'll give you the *Reader's Digest* version. Dom is out of surgery but still unconscious. It's apparently not exactly a medically induced coma, but they're keeping him sedated for pain management. He's in critical but stable condition awaiting the arrival of a pulmonary surgeon from the Mayo Clinic."

"That's a lung doctor, right?" Kodiak said.

Skipper nodded. "Yes, apparently, the bullet did quite a bit of damage to the superior lobe of his right lung. That's the upper portion."

Kodiak, the retired Green Beret and arctic warfare specialist, said, "Thanks. I'm the pretty one, not the smart one."

Mongo, the mental and physical heavyweight of the team, said, "Where's Anya? I think she may give you a run for your money in that department."

Kodiak surrendered. "Okay. Except for her, I'm the pretty one."

"Whatever you say," the giant quipped.

Skipper cleared her throat. "Excuse me, guys. Remember me?"

Kodiak said, "Sorry, you're prettier than me, too. I guess I'm not as close to the top of the list as I thought."

Skipper scowled. "That's not what I was talking about. I'm trying to get us back on track to find whoever shot Dominic."

"Please continue," I said.

"Thank you. In the packet I sent, you'll see the initial local police report. The shot apparently came from the southeast. That creates an issue with Clark's long-range theory. Dominic's place in Port Royal is only about forty feet from the shoreline to the east and maybe a hundred feet to the southeast."

"That puts the shooter on a boat," Gator, the youngest member of the team and Skipper's husband, said. "How are we going to catch a sniper on a boat that nobody saw and could be anywhere in the Caribbean by now?"

Skipper said, "First, calm down. Second, he couldn't technically be *anywhere* in the Caribbean if he's on a boat. That's a pretty big sea down there."

Gator, who was well on his way to becoming a world-class sniper himself, said, "I stand corrected, but there are also about a gazillion islands he could be on and a few thousand airplanes out of there. I think that justifies my *anywhere* comment."

Skipper smiled. "I'm starting to think you're the pretty one *and* the smart one, baby. But you always forget that I've got eyes everywhere. I just happen to have some high-res satellite imagery from earlier today of the beautiful island of Bimini."

"Let's see it," I said.

The monitor above her head came alive with crystal-clear color video. The turquoise water surrounding the islands consumed the bulk of the screen, but a few specks dotted the field of blue.

Singer, our official sniper and moral compass, asked, "What time was the shooting?"

Skipper scanned her screen. "According to the police report, it was just after eight a.m. eastern. The video capture you're looking at was taken at seven forty-eight."

"That means we've got a picture of the shooter," Shawn, our former Navy SEAL, said from the back of the room.

"Why do you always sit way back there?" I asked.

"There are too many Green Berets at the table, and I don't want to get any of that on me."

Mongo, Kodiak, and Singer were on their feet in an instant, and the SEAL was engulfed in a Green Beret bear hug before he could fight them off.

Mongo deposited Shawn onto a seat at the table. "There. You're covered in it, and you can sit at the grown-ups' table this year."

Skipper cleared her throat again. "Hello? Briefing here."

We settled, and she continued. "The Royal Bahamas Police Force will conduct the investigation, such as it is. They don't have a homicide inspector on Bimini, so they'll likely send one over from Nassau. I don't make the tactical decisions, but I think now would be a pretty good time for one."

All eyes turned to me, and I said, "It looks like we're headed to Bimini, but I'd like to get a closer look at that satellite imagery if it's good enough to zoom in."

Skipper said, "I'm already on it. I have a program running to search for anything that could be a rifle on deck of anything afloat out there. So far, I've got a lot of fishing rods and boat poles, but I'm working on filtering them out. I'll have something for you soon."

I said, "Great. Where's the *Lori Danielle*?"

Our five-hundred-eighty-foot ship, the RV *Lori Danielle*, had come to us through a series of bizarre events and transactions that left her the property of the Bonaventure Trust. Although, on her docile surface, the L.D. was every bit an ultramodern research vessel, beneath her academic facade lay a warship unmatched by most navies of the world. She was not only the fastest ship of her size on the planet, but also the deadliest non-military vessel on any ocean. If we were going to chase a killer through the Caribbean, there could be no better base of operations than the *Lori Danielle*.

Skipper said, "She's in Bermuda doing coral reef surveys."

"Let me guess," I said. "It's another of Dr. Turner's projects."

"Sort of. She's running it, but it's funded by something called the Oceans of the World Foundation. They're studying why the reefs in Bermuda are so healthy while the rest of the world's coral seems to be struggling."

"Sounds like a good project to me," I said, "but I'm afraid we'll have to disappoint young Dr. Turner yet again."

Although Masha Turner technically worked for the Bonaventure Trust, she operated more as an independent researcher than a member of our team. She, of course, bore no tactical responsibilities, but when we weren't using the ship to chase bad guys, hers were the loving hands into which we entrusted the vessel.

Skipper asked, "Shall I break the news, or do you want to do it?"

I already had my phone in my hand, and the line was ringing.

"Hello."

"Dr. Turner. Chase here."

She sighed. "I'm hanging up now."

"I know, you hate to hear my voice, but the reefs of Bermuda will still be there when we're finished with your floating laboratory."

She said, "I should've known it was too good to be true. Everything has gone flawlessly for weeks, so I suppose it's time. When and where?"

"Bimini, now."

"Oh, that's not so bad. Can the team and I stay aboard? I've been wanting to start a stingray study in Bimini for a while."

I hesitated. "Uh, well, you can stay aboard until we need to go tactical. I'll need to put you ashore when and if we have to start shooting."

She said, "Oh, yeah. Of course. We'll need to be ashore anyway. I just wanted to catch a ride."

"In that case, we'll see you in Port Royal in a couple of days."

She said, "Conditions are a little rough, so it'll probably take more than a couple of days."

I said, "Clark's father has been shot, and we're going after the shooter."

Dr. Turner said, "Oh, no. Is he, uh . . ."

"He's alive, but it's touch-and-go for now."

She said, "In that case, I'm sure Captain Sprayberry will push her as hard as the L.D. can stand. Have you talked with him yet?"

"No. I thought I'd break the news to you first, but I'd appreciate it if you'd transfer me to the bridge."

"No problem, and please tell Clark we'll be praying for his dad."

"Thanks, Masha. I'll pass it along."

After a few clicks, a gruff voice bounced through the line. "Bridge, Captain."

"Barry, it's Chase."

"Oh, thank God. Please tell me I can pull off this research garbage detail and that I get to shoot somebody. When and where?"

I laughed. "With any luck, I'll find you somebody to blow out of the water. I need you in Bimini yesterday."

I listened as Captain Barry Sprayberry pulled the handset away from his face and barked orders. "Recall the divers and all overboard equipment immediately. Navigator, plot a hasty course for Bimini, and prepare to make way." He came back on the line. "We'll be underway within the hour—sooner if these brats can get their act together. Young guys are sharp on paper, but ask them to heave a line, and they worry about breaking a fingernail."

I said, "Have you thought about bringing on a good hand or two to whip them into shape?"

"What are you talking about?"

"I just happen to know a couple of British Special Boat Service guys who are getting close to retirement and could use a gig under a hard-charging captain like you."

"SBS guys," he said. "I'll take all you've got and a dozen more. When can they be here?"

"I'll make some calls," I said. "And I'll see you in Bimini . . ."

While I let the question linger, he growled. "Navigator, report!"

I couldn't hear the navigator's response, but Barry said, "Twenty-six hours if the weather holds. Thirty if it gets worse. Plan on it getting worse, but I've got a pretty good horse under me, and she ain't afraid to run on rocky ground."

"Why does everybody keep bringing up horses?"

He laughed. "Sorry. I forgot about your little phobia."

"It's not a phobia. It's a supreme degree of hatred."

"It's not nice to hate," he said.

"It's not nice to get thrown on my head every time I climb in the saddle, either."

"See you in Bimini. Have Skipper send me the coordinates."

"Port Royal," I said. "It's Dominic. Somebody put a bullet in him, and we're going to return fire."

With the ship minutes away from steaming south, I said, "I want Dr. Mankiller and a forensic team if we can put one together."

Skipper picked up the phone. "Consider it done."

Turning to my second-in-command, I asked, "Mongo, is the armory aboard the *Lori Danielle* ready and topped off?"

"It is, but we're loaded for hardcore bad guys, not police work."

"In that case, put together whatever you need, and I'll get Gordo on the line."

"Roger, boss."

He pulled the rest of the team from the table and headed for the subterranean armory beneath the house. Within an hour, they'd have every piece of equipment we could possibly need ready to be strapped down inside the airplane.

Before they made it through the door, though, I grabbed Gator by the arm. "You're with me."

"Yes, sir."

My next call was one I'd been looking forward to making for almost two years.

When the aircraft commander picked up, he said, "Gordo."

"It's time to put the Big Girl to work."

He said, "Oh, you know I like it when you talk dirty to me. When and where?"

"You're the third person in the past three minutes to ask that question, and I love it. The when is now. The where is South Bimini. Can you get in there?"

He laughed. "That's a mile-long strip of coquina. I can land and take off half a dozen times without running out of runway on that little piece of Heaven."

"Is your crew ready to go?"

He said, "Tubbs is fly-fishing on the river, and Slider is probably sleeping on the airplane. He won't let that girl out of his sight since she came out of the rebuild."

The Lockheed Martin C-130J that Gordo had affectionately dubbed the "Big Girl" had been an asset of the Special Operations Group of the CIA before we ditched her in the Celtic Sea following a little sabotage, and they wrote her off as a loss. The British government towed the floating fuselage to a shipyard, dismantled it, and sent it back home to Lockheed in pieces. The Triad somehow came up with the eight-figure check to rebuild her just like Colonel Steve Austin—better, stronger, and faster than ever before.

The airplane that came out of the Lockheed hangar after eighteen months of nonstop love looked like a typical J-model Super Hercules, but just like the *Lori Danielle*, she was far more than meets the eye. The airplane was, in fact, one of the most capable medium-lift tactical airframes in existence, with the ability to defend herself against attacks from any angle and engage ground targets with nearly the lethality of the Spectre gunship.

I said, "Wake him up, load the pallets, and spin the turbines."

I turned to Gator, and he said, "Thanks for getting me out of armory duty."

"Sometimes it pays to be a driver," I said. "Get the Twin Otter preflighted and ready to rock. The Big Girl is great as long as there's something hard to land on, but something tells me we're going to need the amphib."

He stood. "I'm on it. What about the Mark Five?"

I pointed to the junior member of our team. "See? That's why you're my favorite. Great thinking."

## Chapter 4
## *The Intern*

Gator darted from the op center to care for the amphibious Twin Otter, his favorite of our flying machines, and Skipper gave me a scowl.

"What's that look about?"

She asked, "Why did you tell him he's your favorite? I love him, but really?"

"Don't be silly," I said. "Everyone knows you're my favorite. He's obviously just an extension of you in my eyes."

Her expression softened. "Obviously."

I have no idea what made me do it, but instead of driving to the airport, I walked. Perhaps my mind needed time to process the complexity of the situation we'd fallen into. Along the way, something pulled me inside the stables that Richter, the gorgeous black Arabian gelding, called home. He was standing in the center of his stall with his eyes closed, as if he were in the deepest meditation possible. I wondered if he was thinking about doing something horrible to me, but more likely, he was just catching a nap. I envied that ability, but I had to chuckle at the thought of me standing in the middle of a horse stall, sound asleep.

I made no effort to wake him. Simply watching as he stood in such apparent peace, it occurred to me that I was part of the reason he could feel such assurance. No predator would encroach on his home. He'd never spend a day in hunger, fear, or without a place to stand and sleep. I wanted the same for everyone in my life, especially Pogonya, and I wanted every American to know that people like the brave men and women around me fought, sacrificed, and trained endlessly to give them exactly what Richter was feeling in his placid moment.

We couldn't do it. We couldn't feed, house, and protect everyone, but we'd never stop giving everything we could to provide for those who depended on us for their freedom to sleep in peace. We'd fail, but that would never prevent us from trying, and that in itself is victory.

My determination to leave the warhorse sound asleep crumbled in my clumsiness as I tried in vain to silently pour sweet feed into his bucket. He opened his eyes, and although he didn't appear unhappy to have been pulled from his slumber when he smelled the oats and corn covered in molasses, to my surprise, he didn't move to devour the treat. His first steps were toward the door of the stall, toward me, and he rubbed his face against my shoulder in what I believed was his way of thanking me for both the sleep and the candy that awaited him in the plastic bucket hanging from a hook. I'd never get a nuzzle from the people I protected, but knowing they were free and safe was nuzzle enough.

The well-orchestrated performance at the airport made me proud of the team of remarkable professionals I'd assembled. Every man and woman knew exactly what was expected of them, and they exceeded those expectations with every stride. The airplanes were loaded, weighed, fueled, and inspected for their readiness to carry us into the world that demanded more than any of us could give alone. Combined, however, we were a force far greater than the sum of our parts. We were unstoppable determination melded with immeasurable skill, and that combination made our team one of the best on the planet at accomplishing any mission in the face of opposition anywhere on Earth.

We huddled up at the main hangar, and I was the quarterback.

I started my briefing as most of them began. "Nice work, guys."

Instead of reveling in the praise, the team mostly ignored the compliment and waited impatiently for the order to go to work. We were still a few steps from the command of execution, but it would soon come, and execution was exactly what would happen.

"Gator is taking the Twin Otter. Shawn, I want you to pick a crew-mate and bring the Mark Five. I'll fly with the rest of you on the Big Girl, and we'll hit the ground running. The *Lori Danielle* will rendezvous with us tomorrow night. Any questions?"

Heads shook, and Shawn tugged at Kodiak's sleeve. I approved of his choice. The pair would not only deliver the hardcore fighting machine of the patrol boat on time, but they'd also crush anything or anyone who got in their way on the nearly four-hundred-mile trek across the punishing Gulf Stream waters lying between St. Marys and Port Royal.

"It would appear that we're missing Dr. Mankiller and her techs," I said. "Has anybody seen them?"

Singer motioned toward the runway. "They're coming. I just saw the lab door closing across the field."

The half mile separating our main hangar from Dr. Mankiller's lab was a barrier greater than most mortal eyes could overcome, but not our sniper's. Eagles in the sky envied his vision, and I was more grateful every day for what he brought to both the team and to me personally.

Celeste Mankiller and her forensic tech arrived in the specialized vehicle that bore little resemblance to the golf cart it had once been. The team lifted a dozen Pelican cases from the back of the cart as the most brilliant technical services officer I've ever met stepped from behind the wheel.

She said, "I believe you've met my new tech, haven't you?"

My daughter smiled up at me, and I shook my head. "Seriously?"

Pogonya threw up her hands. "You said I couldn't spend the summer on South Beach with Maebelle, so I accepted an internship under Dr. Mankiller."

I pointed toward the Hercules. "Get on the airplane, but if you get shot, don't come crying to me, *intern*."

Although she wouldn't hear it from me anytime soon, I'd never been prouder of the daughter I spent fifteen years without.

Gordo and Tubbs, our former Air Force Special Operations pilots, disappeared into the cockpit to bring the beast of an airplane to life, and the rest of us followed Slider, the loadmaster and engineer, up the ramp. With a swing of a lever, the ramp closed, and the space became a time machine that would transport us into our waiting future . . . whatever that might be.

The last time our team had been aboard that particular airplane, we didn't quite make it to our destination. Instead, we made a brief stop on the Celtic Sea, where the airplane was never intended or designed to land. I had every confidence that the evening's flight would not end the same way. The gelatin in the fuel tanks deposited by a saboteur on that previous flight wouldn't be an issue again. The fuel she carried that evening came from our tanks and trucks, with extensive safeguards in place to protect not only the airplane, but more importantly, her crew and passengers.

The list of upgrades the airframe received was extensive, but at that moment, my favorite was what Slider called "the comfort pallet." It was a collection of oversized, airline-quality, first-class seats bolted to a cargo pallet and secured to the deck. The previous seating arrangement had been little more than netting affixed to metal frames running along each side of the cargo bay with rugged nylon straps used as seat belts.

Slider passed out earplugs instead of the usual green David Clark headsets. "These are a little more comfortable than what we had back in the Stone Age. They're noise-canceling and designed to connect with your bone-conduction devices. Three taps will put you in Gordo's and Tubbs' ears. Two will get my attention. The rest of the time, you guys will be on open comms unless you turn them off. If you want to talk one-on-one, each of you should press and hold the button until you hear the tone."

We slipped the devices into our ears and quickly learned how to make them do exactly what we wanted while keeping the Big Girl's ferocious noise at bay.

* * *

The Royal Bahamas Police Force wasn't as welcoming as I'd hoped, but my U.S. Secret Service credentials proved to be a key just heavy enough to open the door I needed to step through.

Chief Inspector Marcus Belafonte glared at my cred pack. "Special Agent Fulton, you must understand this is highly irregular, but in light of your position and as a matter of our great respect for Sir Dominic, you may view the scene."

His accent was lighter than I expected, but he wore the authority bestowed by the Prime Minister like the cloak of Sherlock Holmes and the gun belt of Marshal Matt Dillon.

"I appreciate your kindness, Chief Inspector. Please know that finding the man responsible for attempting to assassinate Sir Dominic —who is an American citizen—is my only interest. When I am successful, I'll ensure that you and your team get the credit. I neither need nor want the publicity associated with any of this."

"Is that so?" the inspector said. "In that case, you wouldn't mind if my man accompanied you through the residence tonight."

"Of course not," I said. "I'm sure my forensics team would appreciate the assistance."

"Forensics team? I said you could have a look. I did not authorize the collection of any evidence."

I checked my watch, thumbed a button on my phone, and tossed it to the inspector. "It's a quarter past eleven p.m. in D.C., but the President will answer. You can tell him."

He caught the phone as fear and disbelief came over his face. The phone ringing on speaker must've felt like a nuclear bomb in his hands when Skipper answered and said, "Good evening, Dr. Fulton. This is the White House duty officer, Lieutenant Commander Woodley. The President is occupied, but I will coordinate with him as soon as possible. What may I do for you, sir?"

I said, "Sorry to bother you, and especially the President with such a trivial issue, Commander, but I'm here with Chief Inspector Marcus Belafonte, and he—"

The inspector cut me off. "This is Chief Inspector Belafonte. Please forgive the intrusion, madam. There is nothing pressing from the islands. Please know that the Prime Minister's Royal Bahamas Police Force is at your service. Good night, madam."

My forensics team and I continued, unescorted, through Dominic's beachfront home, where I'd drunk more Caribbean rum than anyone should, and spent countless hours being regaled by my friend's semi-true stories. When I came to his favorite chair overlooking the sea through a wall of glass and screen, my stomach turned, and rage boiled inside my chest.

The wall behind his chair could've been an abstract study in crimson by some sadistic artist from the Renaissance.

Dr. Mankiller directed Pogonya to photograph everything in sight, and she followed her instructions to the letter. I watched carefully for any sign of Pogonya succumbing to the grotesque nature of the horrific scene, but she never faltered, even though her father did.

Celeste moved, observed, and took note of every detail in her practiced, meticulous fashion until she came to a hole in the wall about the size of a pencil. She withdrew a penlight and magnifying glass and leaned in to examine the bullet's entry into the Sheetrock.

I watched but said nothing as she worked. Soon, a small metal probe appeared from inside her pocket and then disappeared into the hole.

"Hmm," she said. "That's interesting. It went all the way through. Is that inspector guy still here?"

"I'll find out," I said, and jogged for the front door.

The man was perched against Dominic's banister, smoking a cigarette.

"Chief Inspector, Dr. Mankiller needs you inside if you wouldn't mind."

He crushed out the smoke, pocketed the remains, and pushed himself from the railing. "Of course. And please, just call me Marcus. Chief Inspector is so formal."

I hadn't made a friend, but I'd secured a powerful, even if reluctant, ally.

Dr. Mankiller asked, "May I see the projectile your men recovered?"

Marcus studied his boots. "I'm sorry to say that we did not recover the projectile."

"Even better," Celeste said. "We'll find it."

She whispered to Pogonya, and the intern bolted from the room. When she returned, she held out a small leather case. Celeste took it, pulled a probe from inside, and inserted it into the bullet hole. "Time to go hunting."

Marcus and I followed the two women from the room and around the exterior of the house until we found the tiny laser beam projecting from the hole in the wall. The pinpoint of green light struck the white sand ten feet away, and Celeste said to Pogonya, "Welcome to the archaeological phase of your internship. Start digging."

I don't know how many sandbags she could've filled with what she moved, but I didn't envy her task. Twenty minutes into the exercise, Pogo slipped a pair of forceps from her shirt pocket and lifted a bullet from the excavation.

I slapped Marcus on the back. "No wonder your men didn't find it. They needed an ambitious intern like ours."

The bullet found a home inside an evidence bag, and the inspector reached for it.

Celeste pulled it away. "Oh, no, you don't. You can take that up with Dr. Fulton while I measure, weigh, and photograph this thing."

Although the trunk of a car made a poor lab, Celeste made the best of it. She analyzed the bullet from every imaginable angle and with every tool in her kit. When she was finished, she stood, stepped around Marcus, and mouthed, "It's Russian."

## Chapter 5
## *Sir Dominic*

Chief Inspector Marcus Belafonte made his move. "We will, of course, assume custody of the bullet. Once our laboratory has examined it, it may be possible for us to return it to you for analysis."

Although I had no further need for the projectile, I wanted the inspector to believe he'd won a mighty battle. "I don't know, Marcus. It would be best if we hand-carried it back to the States so the FBI crime lab can do a full analysis."

"This is out of the question. This is a crime that took place on Bahamian property, and . . ."

He continued blabbering on, but I turned my focus to Celeste, and she nodded behind a knowing smirk.

With both hands in the air, and while Chief Inspector Belafonte continued his monologue, I said, "Okay! I don't like it, but you're right. The bullet is yours. The U.S. government would ask that you sign a chain-of-custody form. Mr. Fontana is an important man, and we can't let procedural technicalities prevent this case from concluding properly when *we* catch the shooter."

The inspector frowned. "Sir Dominic is, indeed, an important man, especially here in The Bahamas, where the perpetrator of this crime will stand trial."

I didn't waste my time or his by explaining that there would be no trial in The Bahamas, or anywhere else for that matter. Apprehending the shooter and bringing him to justice wasn't on my to-do list. I'd catch him, but there was absolutely no possibility that I'd turn him over to any government or individual before I'd extracted everything he knew about who hired him, why they hired him, and who else was on the hit list.

Celeste dropped the small plastic bag into Marcus's hand and produced a chain-of-custody form as if from thin air. He read the form carefully before filling in his information and scribbling his signature on the line.

Marcus pocketed the evidence bag. "Thank you for understanding, Chase. I'm pleased that we agree."

"I couldn't agree more, my friend. We're on the same team. That brings up one more little technicality I need to make you aware of."

He cocked his head as if I'd piqued his interest, and I said, "The rest of my team will be here tomorrow. In addition to our C-One-Thirty cargo plane and the amphibious search aircraft already on-site, there will be a Mark Five patrol boat and a five-hundred-eighty-foot research vessel christened the *Lori Danielle*. Of course, your status as chief inspector negates the necessity of my filing all the paperwork for operations in the waters of The Bahamas, right? I mean, you wouldn't want to delay finding Sir Dominic's assailant."

The inspector recoiled. "You're bringing an army?"

I furrowed my brow. "The army is already here, Marcus. I'm bringing a navy."

I laughed first, but he soon joined me. "Just don't kill anybody in Bahamian waters without first letting me know. Can you do that?"

I stuck my hand in his. "I think we can live with that arrangement. Remind me again how far your waters extend from shore."

He froze, and I laughed again.

The inspector and his driver left the scene, but only after they watched us do the same.

As always, Skipper arranged for a house that would serve as temporary lodging until the *Lori Danielle* arrived. And as always, it was perfect. The team was sound asleep when Pogonya, Celeste, and I crept inside and found our beds.

My phone yanked me from sleep a few hours later, and I thumbed the button.

"What did you find out, College Boy?"

I yawned and stretched. "How's your dad?"

Clark said, "He made it through the night, but he's still unconscious. They're keeping him that way until surgery this afternoon."

"That must mean the pulmonologist arrived."

"Pulmonary thoracic surgeon," he said. "She insists on *not* being called a pulmonologist. I don't care what we call her as long as she can save Dad's life. Now, quit stalling and tell me what you found."

"We found the bullet."

He huffed. "You mean the local cops didn't even find the bullet themselves?"

"The locals are doing the best they can with what they have, but their assets are few. It was a Seven-N-One round."

"A Russian bullet?"

I said, "Exactly. It was the sniper variant, one hundred fifty-one grain, full metal jacket."

"Intact?"

"Pretty much. It looks like most of the deformation happened inside the wall of Dominic's house and in the sand."

"That explains why it didn't blow Dad's shoulder apart, but I would've expected it to mushroom on impact with the ribs."

I said, "I can't explain it. I'm just telling you what we found."

"Have Celeste and that big brain of hers figure out the angles and energy. It would be nice to know how far away the shooter was. The farther, the fewer."

I said, "I'm sure she's already on it. Do you know off the top of your head what the maximum range of the Seven-N-One is?"

"Depends on what they shot it from and who pulled the trigger. If it came out of a Dragunov SVD, which is the Russian sniper rifle that it was designed for, it's good for eight hundred to a thousand yards in the hands of a good shooter."

"What if it was in the hands of somebody like Singer?" I asked.

"That's exactly my point about distance. The farther, the fewer. There aren't many guys around who can make a single-shot kill from beyond a thousand yards with that setup."

"How few?"

Clark said, "A cat named Vladimir Ilyin made a confirmed kill with one from almost fifteen hundred yards in the Soviet-Afghan War. He wasn't shooting from no boat, though. He would've been sandbagged in and lying prone. God only knows what kind of wind or weather he was in, but there's a better than good chance the conditions in Afghanistan were better for long-range shooting than they were in The Bahamas yesterday."

"I checked the wind," I said. "It was nine to twelve knots all day."

"See? A twelve-knot wind over water is bad enough, but even old Vladimir Ilyin couldn't do much from the deck of a rocking boat."

"You still didn't answer my question. How many people could pull off a greater-than-a-thousand-yards shot from the water with that bullet?"

He said, "I can't come up with any names, but the list is short."

"I'll have more information for you in a couple of hours," I said. "Oh, there's one more thing. The chief inspector keeps calling your dad Sir Dominic."

"They do that. It's a courtesy and respect thing for rich guys who support the local economy. Dad's probably pretty charitable with the police force, and if he's not blown it all on twenty-year-old Cuban girls and thirty-year-old scotch, he should have a nice stash somewhere."

My phone clicked. "Gotta run. Skipper's calling."

"See ya."

"Hey, Skipper. Please tell me you found the shooter's boat."

She said, "That depends."

"That sounds a lot like a no to me."

She groaned. "Yes, it's a no, but not the kind of no you're thinking about."

"I just got off the phone with Clark, and I understood every word he said. That's weird enough, but now that I have no clue what you're talking about, I'm beginning to question my comprehension skills."

She said, "I need to know the angles. Celeste is working on it for me, but she doesn't have anything yet. There are too many variables."

"Okay, so what do you know that we didn't know last night?"

"We know it was a seven six two by fifty-four Russian sniper round."

"We knew that last night," I said. "I've only been asleep for a few hours."

"You're still in bed?"

"Yes."

"Oh, then you have no idea what's going on yet."

"So, tell me."

Skipper said, "Everybody else is up and working. Gator's flying a grid and shooting aerials to compare against the satellite photos from the time of the attack. I'm running the ballistics through every database on Earth."

"Any hits yet?"

"The round was definitely fired from a Dragunov SVD, or at least through the barrel of one. Since I don't have the casing, I can't say what kind of action the barrel was affixed to. As far as I know, though, nobody makes a better action for that barrel than Dragunov, so there's no reason to suspect it was a custom-built rifle at this point."

I said, "All right. I'm up now. I'm going to join the rest of the team and actually do my job. Where's the ship?"

"She's making good time. The weather actually improved a little, so she'll be there before dark."

"Great news. Thanks, Skipper. Do you need anything from me?"

"No, I've got it under control. I was just calling to make sure you were alive since no one has seen you this morning."

I shoved two pieces of toast down my throat and drank what was left in the pot of cold coffee before stepping into the morning sun.

Singer emerged from a clump of trees near the water. "Morning, Sleeping Beauty. I wondered when you were going to join us."

"What were you doing out there?"

He said, "I was just thinking about how I'd take the shot."

"Any ideas?"

He turned to the west. "Wanna take a ride over to Dominic's place with me?"

We made the three-minute drive and ignored the police tape flapping in the wind. Singer leapt onto the AC unit and propelled himself onto the roof in one motion. I followed, but my approach was far less graceful.

"It's the prosthetic."

Singer laughed. "Yeah, that and the extra piece of chocolate cake."

Watching our sniper think has always been more intriguing than watching him shoot. I'd love to know how the gears in his head work, but I'll never have his wisdom or experience.

He stood on the peak of the roof and stared to the southeast with one hand raised against the sun. After several minutes of scanning the scenery, he shook his head. "I just don't see it. There's no way he could've been far enough away for no one to see or hear him and still make the shot."

"So, what's your theory?"

He straddled the roof, letting each leg dangle off either side. "The best shooters in the world couldn't make a thousand-yard shot from a boat out there and expect to hit the front door, let alone hit a man in the chest."

"Could you do it?"

He shook his head. "I don't mean to sound cocky, but I count myself among the best shooters in the world, and to answer your question, no, I couldn't do it. It's impossible."

"It's obviously not impossible," I said. "Somebody did it."

Singer stared back out over the azure water with eighteen-inch swells rolling across its surface. "Yeah, somebody did, but not the way we think."

"You're starting to sound like Skipper. What do you mean?"

"What time was Dominic shot?"

I scrolled through the electronic notes in my phone. "Just after eight a.m."

"And when was low tide?"

I opened the app and pulled up the historical tide data for Bimini. "Seven fifty-three a.m."

Singer smiled. "I know how he did it . . . And yeah, I could've done it, too."

# Chapter 6
## *Young Jedi*

Gator made a textbook water landing and beached the Twin Otter in front of our rented house beside the Mark V patrol boat. After tying off the plane and trotting up the beach, he put the memory card from the aerial camera in my palm. "I don't know what you're going to see. It just looks like a lot of blue ocean to me."

I bounced the plastic card in my hand. "We won't see anything valuable on this one, but when you go back up this evening, all of that's going to change."

"What are you talking about?"

I said, "Let's get your mentor in here and your lovely bride on the phone. They'll explain it to you."

I uploaded the video and stills from Gator's card and called Skipper on speaker.

"Op center."

I said, "You should have a bunch of video files and still shots as soon as the upload finishes, but let's break down your and Singer's theory for the flyboy."

"Hey, baby. How was the flying?"

"Bumpy and boring," Gator said. "And apparently a waste of time."

"Not necessarily," she said. "I'll have to take a look, but I'll need you to make a couple more passes at low tide this evening. Think you can pull that off?"

"I wish I'd known that before I put two hours on the airplane and burned all that fuel."

I said, "Don't worry about that. Every minute you spend in the air makes you a better pilot, and that's well worth whatever it costs."

He shook his head. "You know something? I've got the best job in the world."

I said, "No, sir, you do not. I do, because I've got a whole gang of guys like you who make what I do a little easier every day."

Skipper chimed in. "Would you two either get a room or let me continue, please?"

"We've already got a room," I said. "So, continue."

She made a noise I was incapable of describing. "Gross. Let's get back to work. The files are here, so, Singer, why don't you go over your theory with the less tactically knowledgeable of the group while I take a look at what we've got?"

The sniper said, "There's only one way this guy could've made that shot from far enough away to escape without being immediately identified."

Gator said, "The only way I could've done it would've been from that reef out there. It might be possible to ground a skiff on it and get stable enough to make the shot. Otherwise, it would be a carnival game of shooting for teddy bears."

Singer smiled, turned to me, and pointed at his protégé. "And that's exactly why I'll be able to retire while I'm still young enough to see the world without getting shot at."

I shook my head. "Your retirement is disapproved. You may resubmit later for further disapproval. And why didn't I think of shooting from the reef?"

"Because you're not a sniper," Singer said. "You're a tactician, and you're one of the best I've ever worked for."

Skipper came back to life. "What is this, some kind of love fest in the islands? You guys are killing me. My hot little sniper man is right, of course. There's definitely a reef out there, as well as a sandbar that's only visible at low tide."

I said, "So, is this what you were talking about when we were on the roof earlier?"

Singer nodded. "Yeah. I couldn't see the reef or the sandbar, but I figured something solid had to be out there."

Skipper asked, "Is Celeste handy?"

Pogonya came bopping through the door in part of a bikini. Suddenly, I disapproved of far more than Singer's retirement. "That's definitely not work attire."

"I'm not working," she said. "I'm sunbathing until Dr. Celeste needs me."

"She needs you now," I said. "And *you* need some clothes."

She grinned. "You remember when Mama dressed like this for you, no, Chasechka?"

I pointed toward the back of the house. "You're no Mama, and you won't be one anytime soon. Find Celeste, and for God's sake, stop torturing every boy on the island."

"As you wish, Father. But just so you know, the boys don't think it's torture."

"Go!"

Gator said, "I guess parenting isn't as easy as you expected, huh?"

"I'm not parenting," I said. "I'm preventing a mass murder."

He furrowed his brow. "What?"

"If those boys on the beach look at Pogo the way I looked at Anya twenty years ago, I'll kill every one of them."

Dr. Mankiller walked in, dressed far more appropriately than my daughter. "I hear you need me."

"We do," Skipper said from the speakerphone. "Have you made any progress on an angular fan of fire?"

Celeste groaned. "There were so many trajectory changes that it's impossible to get an accurate angle of fire, but I've narrowed it down to fifteen degrees or so. That would mean if the shooter were a thousand yards away, he would've been in an area—"

Singer threw up a hand. "Stop!"

Celeste froze, and Singer turned to Gator. In his best Master Yoda impersonation, he said, "Tell to me quickly how big is fifteen degrees at one thousand yards, young Jedi."

Gator rolled his eyes. "That was terrible, but one degree at a thousand yards is fifty-two point five feet, so that makes the area seven hundred and uh . . . eighty-seven feet. That's nothing. We can search that in five minutes."

Singer frowned. "Point five."

Gator said, "What?"

The sniper raised his eyebrows. "It's seven hundred eighty-seven point *five* feet. Miss by half a foot, and you'll always be a rifleman—not a sniper."

"Yes, sir."

Skipper said, "Chase was right. There's nothing usable in the video footage. The angle of the sun wasn't great, and the water was too deep, but you've got a boat and only eight hundred feet to search. I'm not a sniper, so I rounded up."

I said, "Round up the whole team and every piece of scuba gear you can find. We're going swimming."

The Mark V patrol boat is less of a boat and more of a massive hunk of floating tactical sexiness, but she's eighty-two feet long and weighs a hundred thousand pounds. Snooping around on top of sandbars and coral reefs only a few feet beneath the surface isn't her wheelhouse, but she had some nifty gadgets that would come in handy, and she could get us close.

Shawn had spent more time at the controls of a Mark V than the rest of us combined, so he was the default operator. Gator stood close by his side, learning every move the SEAL made.

"Bottom's coming up," Shawn said as the depth on the sonar screen decreased. "I intend to make a slow pass parallel to the reef with the side-scan sonar wide open so we can get a feel for what's out there."

"Don't intend. Do it," I said.

"Old habits die hard."

I slapped him on the shoulder. "You're at the helm. That makes you the master and commander. I'm just here to swim when you tell me the pool's open."

We cruised along the interior of the reef at five knots, with the side-scan sonar painting a beautiful portrait of the wall.

Gator studied the screen. "I don't see any scars from a boat on the tops."

I'd grown so accustomed to having Gator impress me that it felt like a kick in the gut when he failed such an elementary task.

Shawn groaned. "Should I tell him, or do you want to drag him behind the boat by his heels for a while?"

Singer stepped up. "Think about it, kid. If you were the sniper and you wanted to ground your boat on this reef, make a shot toward the beach, and get away, which side of the reef would you use?"

Gator palmed his face. "I'm an idiot."

"You're not an idiot," Singer said. "You've just never killed anybody from a boat at a thousand yards while aground on a reef . . . yet."

Shawn took us all the way around the reef, and a massive object appeared on the sonar.

Gator stabbed the screen with a fingertip. "What on Earth is that?"

I checked my watch. "That's something we're going to take fifteen minutes to see. I've been here before, but you wouldn't believe me if I told you without showing you."

I pulled on a BCD and tank. "Pogo, gear up. You're coming, too."

She shucked off her T-shirt, revealing the same bikini as before, and I said, "Nope. Put the shirt back on. We'll get you a dry one when we're back aboard."

We splashed into the water and descended to the sandy bottom fifteen feet below. I led Gator and Pogonya toward the hulking object until we were within a few feet, and I gave my best ta-da presentation. The two swam around what remained of the wreck, appearing mesmerized by the sight.

I let them gawk and swim for ten minutes, but with far more pressing matters at hand, I tapped my tank to get their attention, then motioned back for the boat. We climbed aboard, found a dry T-shirt for Pogonya, and I waited for the questions to fly.

To my surprise, the first one wasn't a question at all. Gator said, "That looks a lot like the remains of a Curtiss C-Forty-Six."

I nodded. "Good eyes, Gator. That's exactly what it is. Somebody dumped it here back in eighty-six after spotting the DEA waiting on the runway. The load apparently shifted, threw them out of the balance envelope, and they ended up on the bottom. Nobody survived, so they never figured out exactly who the cargo belonged to. It's rumored that it could've been Pablo Escobar's."

"It just looked like a rusted-out old airplane to me, but it was still extremely cool," Pogonya said. "Can we dive it again before we leave? I'd like to explore the inside if I can get in there."

Gator said, "I'll take her back down if we have time."

"We'll see," I said. "I just didn't want you to miss it while we were this close. If we don't have time on this trip, we'll come back after we bag our shooter."

Shawn asked. "Can we go now?"

"You're the captain," I said.

He laughed. "Obviously not, but okay."

We rounded the reef and ran parallel to its eastern edge.

"How far offshore are we?" Singer asked.

Gator pulled the range finder from his pack and sighted on Dominic's house. "Twelve twenty-five from the front window. That's a long shot, even from a solid foundation."

Singer said, "It sure is. The current is running to the north, right?"

Shawn nodded, and the sniper said, "Drop us at the south end, and we'll drift it. With any luck, we'll find a scar."

Shawn maneuvered the Mark V to the southern end of the angular fan Celeste calculated, and I said, "Let's add another five hundred feet, just as a margin of error."

Pogonya said, "Dr. Celeste doesn't make errors."

I said, "Dr. Celeste isn't a sniper, and everybody who isn't a sniper makes errors. Ain't that right, Gator?"

He ignored me and said, "You'll probably want to put the wet T-shirt back on."

Shawn positioned us perfectly, and the whole team stepped off the back of the Mark V. The reef lay twenty feet to the west, and we approached together before splitting into two-person dive teams. Singer and Gator paired off and led the expedition, just as expected. Kodiak and Mongo formed an awkward-looking pair, but no predator would dare make an attempt on anything Mongo's size. That left Kodiak in good hands, and Pogonya and I brought up the rear.

We were only inches beneath the surface as we glided along the top of the reef, looking for anything that could've been recent damage. After estimating fifteen hundred feet of drifting, none of us saw anything that remotely resembled fresh damage to the reef. If a boat had intentionally grounded on the coral, we either missed it or it was somewhere else.

We surfaced to find Shawn waiting fifty feet away. I let my regulator fall from my mouth and yelled, "Nothing! Let's do it again and lengthen the line."

He powered toward us, and we climbed aboard.

Shawn drove until we were at least another five hundred feet south of our earlier entry point. "Do you want me to go this time?"

I turned to Celeste. "Are you okay on the boat by yourself?"

She said, "Sure. I've been watching Shawn. I'll stay with your bubbles and pick you up at the north end."

We went back into the water, but we had an odd number of divers for the second splash. Given the choice, none of us would ever dive without a buddy, but Shawn's prowess in the water, coupled with the fact that we'd all be well within sight of each other in extremely shallow water, relieved my concern.

Just as before, Pogonya and I tailed the formation about thirty feet behind Shawn, with the other two teams equidistant in front of him.

After two minutes in the water, Pogonya grabbed my shoulder and pointed to the left. Two Caribbean reef sharks were pursuing a sea turtle with no haste in their movement. I didn't believe they were hungry for turtle soup, and that it was likely coincidental, but the look in Pogonya's eyes through her dive mask made it clear that she wanted to chase them, perhaps to rescue the turtle.

I glanced to the north and counted fins. Everybody was there, so I tapped my knife against my tank to get Shawn's attention. I gave him the hand signal for sharks and let him know Pogo and I were taking a side quest. He gave me the okay signal and continued drifting northward.

After I pointed toward the sharks, my daughter morphed into a mermaid. I could barely keep up with her, but we were closing on the pair. They were graceful and elegant, gliding effortlessly through the gin-clear water, and showing no concern for the two humans finning for all we were worth and closing in from astern.

Seeing such beautiful animals in their world, a world we could only visit temporarily, was an incredible experience, especially since I was doing it with the most important person in my life. Her eyes gleamed in fascination as we drifted only a dozen feet behind the sharks that had apparently abandoned their turtle, which was nowhere to be seen. I credited him with a brilliant maneuver to evade the predators, but more likely, he merely spotted a tasty bit of seagrass he couldn't resist. Pogo, on the other hand, spotted something *I* couldn't resist.

She shook my arm and pointed to the west, even more excited than she'd been about the sharks. In the distance, I saw exactly what we'd been looking for all along.

# Chapter 7
## *A Fistful of Sand*

The typical dive gear we used on missions included full face masks with electronic internal communication systems. In the clear, shallow water off Bimini, we were using the same recreational dive gear any tourist would wear when they stepped into the water with a local diving charter. Our communication was limited to hand signals and tapping on our tanks with anything hard enough to make noise. If I could've called the team, I would've had them by my side in minutes, but without the technology to gather the crowd, it was just Pogonya and me.

I motioned for her to follow me, and I finned for the gleaming object she discovered when the sharks made their departure. We arrived at the site, and I couldn't believe my eyes. It was simple, effective, and absolutely brilliant.

I tied a line to one leg of the structure and inflated my surface signaling device. The orange sausage rose to the surface above us and stood erect in the bright midday sun. Pogo and I surfaced beside the waving tube and waited for the rest of the team to emerge from their drift over the reef a few hundred feet away.

She pulled her regulator from her mouth and let it fall into the water with the mouthpiece down, just as I had taught her, to avoid having the reg spew compressed air in every direction. She said, "What is that thing?"

I pointed toward several boats anchored in the area. "It's called a tuna tower. Most of those boats have one. It's a metal structure bolted to the boat's deck so fishermen can climb up and get a better look at the water from above. They're supposed to be used to spot fish. This one was a shooting platform."

She pulled her mask down and around her neck, and my pride swelled. Divers on the surface with masks on top of their heads often find themselves without a mask after a wave takes theirs for a joyride. That doesn't happen when a diver lowers their mask around their neck. My little girl may have had terrible decision-making skills when selecting swimwear, but she already made excellent decisions in the water.

"But it's too deep, even at low tide. There's no way that thing would've been sticking out of the water."

I said, "The top would've been dry when it was standing up instead of lying on its side the way it is right now."

All we could do was wait, or at least, that's all I thought we could do. In those small moments together, Pogonya was teaching me more about life than I ever believed I could teach her.

"I know you really want the rest of the guys to get here so you can show them what we discovered, but I think it's pretty cool that you and I found it together."

I asked, "How deep do you think it is right here?"

She said, "I don't *think*. I *know*. According to my dive computer, I was at twenty-four feet when we knelt on the sand beside the tower."

"All right, little Miss I Know, let's play a game. No regulators. First one back to the surface with a handful of sand wins, and the other buys dinner. Go!"

She grabbed her inflator hose and yanked it to open the valve above her shoulder, allowing the air inside her buoyancy compensator to escape, but the race was already over before her head descended beneath the surface. I squeezed the buckle on my BCD and raised both arms, slipping from the vest and beginning my descent to the sandy bottom. After hitting the bottom, I grabbed the sand and kicked away. On my ascent back to the surface, I passed Pogo on her descent, her deflated BCD still strapped tightly in place and bubbles escaping her lips.

The look on her face was far from defeat. It was the look of the tactician our sniper had declared me to be. Instead of surrendering to my obvious victory, my daughter reached out, ripped open my clasped right hand, and let my prize fistful of sand fall back to the bottom. With a wink and nod, she rolled upside down, finned twice, scooped up a few ounces of sand, and kicked for the surface.

I wanted to be mad at myself for being outwitted, but instead of anger, my chest filled with pride, again, and I followed the winner back to the surface.

She inflated her BCD, and I slipped back into mine as she sprinkled proof of her victory into the water. "I think I'd like lobster for dinner . . . since you're buying."

"I think you cheated."

She looked and sounded so much like her mother when she said, "You made the rules, and I followed them. No regulators, and the first one back on the surface with a handful of sand wins. Where's your sand, Pops?"

The rumble of the Mark V's engines caught my attention before I could defend my position on our contest rules, and I looked up to see the boat headed north.

"Are they leaving us?" Pogonya asked.

"No. They're going around the reef to avoid damaging it by cutting across and risking hitting the coral with the keel."

She pointed into the sky east of the island. "Look. I think that's Mama."

The glistening white Cessna Citation turned onto final approach, perfectly aligned with the runway at South Bimini Airport.

I said, "I think you're right. She'll probably want lobster, too."

Pogonya grinned. "She didn't earn it like I did, but if I let her wear my bikini, I bet you'd give her anything she wants."

I planted a palm on top of her head and dunked her. When she resurfaced, I said, "She gets whatever she wants without a bikini."

Pogonya's eyes widened. "Oh, my God. That's a terrible thing to say in front of your daughter."

"No! That's not what I meant. I didn't mean without wearing the bikini. I meant—"

She splashed me. "You love her, don't you, Father?"

"Where's your sand?"

She frowned. "You saw me drop it after I won. You're just avoiding the question."

I held up my left hand—the one Pogo hadn't ripped open—and unclenched my fist, revealing a clump of dripping sand. "It looks like you're buying dinner, unless you've got a witness to substantiate your claim of ever *really* having sand before you *allegedly* dropped it."

She shrugged. "Fine. I'm telling Mama you said you don't want to see her in a bikini."

"You play dirty."

She smirked. "I think I'll have two lobsters tonight. Winning always makes me hungry."

The boat pulled alongside, and Shawn leaned over the rail. "Everything okay?"

"Pogo found the perch," I said. "It's a tuna tower on its side."

Shawn pulled on his mask and fins and stepped overboard. He could hold his breath longer than most people could sleep, so I stuck my regulator back in my mouth and followed him to the bottom. We swam the perimeter of the metal frame, and he pointed to the two legs of the tower, where plates should've been, that would've held it to the deck of a boat. The ends of the legs were mangled and flared as if a sea monster had chewed them off.

We'd been underwater for close to four minutes when the SEAL motioned toward the surface. He took his time inspecting the tower on the way up, and I met him on the swim platform of the Mark V.

He caught his breath and pulled off his mask. "Whoever the shooter was, he blew the feet right after taking the shot so the tower would lie down and rot away. That's not stainless steel. It's galvanized. It wouldn't last two months out here before turning into dust."

Singer said, "Would you mind catching the rest of us up on what's going on?"

I described the tuna tower, and Shawn said, "Whoever rigged the legs to blow was an overachiever. He wanted to make absolutely certain that thing would lie down."

Singer asked, "Are you sure it's tall enough to get a shooter above the surface?"

Shawn said, "From what I saw, it's made up of five sections, each one four feet long."

Pogonya said, "That's only twenty feet, and my dive computer says it's twenty-four feet deep here."

Singer gave Pogo's ponytail a tug. "Not at low tide, it's not."

Gator said, "Then it looks like we found our sniper's perch, but what does that really give us? It's not like we can pull fingerprints off of it."

"Maybe we can," Mongo said.

Celeste jumped into the conversation. "I don't know where you learned forensics, but there's no technology in the world that can lift prints from metal that's been in salt water for any length of time."

Mongo said, "Not all fingerprints are ridges and swirls, Doctor. Sometimes, a man leaves his mark with craftsmanship, and that's even better than a fingerprint."

Celeste still wore the look of a skeptic. "What are you talking about?"

Mongo said, "I need to take a look."

Gator tossed him his mask and fins, but the big man said, "No, I'll need a tank. I'm not a youngster anymore, and I'm definitely not a SEAL."

The big man suited up, and I followed him into the water. The way Mongo's brain worked was otherworldly. He understood concepts and ideas that baffled small-brained folks like me, so getting to watch him work was always a treat.

We descended slowly, and he ran a gloved hand across every inch of the metal framework, seeming to pay even closer attention to the joints where the sections of the tower came together. After several minutes of thorough inspection, he shot a thumb toward the surface, and we rose to the top.

He asked, "Can we get that thing aboard the boat?"

I shook the water from my hair. "There's no way to get it onto *this* boat, but we've got a boat on the way that'll snatch that thing off the bottom like a child's bathtub toy."

He furrowed his brow. "We can't get the *Lori Danielle* in this shallow water."

"No, but we can take the tower to deeper water."

"I like what you're thinking," he said. "Let's do it."

Shawn said, "If you can get that thing off the bottom, I'll tow it anywhere you want to put it. We draft just under six feet, so there are plenty of routes out of here and into any depth you want."

"Let's get it out of here while the tide is still high. Plot a course into at least fifty feet of water, and I'll have the tower rigged in ten minutes."

Mongo and Gator pulled six lift bags from the lockers and stepped off the stern of the boat.

I took Pogonya by the arm. "We're going in with them, but you're just going to observe. We're rigging lift bags to each of the four corners of the tower, as well as one pair in the middle. Watch and learn, and no matter what happens, do not get underneath the tower once we lift it off the bottom."

The grin on her face was all the response I needed.

By the time she and I reached the bottom, Gator and Mongo had already rigged the first two bags at the base of the tower with enough air to hold them in place without lifting the legs from the sand. Pogonya watched as I helped rig two more lift bags to the top of the tower that was still lying on its side. It only took Gator a couple of minutes to rig the two smaller bags for stability at the center of the structure.

With all the bags in place, with a squirt of air in each, I motioned toward the surface.

Once our heads were above water, I called to Shawn. "Find us a good route yet?"

He gave the thumbs-up signal. "Ready to go, boss."

Kodiak tossed a towline rigged to a bridle at the stern of the Mark V, and Mongo caught it with one giant hand.

"Here's the plan," I said. "We'll each take one corner and get barely enough air in the bags to get this thing light. Pogo, this part's for you. As the bags get closer to the surface, the air inside will expand, and we'll have to bleed it off to keep from rocketing to the top. Slow, gentle movements. Got it?"

She said, "Wait. I'm doing this?"

"Yes, you're doing it, but I'll be right beside you. Kodiak's coming in to help."

"Okay, but I've never done anything like this."

"We all had our first time, but none of us did it in crystal-clear, eighty-five-degree water. You've got a big advantage. Just don't get underneath it. If it starts falling, or if it runs away to the surface, kick away backward and keep your eyes on the load."

"But you'll be with me, right?"

"I'll never leave your side," I said. Regardless of how she heard those words, they were my solemn vow that would endure as long as I lived.

Kodiak joined us, and we descended onto the corners of the tower. I hovered slightly above Pogonya so everyone could see me and I could see them. Once I gave the hand signal to inflate the bags, each of the three experienced divers in the water stuck their alternate air source beneath the mouth of the bag in front of them and released a short burst of air. Each bag grew and pulled tighter against the lines secured to the tower.

Pogonya got a little carried away and released a long burst of air into her bag, sending her corner climbing from the ocean floor. I reached for the exhaust line and pressed the plastic handle into her palm. She gave it a gentle pull, opening the valve at the top of the bag, and the air she'd blown in escaped.

Everybody on the mission clearly expected exactly what happened, and they all appeared confident that she'd nail it on her second attempt. I gave the inflation signal again, and she released one short blast, making her lift bag look just like everyone else's.

I swam to the center and blew just enough air into the stabilizing bags to let them do their job. Back beside Pogonya, I gave the inflation signal again. My three commandos and one trainee let another puff leave their alternate air sources into the bags, and the tower left the sand. I positioned Pogonya's hand on the release line and signaled for her to watch the other three.

As we rose, the air inside the bags expanded, and everyone vented just enough to keep the tower moving slowly to the surface without climbing out of control.

With the tops of the orange lift bags breaching the surface, I motioned for the team to ascend.

"Nice work," I said. "Now, let's top off the bags and get this thing moving before we get too much attention."

Kodiak pointed at the Mark V. "We've got a fifty-ton, eighty-foot combat vessel in a lagoon. I think we've already got everyone's attention."

We filled the bags with air to keep them on the surface, and Mongo double-checked the towline.

Twenty minutes later and almost two miles away, we reversed the process and sank the tower in eighty feet of water. Although the weather forecast was perfect, we anchored the tower to the ocean floor, ensuring it would still be there when the *Lori Danielle* arrived.

## Chapter 8
## *A Dying Beast*

Pogonya had her lobsters, but they weren't from Maine. They were from hidey holes in the shallow reef where she and I dived, poked, and prodded until we bagged our limit that afternoon.

She licked her fingers clean. "This is exactly what I was craving."

I wiped the corners of my mouth and watched her devour all three spiny lobster tails on her plate. "Good. You won them fair and square. Well, maybe not fair, but possibly square."

It had been Anya's Citation we saw approaching South Bimini Airport, and she positioned herself beside our girl and directly across the dinner table from me. "This is strange thing to say. What is fair or square about lobster?"

I pointed with my finger dripping with melted butter. "*Your* daughter cheated during our freediving competition today, but she pulled a technicality and claimed that I didn't define the rules clearly enough to declare her behavior unfair and disqualifying."

Anya said, "Good. Important part is winning. Rules are sometimes optional."

Celeste lifted a forkful of plantains. "For you, rules are always optional."

"Is same also for you," the Russian said. "We have this in common because we are women with, uh, how do you say . . . certain attributes. This is correct word, yes?"

Gator looked up. "Are you asking me? No! Absolutely not. You are not dragging me into this. I'm just trying to have dinner. In fact, I'd like to change the subject."

"Please do," I said.

He put down his fork. "What are we doing with that tower? I get that we're going to haul it aboard the *Lori Danielle* when she gets here, but then what?"

Singer said, "Patience, my boy."

Gator shook his head. "Don't start that Yoda stuff again. You're terrible at impersonations, and it's hard enough to learn the complex stuff you try to teach me without it coming out of your mouth in code."

Our sniper relented. "Okay, no more Yoda, but I'm great at impersonations. You should hear me do Tigger. 'Cause Tiggers are wonderful things."

"Please don't," Gator said. "Just tell me what we're going to do with the tower once we get it out of the water."

My phone chirped, and I wanted so badly to ignore it, but there was far too much going on for me to neglect whoever was calling. "Hello, this is Chase."

"Where do you want us?"

It took me a few seconds to realize the voice belonged to Captain Barry Sprayberry. "Hang on a minute. I'm handing you off to Shawn. He has the coordinates for you."

I tossed the phone to our SEAL, and he snagged it. After delivering the information, he threw the phone back, and I stuck it to my ear. "Here's the plan. I want to . . . Barry? Are you there?"

Shawn said, "He hung up, and he didn't sound happy."

Barry answered on the fourth ring. "I thought you'd be calling back."

"How'd you get here so fast?"

He said, "The weather improved. What's the plan?"

"First, I need you to lift a tuna tower off the bottom at the coordinates Shawn gave you. It's anchored, so don't try to snatch it up tonight. We'll go back down tomorrow morning and cut it free. We need it on deck without any more damage than it already has. We also want to preserve any welded joints, so you'll need to lift only with straps, not chains."

"Thanks for telling me how to haul something off the bottom. I'm pretty sure I can handle it."

"You're in a mood," I said.

"It's these kids you sent me. I don't know if I'll ever make sailors out of them."

"I didn't send you anybody. You interviewed them, vetted them, and hired them. I just signed the authorization."

"Exactly," he said. "You're responsible. How's it coming with the Special Boat Service guys?"

"I'll try to have some good news for you tomorrow. We're having lobster we caught this afternoon. You should join us."

He groaned. "I'm the skipper of a nearly six-hundred-foot warship masquerading as a research vessel. I don't have time for fancy dinners with my boss."

I tried not to laugh. "Suit yourself. At least send the chopper for us in an hour or so. We'll be at the airport."

Without another word, the line went dead, and I was left hoping we'd have a ride to the ship sometime before dawn.

Barbie "Gun Bunny" Brewer touched down in the Boeing Vertol an hour later, and the whole team climbed aboard. Having a chopper the Vertol's size and strength was a force multiplier for us. We could move more weight farther and faster than ever before, and we could do it under the protection of a pair of General Electric M134 Miniguns in the hands of Ronda No-H, one of the best door-gunners in the business. The gunner doubled as the CFO for our organization, but too much time behind a desk instead of a bad-guy-killing Gatling gun was torturous for her. According to her, she'd take a trigger over a ten-key any day. Everyone on the team had at least dual roles, but few compared to the dichotomy of Ronda's extremes.

We were aboard the *Lori Danielle* in minutes, and the action on the weather deck intrigued me. I wasted no time getting down there and found Captain Sprayberry with his arms folded, overseeing the operation.

"Good. You're here," he said. "You can be in charge of this goat rope."

"What are you doing?"

He grunted. "One of *your* hotshot ship handlers blasted sand all over your tower trying to hover us in place. I almost sent him overboard with a spoon and a snorkel to clean up the mess, but I was afraid I'd rip his head off if I had to look at him."

"Is there more going on than the personnel issues?" I asked.

He squared off in front of me. "It's your fault."

"What's my fault?"

He held up his hands. "I'm sorry. I shouldn't have said that. I've just got my hands full, and . . ."

"And what?" I asked. "Barry, whatever it is, we'll fix it."

He spun on a heel. "Let's just get your tower out of the water. It'll be fine."

I laid a hand on his arm. "Do you have someone on the bridge you trust right now?"

He nodded. "The XO has the watch. He's pretty much all I've got left."

"I'm going to put Mongo and Shawn on this detail, and you and I are going to have a talk."

He shook me off. "You've got a lot going on. My stuff is minor compared to what you're dealing with. I'm sorry. I shouldn't have said anything."

I ignored whatever he said and called Mongo and our SEAL on deck. When they showed up, I said, "One of the new crew got a little overzealous with the Azipods and dusted up our tower. I want the two of you to manage the cleanup while the captain and I take care of some business."

Mongo said, "No problem, but while we're on it, I don't see any reason to wait until daylight to haul it up. We can have the rig on deck in less than an hour. We're in eighty feet of water. It's not like we're raising the *Titanic*."

Barry's mention of his trusted executive officer reminded me how valuable Mongo was to our operation. In my absence, he could do almost anything I could do, but he'd do most things better. He didn't have my flying skills, but outside of that, I'd never be his superior.

The captain's cabin aboard the revamped *Lori Danielle* was far roomier and more luxurious than it had been before the refit, but it still wasn't an executive suite.

I settled onto the same couch he had when we met. "All right, the gloves are off. Let's hear it. What's going on?"

He poured two cups of coffee that may have qualified as the best brew on the ocean and held one toward me.

I accepted and took my first sip. "How do you find such amazing coffee?"

"When a man spends his life at sea, he makes a few connections. Some of mine just happen to be in parts of the world that produce some darned good coffee beans."

I raised my mug. "Here's to such places."

He raised his in return. "And to the people of those places."

I sat in silence, sipping my coffee and waiting for him to throw the first punch.

It finally came.

"Two years is a long time, Chase. Men get antsy. Especially good men who are hungry to do more than sit in one spot in the middle of the ocean while some scientist studies a pimple on a fish's butt."

"I get it," I said. "And you're right. It is my fault. When Penny was murdered, I fell apart, and I expected the rest of the world to carry on without me. I neglected everybody and everything in my life. Now, you're paying the price for my neglect, and I'm sorry."

He stared into his mug. "They didn't just leave me. They left us, Chase. A crew like the one I had needs to get shot at, and they need to shoot back. They don't need to sit on their hands on a research tub."

I planted my cup on the corner of his desk. "Why did you stay?"

He sighed. "What am I supposed to do? Go run a freighter on the Great Lakes or push barges somewhere? This is my boat. I helped design her. She's part of me, but I know how those boys felt. You know I hate research work, but I love this ship. And I love working for you."

"You don't work *for* me, Barry. We're colleagues, you and me, and I want you to know how much your loyalty means to me."

He crossed his legs. "Loyalty's one thing, but this ship turned soft. She's not ready for a fight. Most of the crew have never even seen a real fight yet. I've got a bunch of merchant marines who could probably do just fine on a cruise ship or a freighter, but that ain't what the *Lori Danielle* is. She's a goddess of war, Chase, and you're using her to take pretty pictures of fish and scrape microscopic organisms from a reef."

"You're right. Let's fix it. Do you still have contact with any of the old crew?"

He nodded. "Most of them, but getting them to come back won't be easy."

"Maybe not," I said, "but this is a billion-dollar operation. I'll give you whatever you need to get them back. If they won't come, we'll pillage the Navy for what you need."

"That's a great thought, Chase, but it's not that easy."

I stood and poured myself a second cup of coffee. "It's a blank check, Barry. I need you and this ship ready to fight. I'll give you the tools to get her there, and when you do, I promise to give you plenty of opportunities to let the goddess draw her sword."

"Were you serious about the Brits? The SBS boys?"

"Absolutely, and I'll put you on the phone with some of them tomorrow."

He didn't stand, but I'd said all I could, so I left him sitting behind his desk with steam still rising from his mug.

My boots hit the weather deck only seconds after the crane operator gently positioned the tuna tower onto wooden dunnage on the steel deck. The structure lay on its side with two mangled legs curling upward like the talons of a beast that had given its life in a desperate fight for survival. I couldn't let my organization become such a defeated beast. We didn't fight from the flats of our backs, and we certainly weren't going to start that night.

## Chapter 9
## *Better Left Alone*

Dawn broke over Bimini a few hours after the sun showed her face on the Queen's realm across the Atlantic, and I was determined to keep my word to the captain.

The combat information center aboard the *Lori Danielle* was essentially the shipboard version of the Bonaventure op center. From within its high-security confines, I probably could've had most world leaders—or at least their second-in-command—on the phone in minutes from anywhere in the world, but I couldn't do it alone. I needed the last piece of the puzzle that made up our team, and thankfully, she would be on deck soon.

Anya and Gator took off from South Bimini half an hour before I rolled out of my rack, and they'd be back on the island with Skipper, our analyst, by the time I'd had breakfast and a shower.

* * *

I was almost correct. A morning thunderstorm hanging over St. Marys slowed the trip for Anya and Gator, but Skipper and I stepped through the door of the CIC ninety minutes later.

"Let's give our old chap, Captain James Millgood, a ring, if you please."

Skipper rolled her eyes. "You're not going to keep doing that horrible British accent, are you? If so, you're on your own."

"Okay, I'll behave."

She nestled onto her perch and made the call. When the line finally connected, a gruff voice said, "Oi."

"Captain Millgood? This is Chase Fulton from the States."

He hesitated long enough for me to question whether Skipper had dialed the right number, but finally, he said, "Ah, Chase! How're you getting on, mate?"

"I'm doing all right, Captain. How are things across the pond?"

"Dreadful," he said. "I'm a pensioner now and bored outta me skull. Do tell me you're calling to offer me some work. I can plant only so many flowers. I need a proper job."

"You don't happen to have a license to run a thirty-thousand-ton vessel, do you?"

"Got a stack o' licenses half a meter high, I do. Why do you ask?"

"Remember the *Lori Danielle*?"

"How could I forget her? A grand ol' girl, she is."

I said, "She needs some officers—preferably some salty ones who aren't afraid of a fight."

"You don't say. What about that bloke Sprayberry? He's still her master, yeah?"

"He is, but he's not very happy with me at the moment. I let him and the ship get conscripted into way too much research work and not enough broadside fights. Most of the good officers took jobs on boats with a little more action."

He groaned. "Likes to run out the guns and have a go, does he?"

"You might say that."

He chuckled. "So, you're looking for a research vessel crew?"

"No! That's the problem. We're putting the ship back in the shooting business, and the research crew we have aren't gunfighters. We need hardened seamen who don't mind a few nine-pounders in the rigging."

"Ah, gotcha. I ain't your man, but I think I know a few good chaps who might be spot on for the bill. The crown and parliament cut the

Navy's budget and *offered* early pensions. It weren't really no offer. It were more like orders, but being Brits, they were polite about it."

I said, "Are you telling me there's a pool of British naval officers looking for work?"

"Yeah, mate, exactly. But don't forget about us swimmers. We could use the work, too—especially me and Dingo. Remember him?"

"Who could forget Dingo?" I said. "I'll take you and a dozen just like him if you've got 'em."

"You ain't pullin' my leg, are you? Can you really put us to work?"

"I can't promise you a spot on the ground. You know my team from the op we did together, so you know we're well stocked for soldiers. I can put you on the ship, though. There's always security work on board. As I said, we're putting the ship back in the fight. That means we'll ruffle some feathers, and you and your men are hard to beat when lead starts flying."

"We'll take it," he said. "How many can you use?"

I asked, "Special Boat Service swimmers?"

"Yeah."

"How many you got?"

"Half a dozen, give or take. And I'll get you a roster of good officers when you're ready."

"We're ready now," I said. "How soon can you put that list together?"

"I'll get on it straightaway. Say three, maybe four hours. How's that sound?"

I said, "I'm going to leave you with Skipper. She'll work out the details with you and schedule a follow-up call. We'll talk again later today. For now, I've got a sniper to hunt down."

"Some blokes have all the luck," he said. "Talk soon."

I left Skipper on the phone with Captain Millgood and jogged for the navigation bridge.

Without requesting permission, I barged through the hatch and asked, "How would you feel about some British naval officers?"

Barry looked up from his mug. "They're not greenhorns, are they?"

I told him the story of the defense spending cuts that Captain Millgood described, and he said, "I heard about that. What time can they be here?"

I laughed. "You may want to interview them and take a look at their credentials before we put them on an airplane."

He said, "They're British naval officers, right?"

"According to Millgood, they are."

"So, what time can they be here?"

I helped myself to a cup of his world-famous coffee. "Get with Skipper. She's on the phone with Millgood now, and she'll have everything you need."

He held out his cup for a refill, and I obliged. "Hire who you need, Barry. If we don't have enough money, we'll get it."

He stood and growled at a junior officer. "Hey, you. You've got the bridge. Don't move the ship. Don't touch anything. Don't even change the temperature on the thermostat. I'll be back."

The young man said, "I have the bridge."

Barry followed me through the hatch and said, "Did you hear that? That snot-nosed little maritime academy grad didn't even call me sir when I gave him the ship."

He headed for the CIC, and I assembled our team on the weather deck.

"Get that tuna tower aboard the Vertol, and let's put it ashore. I wanna show it to a few fishermen."

Mongo said, "If we cut off one welded joint, we could walk it around the docks a lot easier than we could parade a bunch of fishermen over to see the whole thing."

"I like it," I said. "Have you inspected the welds?"

"Yes, it's good work and consistent at every joint. The same fabricator obviously did it all."

"In that case, photograph the whole thing while it's still in one piece, then cut out four joints small enough to carry by hand. We'll split up and hopefully make short work of finding somebody who recognizes the craftsmanship."

An hour later, we were ashore and divided into four teams. Singer and Gator took the first piece and headed for the Marina at Port Royal. Kodiak and Shawn took their section to Bimini Big Game Club Resort and Marina. Mongo and Anya headed up north to Resorts World Bimini Beach. And Pogonya and I made our way to Fisherman's Village.

Our borrowed golf cart turned out to be perfect transportation on the island, and Pogonya made a good chauffeur.

"I really love it here," she said.

"Me, too. Maybe we should spend more time on the island."

"I love that idea, but could you start by telling me exactly what we're doing?"

"Sure. We're going to show this piece of metal and the pictures of the tuna tower to some fishermen in the marina and ask if they recognize the work. With any luck, someone will know who built it, and we'll have our first POI."

"POI?" she asked.

"Person of interest. Whoever built this tower built it for the sniper. It's made of a type of metal that would never be used on an actual boat. It's galvanized instead of stainless or aluminum. That kind of metal can't survive in this saltwater environment."

She said, "That was the purpose, I guess. They wanted it to rot out there."

"Exactly."

"Why are you including me in this?"

I threw my arm around her. "It's the family business."

She laughed. "I don't buy it. You're playing chaperone so I don't 'torture' the boys on the beach, aren't you?"

"Well, maybe a little of that, too, but I do want you to learn what we do . . . at least the safe parts."

"And this is safe?" she asked.

"I don't anticipate anyone shooting at us today."

"That's a bonus."

We pulled into Fisherman's Village, and Pogonya reached for the chunk of metal.

I stopped her. "Not yet. Let's take a walk first."

We strolled down the floating docks, nonchalantly inspecting boat towers and looking for anything that resembled the shape of our sniper's tower.

Back at the golf cart, I said, "Tell me what you saw."

She shrugged. "A bunch of boats with a bunch of towers that all pretty much looked the same."

"That's what I saw, too."

I checked in with the three other teams, and none of them had made any real progress either.

"I've got an idea," Pogonya said. She tossed her Georgia Bulldogs cap onto the seat, shook out her chestnut ponytail, and pulled off her T-shirt. The day's bikini top still didn't qualify as dad-approved, but she'd obviously learned a thing or two from her mother about getting what she wanted.

Holding the hunk of metal, and her blue eyes sparkling, she said, "Let me do the talking."

The father in me hated the approach, but the operator approved.

Pogonya got a lot of attention, and nobody refused to talk with her about the tower. We didn't hit pay dirt, though, until we made it to the end of the third row of boats, where a white-haired gentleman sat in his fighting chair, bare feet propped on the transom of a sportfisher that had obviously seen a lot of water.

"Hey, I'm Pogo," my newest deputy began.

The old man obviously wasn't impressed. "You can put your clothes back on, missy, but let me take a look at that metal you've got there."

The look on her face said she wasn't pleased to learn that her charms weren't universal, but she handed the tubing to the old fisherman. He took it in a weathered hand, pulled a pair of filthy glasses from a drink holder on the side of his chair, and slid them up the bridge of his nose.

Pogonya squirmed beside me, and I passed her a twenty. "Run up to the office and grab us a couple of drinks."

The dismissal clearly wasn't what she wanted to hear, but it appeared she understood.

With her gone, the old man said, "I wondered how long it would take for somebody to come asking around about this thing."

"What do you know about it?" I asked.

"You're an American."

I offered my hand. "Yes, sir. My name is Chase."

He ignored me and continued inspecting the welded metal tubing. "Billy Goddard."

"It's nice to meet you, Mr. Goddard."

He shook his head. "I ain't him. Billy Goddard done this work. Why do you reckon he made it out of galvanized steel?"

I said, "Maybe he was testing out a new design and wanted to see how it came together before he spent a bunch of money on stainless steel."

The old man huffed. "You a cop?"

I slowly shook my head. "No, sir. I'm just trying to help a friend."

"Is your friend a cop?"

I made a judgment call. "No, sir. My friend is Dominic Fontana."

The man closed one eye against the sun and glared at me with the other. "Billy Goddard is a drunk, but he's a good fabricator and a decent diesel mechanic. Don't let him near that daughter of yours, but you'll find him at Downrigger most every night. Especially nights when he gets paid."

"What's Downrigger?"

He let out a snort. "Is Dominic alive?"

"For now," I said. "I didn't catch your name."

He handed the tubing back to me. "Good luck to you, son. Be careful. Some stuff is better left to the cops, and *some* is better left alone."

## Chapter 10
### *Only One Heart*

There was no doubt the conversation with the fisherman had reached its end, so I made no further attempt to gather information.

Pogonya met me on her way out of the marina store and said, "That was quick."

"Yes, but productive. I got a name and a location, so you can put your T-shirt back on."

She stuck a bottle of water toward me and shook her head. "We're on a tropical island, Pops. Everybody wears bikinis."

"*Sub*tropical. Let's go."

As she drove us south on the Queen's Highway toward the ferry terminal, I made a conference call to the rest of the team. "Wrap it up, guys. We've got what we need for this morning, but tonight's going to get interesting."

It took just over an hour for everyone to recover to the ship, and we filled the CIC.

"I take it everybody struck out. Am I right?"

Anya said, "We have name. Two people told to us person named Billy Goddard probably built tower. They said it looks like his work."

"Pogo and I got the same," I said, "but we scored a location to go along with it. Apparently, Billy likes to have a drink or twelve at a place called Downrigger when the workday's done."

Anya said, "If we are going to grab him, it would be nice to know what he looks like and if he has friends who might try to stop us."

"Way ahead of you," Skipper blurted out. "Here's your boy Billy."

She brought up a driver's license photo on the primary monitor, and Billy looked a lot like the picture my imagination had already drawn.

Skipper said, "Forty-four years old, divorced four times, and the address on his license doesn't seem to exist. It may actually be a boat slip. I'm not sure."

"Sounds like a swell guy," Kodiak said. "Maybe you should check for charitable giving. I bet he's quite the philanthropist."

"Look at you using big words that you don't understand," Skipper said. "He's supposed to be paying a lot of child support, but based on what I can find, he's not great at keeping up his end of the bargain."

"Any violent history?" Mongo asked.

Skipper typed furiously. "Checking now . . . Two domestic violence charges. One dropped, and the other one stuck. He did ninety days, but that was over ten years ago. It looks like he's been a pretty good boy since then. Other than a D and D, and some minor traffic stuff, I can't find any reason to be afraid of him. He does have a drug bust, but I can't find much about it."

"Associates?" I asked.

Keys clicked, and the computer hummed. "Doing that now."

We waited as she worked, and Skipper finally said, "His boys aren't so nice. Based on cell phone history, he's got four or five guys he spends most of his time with after hours. One is a mystery, but four of them are rough characters."

The screen filled with five pictures of guys who definitely looked like they'd hang out together, but probably not at church functions.

The analyst said, "If you'll give me half an hour, I'll have all of their cell phones tracked so we'll know who's joining him at Downrigger."

"I'll never know how you do it," I said.

She grinned. "You don't have to know. You just have to keep writing me a check every month."

"Count on it."

"I do. Oh, and Downrigger looks like quite the swinging joint. There were forty-nine arrests for bar fights on the island last month. Thirty-six of them were at Downrigger."

Shawn rubbed his palms together. "Sounds like my kind of place. I can't wait."

Mongo said, "I hate to be the voice or reason, but do you think we should let Chief Inspector Bellefonte know we're planning to pay Billy Goddard a visit?"

"I've already thought about that," I said, "and I want to wait. Since I'm not in the know about how Bahamians interrogate persons of interest, it's probably best if we chat with Billy off the record before we involve the police."

Mongo nodded once, and we moved on.

Skipper said, "Here's a sketch of the floor plan and aerial view of Downrigger. It looks like double doors up front, with one big delivery door into the kitchen, and what was probably once an emergency exit on the opposite wall."

"Where'd you get the floor plan?" I asked.

"Yeah, about that. It's all I could find from an accident report twelve years ago when they had a fire. It's not much, but it's better than going in completely blind."

"What time do they open?" Shawn asked. "If we need a little recon done, I could go for a cold one before the sun goes down."

Anya hopped to her feet. "I will go also with you."

"Sure, go," I said. "Try to draw something a little better than that chicken scratch Skipper dug up."

Celeste said, "There's no need to draw anything. I had Skipper load an app I designed onto all of your phones. Just pretend to be on the phone, and make a three-sixty. The camera will record and measure the room. Walk around all you want—you can't overload it with data. The more the better, but it doesn't require much if you get pushed for time. The icon looks like a pencil and a triangle."

As if Pavlov had rung his bell, everybody in the room grabbed their phones, and the room filled with oohs and aahs.

Skipper, the only one not looking at her phone, was on a call. "What time do you open and close today?" A few seconds later, she said, "Thanks. See ya tonight." She ended the call. "They opened an hour ago, and they don't have an official closing time."

I said, "The plan is to catch Billy on his way in or out of Downrigger and invite him to have a little chat with us."

"Are we bringing him to the ship?" Gator asked.

"I'd rather not. Let's just take him for a ride in the RHIB. He's a boat guy. We'll make him feel right at home."

We had four rigid-hull inflatable boats aboard the *Lori Danielle*, two of which were large enough to carry the entire team, as well as our guest of honor.

"Are you going to interrogate him?" Skipper asked.

I said, "I'm certainly not going to let your husband do it. He'd set him on fire and try to put him out with gasoline. Maybe a more subtle approach would be best."

Anya beamed. "I can be subtle."

I motioned for the door. "Take your little friend, the SEAL, and scope out Downrigger. I'll handle everything else."

She pouted. "I will be close if you need maybe assistant."

"I'll keep that in mind," I said. "Let's check on Dominic."

Almost before I could finish the sentence, Skipper had Clark's weary face on the screen.

"How's your dad?" I asked.

"He's in surgery now. Is Anya there?"

She stepped back through the hatch at the sound of her name. "Yes, I am here."

Clark said, "Thanks again for going to get Mom. It means a lot to all of us. We really appreciate it."

Anya shrugged. "Is what family does."

"I know," Clark said, "but it was really nice of you."

"You are welcome. And I will take her back to Colorado when Dominic is on feet and again chasing girls who could be his granddaughters."

Clark's crooked smile made its first appearance of the conversation. "We'll see how the surgery goes." He checked his watch. "He's been in there almost three hours, and the surgeon said to expect four."

"Do you need anything?" I asked.

He scowled. "Yeah, College Boy. I need, in my hands, the head of the guy who pulled the trigger. Think you can make that happen?"

"I'm doing my best."

It took a few minutes to bring Clark up to speed on what we learned, and he said, "That's pretty elaborate. What do you make of it?"

I shrugged. "We'll know more tonight after we talk to Billy Goddard, but I'm with you. They went to a lot of work to hit one guy. They could've poisoned his cocktail or stuck a needle in him on the island. I can't come up with any logical reason they'd work so hard to put a Russian-made bullet in him from offshore."

"It's a message," he said.

"What's the message?"

He shook his head. "Somebody knows . . . Keep me posted."

"We will, and you do the same. Make sure your mom knows she gets absolutely anything she wants or needs. Don't let her sleep in a hospital chair."

Clark laughed. "You try telling Wanda Johnson she has to leave the hospital. I'm scared of that woman."

"That woman is your mother, and you should make sure she sleeps in a good bed."

"I know who she is, and that's part of the reason I'm scared of her. She'll sleep where she chooses, but I'll tell her you said she needs to do what she's told."

"Don't you dare tell her that," I said. "I'm afraid of her, too."

Clark's image on the screen jerked and was promptly replaced by the well-coiffed Wanda Jean Johnson. "Are you boys talkin' about me?"

I straightened. "Yes, ma'am. I was just telling your son how much I wanted to make sure you slept comfortably and didn't try to camp out in the hospital."

"Aren't you precious?" Wanda said. "I've already arranged for a second hospital bed in Dom's room. I'll be just fine, darling. I've got a suite at the Aurora across the street, where I can freshen up, but in the condition he's in, I can't leave that man all by himself in that room. He needs me there."

"Whatever you say," I said. "Just know that we'll take care of whatever you need."

"You're sweet, but it's all taken care of. Besides, I can stay at Mud Pie's house if push comes to shove."

I lost my composure, and it took longer than it should've for me to stop laughing. "I almost forgot about you calling Clark Mud Pie. I needed that. Thank you!"

Wanda said, "Oh, here comes the doctor."

Clark reclaimed the phone. "I'm going to turn off the camera, but I'll leave the speaker on."

The screen went dark, and a slightly Indian-accented feminine voice came through the speakers. "There was more damage than we originally believed based on the MRI, but the surgery went well. We saved about sixty percent of his lung, maybe a little less, but that doesn't mean he will be running the Miami Marathon anytime soon."

Wanda said, "But he's going to be all right?"

"Yes, he should recover nicely, but he *is* a man of, shall we say, a certain age. His recovery will be slightly slower than he might want, and he probably won't feel like walking eighteen holes very soon."

Wanda huffed. "Let me tell you, that man prefers eighteen-year-olds to eighteen holes."

The surgeon failed to stifle a chuckle. "Well, be that as it may, he will have to slow down a little. Maybe keeping him from wandering will be a bit easier now."

Wanda let out a guffaw. "Sweetie, that man will find a way to pinch a pretty girl on her butt at his own funeral. We've been divorced almost as long as I've been alive, but I still love him. I just can't help it."

The surgeon said, "Family dynamics are always interesting. Your husband—or former husband—will be in recovery for a couple of hours, but if all goes well, he will be back in his room after that."

I whispered to Skipper, "Cut the call. I'll text Clark."

Just as our meeting was breaking up, Captain Sprayberry stepped into the CIC. "Oh, sorry. I can come back."

I said, "No, no. Come on in. We're finished."

He closed the door behind him. "Have you heard from Clark?"

I caught Barry up and asked, "What brings you up here?"

"Job interviews using something called Skype."

Skipper sighed. "It's not really Skype. That's just what I called it. It'll be a secure satellite video link. Just think of it as FaceTime."

Barry leaned toward me. "I don't know what that means, either."

We surrendered the room to the captain so he could hire a new set of officers that both he and the ship deserved.

Every meal aboard the *Lori Danielle* was better than most things we could've found ashore, and lunch was no exception. We ate like a big family, and Singer prayed the most beautiful prayer of thanks for Dominic's successful surgery, bringing a tear to every eye in the room.

When our recon team made their triumphant return, Skipper turned the footage from the app on Shawn's phone into a three-dimensional rendering of the inside of Downrigger bar.

I studied every nook and cranny. "It's almost like it was built for an extraction."

"Are you planning to pull him out?" Shawn asked.

"Only if we have to. I'd much rather take him by the arm and lead him to the boat. We don't want to cause a scene."

Skipper said, "I have three of the five phones under surveillance, but I can't find Billy's or the other guy's. It's weird. I can't even find the other guy's name."

"Stay on it," I said. "You'll find them. Have you tried calling Billy's phone?"

She cocked her head. "Really? Oh, gee . . . Why didn't silly ol' me think of that? Yes, of course, I tried calling his phone. It went straight to voicemail. And no, I didn't leave a message."

I changed the subject. "How did the interviews go?"

"From the sound of it, we're getting a whole new flock of officers."

"Flock?"

She said, "Yeah, I don't know what a group of officers is called, but we're getting one."

I left the CIC and headed for my cabin, but Anya stopped me in the corridor. "I want to tell to you something."

"Okay, let's go to my place. I've got almost two hundred square feet. It's practically a palace."

She sighed. "Yes, I know this. I have been inside your cabin many times, but mine is bigger. Perhaps we should go there instead. I can make tea."

"Yours is bigger? And you've got a teapot? I need to talk to whoever's in charge of accommodations on this ship. I need an upgrade."

Anya made tea, and we sat on the edge of her bed.

I said, "Your place is a little bigger than mine, but I have a much better porthole."

She blew across the surface of her steaming tea. "But maybe you would rather see what is inside this room instead of what is outside."

"Are you flirting with me, Ms. Burinkova?"

"You are father of my child. I can flirt with you whenever I want."

I sipped my tea. "Yes, you are, and yes, you can. What did you want to tell me?"

"Did you hear on video telephone call how Wanda still loves Dominic?"

"Yes, I heard. It's kind of sad when you think about it. She still loves him after everything he put her through for all those years. She's a beautiful—and wealthy—woman. She could've had her choice of men."

Anya said, "Dominic has only one heart. He never had one of his own, so Wanda gave to him hers many years ago. When a woman does this for a man she truly loves, she never takes it back. Trust me. I know exactly how that feels."

# Chapter 11
## *Billy Boy*

With the team assembled in the CIC, Skipper kicked off the briefing. "If you'll take a look overhead, you'll see the most recent satellite imagery of Downrigger and the surrounding area. It's a few days old, but it doesn't matter. I'll have a pair of drones airborne when we go hot tonight. As you can see, ingress and egress shouldn't be challenging in the RHIB. The place sits right on the water."

Shawn squinted and studied the monitor. "That looks like pretty good tree cover to the south. That would make a nice spot to avoid being seen from the back of the bar or the street."

"I like it," I said. "The less attention we can garner, the better. I want this to be an in-and-out operation, nothing ugly."

"That's no fun," Kodiak grumbled. "Ugly is what we do best."

I couldn't disagree with him, but I said, "We'll get to that part, I promise. Let's just bring our boy on board nice and gently, then see how hard he wants to be pushed."

Mongo asked, "Any luck on pinging Billy's cell?"

Skipper said, "Some. I got a hit earlier, but it wasn't fresh. It was the last time a cell tower pinged the phone. I plotted it on the graphic on monitor two."

"When was the ping?" Mongo asked.

"Yesterday afternoon, and it only lasted a few minutes. No calls or texts since then."

I asked, "Are there any security cameras at Downrigger?"

Shawn said, "Not hardly. The place barely has electricity. It's a real dive."

Anya said, "There are security cameras on building across street, and angles are maybe wide enough to capture some of front of Downrigger. There is electric lock on delivery door into kitchen, but is broken. Door was tied with small piece of rope over hook when we were there."

I chuckled. "Sounds like a real five-star establishment."

"What if he doesn't show up?" Singer asked.

I said, "Then we'll pick up his buddies and ask them nicely to take us to him. That'll be plan B. Plan A is to nab Billy Goddard and get him offshore. We've done this a thousand times, but don't get lazy. The Bahamians frown on firearms, so we'll likely be the only ones with bullets inside tonight. That doesn't mean there won't be knives and fishermen looking for a fight. I'd rather get out of there empty-handed than wearing handcuffs in the back of Inspector Belafonte's car."

Skipper said, "Drones are airborne with four hours of battery life. I have two more waiting in the wings if the op runs long. What else do you need from me?"

No one spoke up, so I said, "Keep us updated on Billy's whereabouts if his phone comes back to life. How about his buddies? Are you tracking them?"

"Oh, yeah," she said. "Three of them are already inside and probably on their fifth round. All of their pictures are on your phones and tablets, but as one final reminder, they're bigger than life on the monitors."

We memorized their faces, and I said, "Singer and Gator, get into position. I'll take Shawn and Anya with me in the RHIB, as well as inside Downrigger. Kodiak and Mongo, I want you on the doors with the vehicle ready in case this thing turns into a car chase. Questions?"

Heads shook, and I continued. "When we grab him, I want everybody to collapse on the RHIB. We'll exfil as a unit and recover the vehicle later."

Pogonya spoke for the first time. "I can bring the Suburban back on the ferry so it's not left behind."

I said, "No. You're in the CIC with Skipper. I don't want you anywhere near this thing."

Anya's look made me question my hasty decision, but I didn't waver. I was okay with our daughter tagging along when there was no danger of a fight, but she'd seen one snatch-and-grab on the streets of Pensacola that left her shaking in her boots. She, or maybe I, wasn't ready for another night like that for her.

Pogonya said, "Yes, sir."

Gator, Singer, Kodiak, and Mongo took off in the helo while Anya, Shawn, and I stepped into the RHIB. I watched the Vertol climb into the sky and descend almost immediately for the airport where our Suburban waited to take our two snipers and a little muscle across the channel on the ferry. Although Gator and Singer wouldn't spend their evening on overwatch behind long-range rifles, their eyes were still crucial for observing the world as only snipers can.

The crane operator lowered us over the port side and deposited us onto the placid Atlantic. I cast off the lines, and Shawn took the helm. We were motoring away from the *Lori Danielle* at the same time Gun Bunny climbed off the airport in the helo. All of the pieces were falling into place, but something deep in my gut felt like a fist of razors.

"CIC, Sierra One."

Skipper answered on the open-channel comms. "Go for CIC."

"Verify tracking all Sierra elements."

Instead of our analyst answering, Pogonya's voice filled my ear. "Tracking all Sierra elements. Drones are in position, and video is live."

I tried to hide the pride in my voice with professionalism. "Roger. Sierra Five and Six, report in position."

Singer said, "Sierra Six, roger. We're on the ferry and should be ashore in two minutes."

Shawn piloted the RHIB like an artist. Tiny adjustments to the throttles kept the ride smooth and fast, while his hand on the wheel kept the bow exactly where he wanted it to be.

We rounded the southern tip of the island and turned north. The shallow water was alive with bioluminescence as if the aurora borealis had traversed a quarter of the globe and gone aquatic. Streaks of green wafted across the flats like ancient ghosts haunting the shallows and dancing their immortal ballet beneath our hull. That's exactly how I wanted our night to play out. We couldn't be invisible, so I wanted my team to move with the grace of the wind and disappear into the sea just like the phosphorescent glow playing its primordial rhythm just beneath the surface.

"Sierra One, Sierra Six."

"Go for One," I said.

Singer's confident baritone said, "Five and Six are in position."

"Roger. Sierra Two and Four, say status."

Mongo said, "Sierra Two is in position on the back door."

Kodiak groaned. "Four is in the slot, and all's quiet on the eastern front except for some miniature street party half a block north. The front door of the bar is blocked by a black work truck, but there's three feet on either side."

I said, "Roger. We're thirty seconds out."

Mongo met us beneath a clump of mangroves and tied the bowline to a winding tree trunk.

"Keep one eye on the boat and one on the back door," I said.

Mongo said, "Let me know if he bolts, and I'll snatch him coming through the door."

Shawn, Anya, and I rounded the weathered building and slipped in through the front door. It took several seconds for my eyes to adjust to the darkness inside the bar after having been on the well-lit street where Kodiak's street party was still thumping.

"We're in," I said.

Skipper reclaimed the comms. "Roger. Still nothing on Billy's cell phone. Do you see him in there?"

"Not yet," I said, "but two of his buddies are at the end of the bar."

Anya said, "I am looking for number three. You said he was here, yes?"

Skipper said, "Affirmative. All three of their cell phones are still showing active inside the bar."

Shawn moved to the short hallway leading to the bathroom and kitchen to get a fresh angle on the room, while Anya and I split up and took separate corners.

We studied the room, measuring every face against the pictures Skipper had shown us, but Billy Goddard's face wasn't in the crowd.

Singer said, "Possible primary moving to the front door. He rode up on a bicycle. I can't positively ID him, but give him a look."

Gator said, "I've got a little better angle. I don't think it's our guy, but Sierra Six is right—he's worth a look."

"I have him in front door," Anya said. "Is maybe him. I cannot be certain."

Skipper said, "How can you not be certain? I showed you his picture."

I said, "Stand by. I've got him, too, and he's moving to the bar. Give me his stats again."

Skipper said, "Five-ten, one sixty-five, brown hair and eyes."

"This guy's closer to six feet and heavier," I said.

"Our data is from his driver's license, so it could be a couple years old," Skipper said.

I stepped behind him a few feet and followed him toward the bar. He leaned between the two friends and bumped fists before a beer landed on the bar in front of the guy I was quickly coming to believe was our target.

The three men talked and drank, but what they did next concerned me. Guy number one turned to face the front door, then leaned back against the bar while number two maneuvered to keep the back door in sight.

"This doesn't look good," I said. "I think Billy knows he's got a tail."

"So, you think it's him?" Skipper asked.

"It's him," I said. "He's wearing boots. That explains the extra height."

Shawn made a sidestep maneuver and hip-checked a tall, skinny man coming from the bathroom hard enough to put him into the wall. The ploy worked. Guy number one beside Billy moved toward Shawn and his adversary.

"Nice work," I said. "I'm cutting Billy from the herd. Anya, take the third guy watching the front door."

Shawn said, "I'll clear a path out the back. Come to Daddy."

As Anya and I closed on the bar simultaneously, I raised a hand and yelled, "Hey, buddy. Can I get a beer?" Continuing forward, I extended my arm between Billy and his buddy to his right.

Anya stepped in front of the man and put a hand on the center of his chest. "Hey. I'm Anna. Let's dance." Her Russian accent was gone, but her allure was not.

The man said, "This ain't a dance club, sweetheart."

Anya stepped closer. "So, let's go someplace where we *can* dance."

The man turned, apparently to check on Billy, but I was blocking his line of sight. The momentary glance away was enough time for Anya to deliver a blindingly fast shot to his solar plexus, sending him melting to the floor. The darkness and noise in the bar were enough to let the man slump at the foot of the bar without anyone reacting, and Billy took his first sip of beer without realizing what was happening just a few feet behind and beside him.

I peered toward the hallway to see Shawn grinning, backing up, and motioning for the bigger man to keep coming. The tall man who'd "accidentally" stumbled into the wall beside our SEAL turned to join the party.

I slid a twenty onto the bar beside my target's beer and said, "Let's go for a walk, Billy. We need to have a chat. Don't do anything stupid like your friends."

He stiffened, and I sent a knee shot into the back of his leg hard enough to pin him to the bar. After letting out a hard groan, he looked around me and saw his buddy on the floor. Realization overtook him, and he gripped his beer bottle.

"Pick up that bottle, Billy, and it becomes part of your internal anatomy. Now, walk."

He didn't heed my warning, and Anya made him pay. As he squeezed the bottle and lifted it from the wooden bar, with my head as a target, the Russian's favorite fighting knife came to rest against Billy Goddard's wristbone.

"Feel free to keep resisting," I said, "but I can't promise you'll get to keep your right hand."

He spread his fingers, releasing the bottle as blood trickled down the back of his hand, and his eyes shot toward the front door.

"That's a bad plan, too," I said. "We're not here to hurt you. We just want to talk. But if you want to run or play rough, I've got three men out front and two in the back. In case you haven't put it together yet, the good-looking blonde with the knife is mine, too."

Of fight or flight, Billy still had the latter in his eyes, and for an instant, I almost let him run. Kodiak deserved to have a little fun out front, but the number of people on the street changed my mind.

The second that Billy bolted for the door, I landed a sidekick just below his knee, bending his left leg unnaturally and sending him toward the floor. I caught an arm, and Anya grabbed his belt on the opposite side, keeping him on his feet.

The tip of her blade landed in his armpit, and Anya's accent returned as she gave him the warning that sent chills down my spine every time I heard it. "Keep walking, or I will gut you like pig."

Suddenly, Billy Goddard was the most compliant subject I'd ever escorted through a door.

# Chapter 12
## *You People*

Anya and I cleared the back door of Downrigger with Billy Goddard between us, and Mongo looked like a statue of some Greek god on the crushed shell parking lot behind the bar. He had one knee planted solidly on the first man's neck, pressing him into the ground, and he had the second guy's arm twisted so far between his shoulder blades, it looked as if his arm might pop off at any moment. The giant gave me a wink. "You good?"

"Oh, we're fine, but you seem to have your hands full."

He shrugged. "Not at all. The three of us reached an agreement. You might even call it a covenant. They're going to behave, and I'm going to let them live."

"Sounds like they're getting the good end of that deal," I said as we kept moving toward the waiting RHIB.

Shawn waited at the helm of the boat, and I gave the order, "All Sierra elements collapse to the exfil point."

A little more pressure beneath Mongo's knee sent guy number one into dreamland just before the big man wrapped both arms around the second man's head and neck, singing him to sleep right beside his buddy.

Sixty seconds later, Shawn crushed the throttles, and the overpowered RHIB leapt onto plane, rocketing across the dead calm water to the southwest.

Our detainee wrestled against the flex-cuffs Anya slipped onto his wrists, and he made his first protest after leaving dry ground. "You've got the wrong guy. I'm not Billy!"

"Sure, you're not," I said. "That'd be my story, too. Just lie still, and this'll all be over before you know it."

"No! Please don't kill me. Please!"

"Relax," I said. "Nobody's going to kill you. We just need some answers. Now, shut up and be still. We'll chat when we get where we're going."

He jerked and bucked against his restraints and my boot, so I gave him one last opportunity for comfort. "Calm down, or I'll snap your spine. Your choice."

I pressed my bootheel a little deeper into the flesh of his back, and he suddenly became the same, compliant Billy we'd frog-marched from the bar.

"Okay! Okay! Just tell me what you want."

"I already told you," I said. "Shut up and lie still."

He obeyed, and we shot across the water at fifty knots beneath a moonless sky speckled with countless stars. Although my psychological education should've explained it, I'd never understand why the heavens beckoned to me with such a siren's call, even in moments like those. I should've been focused on Billy Goddard beneath my heel, but my mind and eyes couldn't be pried from the limitless dome of creation overhead.

Seven miles offshore and less than half a mile from our mothership, Shawn cut the throttles and let us drift on the motionless sea. Not a breath of wind touched my face or stirred the blue Atlantic as the engines fell silent, while only the sound of water kissing the drifting hull pierced the night.

"Set him up," I said.

Mongo pulled our boy from his facedown position on the deck and put him into a sitting position on a cushioned seat.

I stuck my phone in his face with the video camera running. "CIC, Sierra One. Subject in custody. All secure. No casualties."

She said, "Roger. Video and audio are good, and I'm recording everything."

I took a knee in front of Billy Goddard. "Look at me. If you cooperate, you've got nothing to be afraid of. We're not going to hurt you as long as you answer our questions and tell us the truth. When this is over, we'll drop you off wherever you want to be, and it'll all be a distant memory. Do you understand?"

He said, "I'm telling you, man, I'm not Billy. You've got the wrong guy."

I backed up. "Oh, in that case, you have every reason to be afraid. If you're not Billy Goddard, you're of absolutely no use to me."

I turned to Anya. "Gut him and throw him overboard."

"No! No! Wait! You don't understand!"

I leaned back into position. "I'm a pretty bright guy, Billy, and I think I understand exactly what's going on. Now, tell me about the tuna tower you built out of galvanized steel that was never meant for a boat."

His breath came hard and fast. "Listen to me. I'm not—"

Instead of simply shuffling backward, I stood, walked to the stern of the RHIB, and ordered, "Gut him!"

Anya drew her knife and planted a knee between Billy's legs.

His hyperventilation morphed into sobbing. "I'm not Billy. I'm his brother, Chuck."

"Hold!" I ordered, and Anya froze.

"CIC, Sierra One. Check for a brother named Chuck."

"Stand by," Skipper said.

Anya hissed. "I hope you are lying. It has been very long time since I have turned man inside out, and I miss this feeling."

If possible, the terror on the man's face grew even more animated. "I swear to God, I'm Charles Goddard, Billy's brother. Billy's missing."

Skipper said, "I've got a Charles Michael Goddard of St. Charles, Missouri. DOB eleven-sixteen seventy-nine."

"Tell me your birthday," I demanded.

The man's voice trembled. "November sixteenth, nineteen seventy-nine. I swear I'm not Billy."

"Where do you live?"

He whimpered. "Missouri . . . St. Charles, Missouri."

I tugged Anya's arm, and she moved aside. "Okay, *Charles*. Or do you prefer Chuck?"

"I don't care, man. Call me whatever you want. Just don't kill me."

I'd made some colossal mistakes in my life, but I was seven miles away from the nearest dry spot of land after kidnapping a completely innocent man and threatening to feed his guts to the sharks. I would've given a million dollars to undo the previous half hour of my life, but like so many other days in my life—in for a penny, in for a pound.

"Chuck it is, then. What are you doing on Bimini?"

He tried to dry his eyes with a shoulder. "I was out of work, so I came down to help Billy for a while. That's it, man. I swear."

"Take it easy," I said. "We're checking your story. As long as you're telling the truth, you've got nothing to be afraid of."

"What are you talking about? I just got abducted by a bunch of—whatever you people are—and now I'm tied up on a boat with some crazy Russian threatening to gut me like a pig."

I shook my head. "She never said that. She doesn't use articles. It's not gut you like *a* pig. It's just gut you like pig."

"What's wrong with you, man? This is insane."

"If I cut your hands free, are you going to behave?"

"Yeah, just keep that crazy woman away from me."

I drew my switchblade and leaned close. "She's the sanest of all of us. Let that sink in."

With the flick of my wrist, he was free, and I slid back a few inches to gauge his reaction to partial freedom. Part of me expected him to lash out and try to fight his way through me, but instead, he slowly pulled his hands in front of himself and rubbed his wrists.

"Tell me about your brother. You said he was missing, right?"

Chuck nodded. "Yeah, he's been gone a couple of days."

"Did you report him missing?"

"Report it to who? This is an island, man, and me and Billy are Americans. Nobody cares if we come and go. We aren't missing as far as the cops are concerned. We're just transient workers fixing boats and doing odd jobs for beer money."

"But you were hanging out with Billy's friends."

"Who else am I going to hang out with? They're the only people I know."

"Why weren't you looking for your brother?"

"We were, man. But it's not that weird for him to disappear for a day or two here and there. He's got this thing . . . I don't know . . . with his brain. He just wanders off sometimes and goes into some world of his own."

"How often does he disappear?" I asked.

"I don't know. Maybe a couple times a year. He'll just go off and go fishing or something. I don't know where he goes. He just goes, man, and when he comes back, it's like he was never gone. He just picks up like nothing happened."

I took a breath to consider everything I'd just learned.

"Did you help your brother build a tuna tower out of galvanized steel recently?"

"Yeah, *he* built one. I'm a carpenter. I'm not any good with metal. I mean, I can't weld or anything. I can measure and cut, but Billy's the fabricator."

"How long ago did he build it?"

"Like two weeks ago. No, wait. It wasn't that long. Maybe nine or ten days."

I relaxed a little. "How much have you had to drink tonight?"

"Part of one beer. You kidnapped me before I could finish it."

"Good. I want you to be clearheaded."

He huffed. "Clearheaded? You scared me to death, and I'm still scared. Even if I'd had a case of beer, I'd be sober right now."

"Tell me about the person who hired Billy to build the tower."

"I don't know. I never met the guy. Like I told you, I just measured and cut. Billy did everything else."

Chuck's right leg tightened, and I reacted the wrong way. Instead of lunging for him, I ducked what I thought was a coming punch. The terrified man wasn't attacking—he was escaping. Or at least attempting to escape.

Shawn hit the water a second after Chuck and had him wrapped up three seconds after that. "What do you want me to do with him, boss?"

"Get his attention."

Shawn took a breath and let his absence of body fat drag both of them beneath the surface. I didn't start a timer, but they were down far longer than I'd want to hold my breath.

When they resurfaced, Chuck gasped, spat, and gagged while Shawn looked like he'd just taken a leisurely stroll through the park. "Mission accomplished. Now what?"

"Let's get him back aboard."

Mongo snatched the man from Shawn's grasp and yanked him over the starboard tube. As soon as he hit the deck, Anya put on her crazy eyes and drew her knife again. "I can do it now, yes?"

It was a show, and I played along. "If he tries again, he's all yours, but not yet."

She slumped and sheathed her blade. "You never let me have any fun."

"Lash him to the deck," I ordered.

Kodiak tied Chuck's feet to the pad eyes designed to carry the lifting bridles for the crane to haul the boat out of the water.

I asked, "We're not going to do that again, are we?"

Chuck scowled, still trying to catch his breath. "Who are you people?"

I said, "*Who* we are doesn't matter. *What* we are is the important thing. So, listen very closely. We might be able to find your brother. Billy's in trouble, Chuck. He's not on one of his wanders."

"What are you talking about?"

"That tower you built was used in an attempted murder, and if my hunch is correct, whoever paid you and your brother to build it is covering his tracks by burying everybody who knows anything about it."

# Chapter 13
## *Now I Know*

Chuck Goddard sat in the bow of our RHIB with terror in his eyes, but it wasn't one of my threats that gave him that look. It was merely the expression of my suspicion.

His voice cracked when he said, "Burying? You mean like killing people? Are you saying Billy's dead?"

I considered my answer carefully before blurting out the thought dancing on my tongue. "No, I'm not saying your brother is dead. I'm saying it's a possibility."

"But you said you could find him."

I shook my head. "No, I said we *might* be able to find your brother. There's a chance that whoever hired him to build the tower has already gotten to him, but we'll do everything in our power to find him and keep him alive."

"If it's not already too late," Chuck said.

"Yes. . . ."

I wanted a private conference with my team, but under the circumstances, that couldn't happen, so I did the next best thing. "Gator, get everything you can out of Chuck's head, but don't hurt him. They're just questions, not an interrogation."

"You got it, boss."

I moved the rest of the team to the stern of the RHIB and spoke quietly while Gator entertained our guest. "I think we have to take him back to the ship."

Mongo sighed. "I agree, but I don't like it. If we put him back ashore, he's a flashing neon sign with a target on his back."

Shawn said, "The brother's dead, isn't he?"

I nodded. "I'm afraid so, but we have to look."

"Oh, I get it," Shawn said. "I just wanted to make sure we're all on the same page."

"It's not a great page," I said, "but I'm pretty sure we're all on it together. Anyone have a good reason not to take this guy back to the *Lori Danielle*?"

Kodiak groaned. "I can come up with a few dozen reasons, starting with the fact that we'd be showing a billion-dollar warship to an unemployed ne'er-do-well who probably can't keep his mouth shut."

"I know, but do we really have a choice?"

"We could give him to police," Anya said.

I said, "That's not a terrible idea, but when he tells Chief Inspector Belafonte what happened to him tonight, we're all either going to jail or getting kicked off the island. And we can't have either of those things happening yet."

Anya said, "Then we have no choice other than taking him to ship."

Shawn hit the starters, and we were soon gliding across the water with the *Lori Danielle* on our bow and growing larger by the second. When we came alongside, the crane operator hoisted us aboard and placed the RHIB on her cradle.

Chuck eyed the nearly six-hundred-foot-long vessel. "This is your boat?"

"It's just a research vessel," I said. "You might say we're using her as a floating hotel."

He let out a laugh. "Yeah, you might say that, but it'd be a lie. You guys are government operatives like the CIA or something, aren't you?"

"We're definitely not CIA," I said. "Now, tell me about the guys you were supposed to be drinking with tonight. Are they all Americans?"

"Yeah. They're just transient workers like Billy and me. They spend most of their time on the island working on boats and doing construction . . . stuff like that."

"Did they have anything to do with building the tower you and your brother worked on?"

"No, that was just Billy's job. Nobody else was in on it."

I said, "That's good, but do you think they'll go to the police about us grabbing you out of that bar?"

He laughed. "Not a chance. They're not the kind of guys who go to the cops, but you can bet your butt they'll be looking for Billy and me."

I pulled Gator aside. "Take Chuck down to sick bay and get him checked out by whoever's on watch. Find him some dry clothes and something to help him sleep."

"Got it."

The rest of us headed for the CIC, where Skipper wasted no time making her first point.

"Are you serious? You brought him back to the ship?"

"We did," I said. "We couldn't put him back on the island until we know where Billy is."

She huffed. "I'll show you where Billy is—or at least where his body is. It's in the shallows around Healing Hole."

"That's exactly where we're headed as soon as the sun comes up."

She said, "Are you planning to tell Inspector Belafonte?"

"If we find a body, I won't have any choice."

"But you're not telling him about grabbing Chuck, right?"

"I don't plan to bring that up."

"Good. Stick to that plan. Do you want me to launch the drones?"

"I do. They have decent night-vision capabilities, right?"

"Better than decent. I'll launch them."

"Don't overwork yourself. You've got a potful of other stuff to do."

She laughed. "Thank you for the concern, but I've got everything under control. The drones are pretty much autonomous once I program the search area and launch them."

"I have no idea what I'd do without you."

She said, "We've been through this before. Without me, you'd be chasing Russian girls all over the . . . oh, wait. It would appear that you already caught one."

I huffed. "I think I'm the one who got caught."

"You don't seem unhappy about having your foot stuck in that particular trap."

I pulled up a chair. "While we're on the subject, tell me what you think, and be honest."

She lowered her chin. "When am I anything other than brutally honest?"

"Excellent point, so let me have it."

She laid a hand on my knee. "I'll make it simple for you, Spy Boy. No one's surprised. It seems to be the natural order of things that you and Anya would end up together, especially now that Pogonya is in the picture."

"Is it too soon, though?"

She raised her eyebrows. "Chase, it's been two years since Penny was murdered. I know you'll always love her, but there's no way she would want or expect you to be a monk for the rest of your life."

"What about the rest of the guys? How do you think they feel about it?"

"See?" she said. "That's what makes you a great leader. You think of the team before yourself. They love you, Chase. Every one of them knows that Anya's last name will be Fulton sooner or later, and to be honest, they already see it that way. So, stop worrying so much, and let yourself be happy. If anybody deserves that, it's you."

I sighed. "I don't know. Sometimes it feels like Penny's going to walk through the door like nothing ever happened."

"Look at me. My husband was murdered, too. I know exactly how you feel. She's not coming through that door or any other door, no matter how much you want her to. I still love Tony, and I always will, but Gator is my husband now, and he makes me feel like the most treasured woman on Earth. Let Anya do that for you. Both of you need that from each other."

I gave her a warm smile. "We've come a long way, you and me—from a pretty good baseball player and a bratty teenager to saving the world."

She laughed. "You were better than pretty good, and I'm still bratty."

I shoved her chair away. "Yes, you are, and I wouldn't have it any other way."

"Go get some sleep," she said. "If you're taking Chuck to find his brother tomorrow, you're going to need all the rest you can get."

She was right, as usual, so I hit the sack with the intention of being ready to hit the ground running before daybreak.

But fate had other plans for me, and fate had a name an hour before sunrise.

"Hey, College Boy. It's Clark. Get your butt back to Miami. Dad's coming out of his coma."

I wiped the sleep from my eyes. "That's great, but why do I need to be there? I'm still trying to find the shooter who put him in the coma."

His answer knocked me from my bunk and into my boots. "Because you're the only brother I've got left, and I want you here."

"Get me permission to land on the helipad, and I'll be there in an hour."

Minutes later, I knocked a fist against the navigation bridge hatch. "Permission to come aboard."

A bright-eyed young officer pulled open the hatch. "Oh, Dr. Fulton, it's you. You don't need permission to—"

"I know, but Captain Sprayberry likes his naval traditions."

"Indeed, he does. What can I do for you, sir?"

"I need to launch the helo. Are you in charge?"

"Uh, well, yes, sir. I'm the officer of the watch, but—"

Captain Sprayberry growled. "What's all the racket about out here?"

The young officer stepped aside. "Oh, good morning, Captain. I didn't mean to wake you."

"I don't sleep. What do you want, Chase?"

I said, "Dominic's coming out of his coma, and Clark wants me there."

The captain said, "Then why are you still here?"

"I didn't want to launch the chopper from your ship without approval from the . . ."

The captain said, "Well, you've got it. Now, go."

Gun Bunny answered my knock as if she'd been awake for hours. "Good morning, Chase. I didn't expect to see you at my door, but I promise I won't tell Anya."

"What she doesn't know won't hurt her."

The pilot laughed. "Oh, but she'd hurt us."

"Then, let's not risk it, and let's go flying instead. I need to be in Miami ASAP."

She spun, grabbed her flight bag, and stepped through the door. "Is Gator coming?"

His door was the next one to feel my fist, and just like the pilot, he yanked it open as if he'd been waiting for the knock. Glancing between Gun Bunny and me, he said, "Yes, I want to come, and it doesn't matter where we're going."

I was getting better at being a passenger, and even though part of me still loved the front seats, I took a seat in the back because Gator needed the stick time, and Gun Bunny was an incredible instructor. I plugged my headset into the cockpit's intercom system so I could listen as she taught and he learned.

"Have we done a rooftop landing before?" she asked.

Gator said, "No, ma'am."

She said, "It'll feel just like landing on the ship, with one big difference. The wind is completely unpredictable on top of a building, so you have to fly it like your life depends on it."

"I always fly like my life depends on it."

She said, "Yeah, well, this time, fly it like Skipper's life depends on it."

The massive Miami skyline came into view with the sun behind us, and it looked like a work of art. What the scene could never suggest was that a man who'd been a part of my life for nearly two decades lay at death's door, and what he remembered when he woke up—if he remembered anything—could change the direction of the rest of my life forever.

"Check the wind sock," Gun Bunny said. "But not just the hospital's sock. Check everything in sight that could be an indicator of wind direction and speed."

Gator said, "That flag's not a bad choice."

"Exactly, but look at the smoke from that stack. It's at least sixty degrees off from the flag and the wind sock. Take it all in, and fly us to the pad."

Gator did as she instructed, and I couldn't resist kneeling between the two front seats to watch the show. He slowed the Vertol to approach speed and gradually bled off energy as we approached the hospital roof.

"You're doing great. Just stay with it, and don't quit. If it doesn't feel right, your bailout is to the left. Nothing on that side is higher than the hospital, so we'll have plenty of room to climb out and try again."

I studied his hands on the controls, and unlike mine during my first rooftop landing, his grip was light and confident. He manipulated the controls with tiny, almost imperceptible corrections and flew us down the imaginary glide slope until bringing us to a hover only inches above the pad.

When the landing gear touched down, Gator fully lowered the collective and sighed.

With her gloved hands resting on her thighs, Gun Bunny said, "I never touched a thing. Nice work. You're a lot better at this than Chase was."

I said, "She's got a point. She's wrong, of course, but she does have a point. You two get back to the ship. They'll need the chopper for the search. Mongo's in charge, and I'll call you when I need a ride."

The look on the man's face at the rooftop door told me Clark had done absolutely nothing to secure permission for us to be there, but in my world, permission is highly overrated, so I pushed by the guard and his protests.

When I finally made my way through the maze of corridors inside the hospital to Dominic's room, Clark met me at the door. "He's awake."

I stepped inside to see the man who'd been my first operational handler—and my friend—sitting somewhat upright, his shoulder and chest encapsulated in a massive bandage.

"Chase," he said. "Clark told me you were coming, but I'm a little groggy, so you'll have to forgive me."

"Nothing to forgive, Dom. It's good to see you awake."

"I think you mean *alive*."

"That, too. What do you remember about the . . . incident?"

"Incident?" he said. "I'd call it an attempted assassination, but if you prefer incident, we'll go with that. I was having coffee and reading the newspaper when the whole world exploded in front of me. Next thing I know, I'm waking up in a hospital in Miami with my son and ex-wife looming over me."

"Forgive me for being all business, but do you have any idea who might want to take a shot at you?"

Wanda said, "I could name a couple dozen jealous twenty-five-year-old husbands who'd like to kill him. Does that count?"

Dominic said, "Wanda Jean, you know I don't mess around with married girls."

She rolled her eyes. "I think you mean you don't *ask* if they're married."

He said, "Don't pay any attention to her. You can't believe anything a seventy-five-year-old woman who looks like she's thirty has to say."

Wanda blushed and squeezed Dom's arm.

The television droned softly in the corner of the room, and Dominic said, "I need my glasses."

Clark handed them to his father, and while staring at the screen, Dom slid them on. He said, "Did you see this story? Somebody killed Parker Kemper's son at Gettysburg."

I looked up at the TV. "We were there when it happened, and it wasn't his son. It was Congressman Kemper himself."

Dominic said, "Yeah, I know it was, but I'm talking about his father. And now I know exactly who tried to kill me."

## Chapter 14
## *Locked and Loaded*

Dominic immediately had my full attention. “What do you mean? Who tried to kill you?”

Before he could answer, his eyes glazed over, and his head drooped against his bandaged shoulder.

I grabbed his hand. “Dominic!”

Wanda gripped his arm. “Dommy . . . Dommy! No!”

Clark pointed toward the monitor still showing a slow, steady rhythm in Dominic’s heart rate and breathing.

He slid an arm around his mother. “Mom, he’s okay. He just fell back asleep.”

Tears streamed down Wanda’s face as she collapsed against the hospital bed. “Oh, thank God. I can’t lose my husband. I just can’t.”

Clark helped her into a chair. “It’s okay, Mom. He’s going to be all right, but he’s not your husband anymore. That ended when Tony and I were kids. I think you need to get some rest.”

She shoved him away. “You don’t get to declare when something’s over. I’ve loved that man since the second I laid eyes on him. You should’ve seen him, Mud Pie. He was so handsome, just like you, with that crooked grin that made me melt where I sat. He was really something, son. He really was.”

Clark slid onto the seat beside her. “Mom, you can’t do this to yourself. You know who and what he is.”

“Let me tell you something, son. You’re exactly right. I do know who and what he is, but I also know what he *was*. He was a spy, and every little girl in the sixties wanted herself an honest-to-God spy of her own. And you know what? I got me one, and I loved him through all of his cloak-and-dagger crap. And I still do. You boys have got to find the man who did this to him, and you better let me look him in the face before you kill him."

Clark opened his mouth to protest, but she pressed a finger to his lips and leaned around him, then stared directly at me. "That goes for you, too. You find him. You hear me, Chase Fulton?"

The monitor continued ticking away, showing Dominic's heart rate at forty-four beats per minute and respirations at twenty-one. "Yes, ma'am. We'll find him."

When Wanda had gathered herself, I tugged at Clark's elbow. "We need to talk."

He turned to his mother. "Will you be okay for a few minutes?"

"I'm fine, son. I'm just fine. Go do what you do."

Clark and I stepped into the hall and checked both directions for ears.

I asked, "What do you think he was talking about? How could a news broadcast about Parker Kemper tell him who took a shot at him?"

"I don't know, but we need him to wake up. I'm going to find a doctor."

I stepped back inside the room with absolutely no doubt that Clark would be back very soon with at least one doctor in tow.

Wanda looked up. "Chase, I'm sorry you had to see me like that. I'm ashamed."

I took the seat beside her. "You've got no reason to be ashamed. We're working this thing, and if the man can be caught, I'll catch him. I promise you that."

"I know you will. You're so brave, just like my little Mud Pie."

"I don't know about that, but Clark went to get a doctor. We need to wake Dominic back up and find out what he was about to say. You might want to go for a coffee or something."

Her face turned to stone. "I'm not walking out of this room until Dommy walks out with me. You understand me?"

"Yes, ma'am."

Just as I expected, Clark burst through the door with a resident who didn't look happy about the situation. "Wake him up. We need to talk to him."

The doctor said, "Mr. Fontana needs to rest. In fact, all three of you—"

Clark held up a hand. "This would be a very good time for you to stop talking and wake him up. Telling us what we *need* to do is not in your best interest."

The doctor was nothing if not devoted to his position. "If you don't step out of the room and give Mr. Fontana time to rest, I'll have to call the police."

Clark looked at me, and I stood, drawing my credentials. I held the badge and ID a few inches in front of the doctor's face. "Do you mean you're going to call the guys with badges? Take a look at mine. If I remember correctly, it says United States Secret Service on it. Do you have the phone number of a cop in this town who can throw me out of this room?"

The doctor didn't flinch. "My responsibility is to my patient, and I will do whatever is necessary to protect him."

"Oh, goodie," I said. "I guess that means you're coming with me to hunt down the man who shot him. I recommend a bulletproof vest instead of that lab coat. Things get a little dicey when you're chasing murderers, *Doctor*."

"What's going on in here?"

The stern, confident voice immediately captured our attention, and I turned to see a man in his sixties wearing a lab coat that looked a lot like the other doctor's.

With my credentials still plainly visible, I said, "We're investigating an attempted assassination, and this man is obstructing that investigation."

The older doctor said, "I'm certain it's a misunderstanding. How can we help?"

I said, "You can wake Mr. Fontana up again so we can continue our conversation. He was about to tell us who shot him when he fell unconscious again."

The physician stepped around me and pulled a stethoscope from his pocket. After several seconds of listening to Dominic's heart, he said, "I don't think waking him up is a very good idea at this moment, but I understand your sense of urgency. If you'll give us a few minutes to call in a cardio consult, I'd like to get my colleague's input before we wake Mr. Fontana again."

"How long will that take?" I asked.

"Give us twenty minutes. Is that acceptable?"

I said, "Not a second longer."

The two doctors left the room, and Clark said, "Get Skipper on Parker Kemper, Sr. We need to know if he has any connection with my dad."

I dialed the number, and Skipper said, "CIC."

"I need everything you can find on Parker Kemper, Sr., especially anything that might tie him to Dominic."

She said, "Parker Kemper? The congressman who was shot at Gettysburg?"

"We think it's his father, but I want you to run a family tree. There's a connection, and I need to know what it is."

She said, "I'm on it now. How's Dominic?"

"I think he's going to make it. He's unconscious again, but the doctors seem to think that's a good thing. Let me know as soon as you get a hit."

"Don't hang up," she said. "I told you I'm on it."

"Oh, sorry. I'm here."

The keys rattled, and Skipper made the familiar, typical sounds she always did when working on a case. Finally, she said, "He's not a senior. He's a second."

"What?"

She said, "Parker Kemper the third was killed at the reenactment at

Gettysburg. His father, Parker Kemper the Second, is a retired State Department attaché."

"Did you say *is*? As in, he's still alive?"

"Yes, as far as I know, he's still alive, and it looks like he lives near Cadiz."

"Spain?" I asked.

"No. Believe it or not, there's a Cadiz, Kentucky. I'm sending you his address now."

"Do you have a contact number for him?"

"I'm looking, but so far, I can't find a cell phone or a landline. That probably means he still has a State Department phone."

"Then get somebody at State to give us his number. I think he's tied to this thing in some way, and I want to know how."

She said, "Okay, but don't wait on the line for that one. It'll take some time. Are you coming back to the ship?"

"No, but I'm sending your husband and his new favorite flight instructor back. Is Anya in the CIC with you?"

"She is."

"Put her on the phone."

"Yes, Chasechka. Everything is okay, yes?"

"No, nothing is okay right now. Dominic's alive and improving, but he's got a long way to go. We've got a new lead, and I need to be in Cadiz, Kentucky, as soon as possible."

"Is no problem. I will be in Miami airport in minutes."

"Don't go to Miami. Go to Opa Locka Executive. Bring Shawn and Mongo. If this thing gets weird, we might need some muscle."

Anya said, "I will bring also knives. I do not have big muscles, but I am stronger than I look."

"Yes, you are. I'll meet you at Signature Aviation."

I shoved the phone back in my pocket, and Clark asked, "Wanna let me in on any of that?"

"Skipper said Parker Kemper the Second—apparently he's the dead congressman's father—lives near a place called Cadiz, Kentucky, and he's retired from the State Department. I think that's who your dad was talking about."

"So, you're headed to Kentucky?"

"Unless you've got a better idea."

"Keep me in the loop," he said.

"And you tell me what your dad says when they wake him up again."

"You got it, College Boy. Be careful. This thing is starting to smell."

"Speaking of smelling, how long has it been since you've had a shower?"

* * *

I watched Anya's Citation touch down with the nose higher than she typically landed, but she taxied to the Signature Aviation ramp at her usual cautious but efficient pace. When the door opened, the nose-high landing attitude suddenly made sense. Gator stood in the doorway.

I jogged up the three steps into the Citation, and he said, "It was her idea. I told her we should ask you if it was okay for me to come, but she insisted it'd be fine."

I gave him a playful shove toward the cockpit. "Do better on your next landing."

He contorted himself back inside the small cockpit, and I stuck my head in behind him. "File for one-Mike-niner. That's Lake Barkley State Park Airport."

Anya's fingers were already programming the GPS while Gator checked the weather for the route.

Without looking up, Anya said, "Is one hour fifty-one minutes. You are ready to go now, yes?"

"Absolutely."

God was apparently on our side because an unforecast tailwind added just over forty knots to our ground speed, putting us in Southern Kentucky fifteen minutes ahead of Anya's calculation. As Gator flew the approach, I leaned into the aisle to get a view of the panel and the runway in front of us. A few seconds before touchdown, Gator pushed the throttles forward, and we accelerated away from the airport.

I didn't like it, but I stayed in my seat. The two pilots in the cockpit were in charge, and I was just a passenger.

We flew a traffic pattern and landed beautifully on the next pass.

Gator poked his head from the cockpit, and I asked, "What's with the go-around?"

"Geese. The runway was covered with them. We had to scare them off before we could land."

The airport was a single runway with no parallel taxiway and a simple wood-frame structure at the north end. The Citation definitely stood out on the ramp. A Cessna Centurion and a Republic Seabee rested on the small parking apron. The only other vehicle in sight was a black Chevy Suburban parked beside the building.

While everyone else filed out and down the steps, I slipped behind Gator and stuck my head into the cockpit, where the jet's owner and pilot still sat, recording times in the log.

I said, "You're not going to like this, but I need you to stay with the plane."

Anya dropped her pen and closed the logbook. "This is terrible idea. If we are walking into trap, there is nothing I can do from here."

"You're right, but if this *is* a trap and it goes badly, we can't make Pogo an orphan."

She scowled. "Then you should stay with airplane, and I will lead team."

"That's not how it works. I'm in command."

"Why did you bring me at all if I am only to guard airplane?"

I said, "If we get shot up, we need somebody to fly us out of here."

She laid a hand against my cheek. "Do not get shot up. If you do, I will kill you."

I leaned close and kissed her playfully. "No, you won't"

She ducked her chin. "Maybe I will."

I made the call, and Skipper answered by saying, "Is the Suburban there?"

"It is. Thank you for that. Nice job. Any luck finding a number for Kemper the Second?"

She said, "No. And it's not the typical no. It felt more like a no-and-don't-call-back kind of no."

"Did you pull some strings?"

"I pulled some ropes, but I still got nowhere. I don't know what's going on at the State Department, but they're circling the wagons around something."

"How about Ginger?" I asked.

Ginger was the only analyst on the planet who may have been slightly better at the job than Skipper.

"She tried, too, and they gave her the same treatment. I don't know what you're about to drive into, Chase, but I recommend you do it locked and loaded."

## Chapter 15
## *Cold War Pussycats*

The Suburban that Skipper arranged was exactly what we needed. Although I hoped the four-wheel-drive system wouldn't be necessary, having that option always increased our capabilities in the field. The vinyl seats were also a plus. Cleaning bloodstains from leather and carpet interior is a nightmare, and my team weren't strangers to wounds inside vehicles. We climbed aboard, and I called Miami.

Clark answered. "I assume you made it to Dump Truck County, Kentucky."

"We did, and it's gorgeous up here. How's your dad?"

"Still unconscious. The doctors refused to wake him back up. Apparently, there's something going on with his heart, and they're afraid any induced stress might kill him. They said something about the trauma from the lung surgery could cause issues in treating a heart attack."

"So, he's been out since we left?"

"Unfortunately, but if he wakes up again, I'll be right by his side, and I'll get the goods on what he thinks he knows."

"Is your mom okay?"

"She's a mess," he said. "And I can't seem to make her understand that she and Dad aren't married anymore."

"Oh, I think she understands it. She's just not interested in admitting it right now."

He said, "You're the shrink. Maybe you're right. Have you made any progress in Kentucky?"

"We just hit the ground. The GPS says we'll be at Kemper's place in twenty-five minutes."

He grunted. "Keep your heads down and your powder dry, and let me know what you find."

"We will."

Over my shoulder, I saw Shawn and Mongo press-checking their weapons. "Good to go?"

Mongo said, "I guess so. Without knowing what we're walking into, who knows if we're good or not?"

I turned to Gator. "All right, driver. Let's do this."

We pulled away from the airport, and silence consumed the ride. I couldn't stop asking myself how Parker Kemper the Third and Dominic were connected and how that connection could get both of them shot.

I dialed the CIC. "Skipper, it's Chase. Sorry to bother you again, but have you found anything putting Kemper in bed with Dominic?"

She sighed. "I assume you mean Parker Kemper the Second. Other than them being roughly the same age and working with the State Department at the same time, I've got nothing. I can't find any record of them working directly together or in the same country at the same time."

"Have you found out what Kemper really did for State?"

"The official record is so vague that it could only be one thing—he was obviously a spook."

I asked, "Does his dossier list his education?"

"He was an economics and accounting major, of all things. He even took the CPA exam in Virginia back in the seventies."

"Did he pass?"

"Of course, but I can't find any record of him practicing anywhere."

"How about Dominic? What did he study?"

"Political science for his undergrad, but he's got an MBA."

"Their educations certainly don't put them on the same playing field."

"I agree," Skipper said. "There's no reason they would've ever even known each other."

"Stay on it. There has to be a connection. When Dominic saw the news broadcast about Congressman Kemper being assassinated, he immediately told us he knew who shot him."

She groaned. "I'll keep digging, but I'm getting close to hitting bedrock. I'm tracking you, by the way. Go to open-channel comms when you get close so I can have audio."

"You got it. We'll be there in less than fifteen minutes."

"Be careful, Chase, and don't get Gator killed. I can't be a widow again."

We drove across dilapidated roads that felt like washboards, between massive fields of tobacco as far as I could see, until the GPS said we reached our destination. Gator rolled to a stop outside a metal gate that looked like it hadn't been opened in years.

"Is this the right place?" Shawn asked.

I said, "According to the address Skipper gave us, it is. What do you think? Should we drive in or hoof it?"

The SEAL pulled out his tablet and brought up the satellite image of our location. "It looks like it's almost a mile to the closest house. There are four barns and a few sheds. I say we drive if we can get that gate open."

Mongo said, "Don't worry about the gate."

He dismounted and ripped the rusted contraption from its hinges. Gator pulled through, and Mongo propped the gate back in place.

When he climbed back inside the Suburban, the big man said, "I leaned it outside the post in case we have to crash it on the way out."

"Good thinking," I said. "Let's go to open-channel comms."

We brought our satellite comms online, and I checked in. "CIC, Sierra One."

Skipper said, "CIC has you loud and clear. How me?"

"I have you the same. We're at the gate and moving into the property. You don't happen to have any live satellite coverage, do you?"

She said, "No, but if you'll check Gator's pack, you'll find the mini drone."

"Have I mentioned that I love you lately?"

"Take that up with my husband. He packed the drone, not me."

"In that case, I love him," I said.

Shawn pulled the pack from behind the seat and tossed it onto Gator's lap. He unzipped the main compartment and pulled out the hard plastic case. Minutes later, we had an airborne surveillance platform at our disposal, and I was starting to feel better about the operation.

Gator said, "I can't drive *and* fly the drone. Somebody else has to do one of the two."

Mongo reached across the seat for the remote control. "I'll do the flying. You stay behind the wheel."

He navigated the drone a thousand feet ahead of us, providing a bird's-eye view of what lay ahead.

"See any signs of life?" I asked.

Mongo studied the screen. "None. There's a pickup truck near the house, but there's no heat signature, so it hasn't been driven lately."

"I'm not digging this," Shawn said. "Something doesn't feel right."

"Tell me about it," I said. "Let's clear that house."

Gator parked behind the pickup, and we climbed out.

I said, "Mongo, you're on exterior security and the drone. We'll clear from the front door."

The big man took up a position at the rear of the Suburban, where he could use both the SUV and the pickup as cover and concealment if necessary, and the rest of us headed for the door. With Gator on his heels, Shawn took the lead, and I brought up the rear.

Shawn gripped the doorknob and waited for my signal. I gave the nod, and he twisted. To my surprise, the door opened and swung inward with a definitive screech of the hinges.

"Better than an alarm system," Shawn whispered.

"Old spooks love their tradecraft," I said. "Let's move."

We cleared the front door and foyer. The living room was next, and it was as barren as the surface of the moon. We pressed our way down the hall and cleared every room along the way.

When we reached the fourth door, a rustling sound came from inside, and we froze in place. The movement was subtle, but it was definitely there. Somebody was behind the door, and we were seconds away from discovering who.

I drew a mental map of the first floor of the house. We'd cleared the entry, kitchen, living room, and two bedrooms. The door in front of us had to be a bathroom. That meant extremely close quarters and very little room to fight if the guy inside wanted a brawl . . . or a shootout.

Apparently coming to the same realization, Shawn lowered his rifle, allowing it to hang snugly against his body. With his left hand, he drew his sidearm and squeezed the doorknob with his right. The thousands of hours we'd spent training together gave us three the ability to move and almost think as one person.

Shawn turned the knob, and the rustling intensified. Shoving the door to its limit, he stepped inside with his pistol at the ready. Gator raised his rifle over Shawn's shoulder and swept left, while I covered the right side of the small room. When we moved in, the rustling became screeching, and a flash of motion appeared just ahead of our SEAL. Most operators would've put a pair of rounds into the attacker, but Shawn's composure made him the perfect point man. Instead of ending the assailant's life, he grabbed him by the throat and powered forward until he had one foot in the bathtub and his attacker's back pressed against the wall.

Gator was the first to chuckle, but it only took a breath for Shawn and me to join him as the fat tabby cat in the SEAL's grip clawed and hissed like a wild beast.

Shawn holstered his pistol and pulled the cat against him, stroking his fur and doing everything he could to calm the animal. Cuddling obviously wasn't what the cat had in mind as he continued fighting against Shawn's affection. Finally, the tabby leapt to the ground and ran toward the kitchen.

I followed and watched as the cat pawed at his stainless-steel food bowl lying empty on the tile floor.

"It's been a while since he's had anything to eat," Gator said.

I pulled open the fridge and tossed several slices of ham into the bowl. The cat lost all interest in us and devoured the meat.

Skipper said, "Sierra One, CIC. Sitrep."

I said, "Sierra Seven just fought off a mountain lion, but he's okay."

"A mountain lion? Are you serious?"

"Well, it looked like a mountain lion when it jumped from the sink, but it turned out to be a hungry house cat. It looks like the place is empty, but we're going to clear the upstairs just to be sure."

I refilled the cat's bowl and left him to his meal as we climbed the stairs. The three bedrooms, one bathroom, and attic all proved to be just as empty as the downstairs.

"Let's check the barns," I said.

We moved down the staircase, and Gator asked, "What are we going to do with the cat?"

"Nothing," I said. "We're looking for a Cold War spy, not a pussycat."

As we approached the front door, I said, "Sierra Two, we're coming out."

Mongo answered, "Roger. You're clear in all directions."

"Well, that was exciting," Shawn said. "I think I may have peed a little."

"Imagine how the cat felt," I said.

Shawn shook his head. "Oh, I know exactly how he felt. If I hadn't been wearing gloves, I'd be a bloody mess."

I checked the screen on the drone controller. "Is there anybody within a mile of this place?"

Mongo said, "There's a chopper in the air to the north, but it's probably a bird from Fort Campbell. Other than that, there's not a soul in sight."

"Good. Leave the drone in a hover and come with us. We can split into two teams and clear the barns twice as fast."

Shawn and Gator headed for the closest barn, while Mongo and I jogged toward the largest of the structures a few hundred yards away. Team One made entry and reported clear before we reached our objective. They moved on to barn number three just as Mongo and I stepped through the door of the massive, isolated structure.

The door slid open easily, and light filtered into the space. It was obviously a barn used for curing tobacco, but it was nearly empty with the exception of a pair of tractors and a few bales of hay stacked along one wall.

We spent less than two minutes clearing the area before heading for the rear door.

"Wait a minute," I said. "Why would there be hay in a tobacco barn? Did you see any horses or cows?"

Mongo raised an eyebrow. "Excellent question. Let's have a look."

We moved back inside the barn, and the giant tugged at one of the bales on top of the stack. It didn't budge, but the whole stack moved an inch to the left.

"That's interesting," I said.

Mongo shouldered the stack, and it continued sliding as if it were mounted on invisible rails. When we'd moved the hay bales three or four feet, an opening beneath the stack appeared, and a ladder led into a pit below.

Mongo said, "Some more Cold War stuff. I'll bet he's got two dozen gas masks and enough food and water to survive for a year down there."

"I'll bet you're right, but let's not make any assumptions. Stand down until we get Gator and Shawn in here." I said, "Sierra Five and Seven, say position."

Shawn answered. "We just cleared barn number three, and we're headed for number four."

"Break off and join us in the big barn. We found something interesting."

"We're on our way."

Minutes later, the SEAL and Gator sprinted into the barn. "What'cha got, boss?"

"A basement," I said.

"In a barn?" Gator asked. "What's down there?"

Shawn gave him a shove. "Really, rookie? Do you think they would've called us in here if they knew what was down there? Just for that, you take point."

Gator shouldered his rifle and descended the ladder, flooding the subterranean space with his rifle-mounted light. "Oh, this isn't good."

He hopped to the floor from several rungs up the ladder, and the rest of us followed him into the pit. We shone our lights on the same point —the body of an elderly man hanging from a rope in the center of the room. His pallor said he'd been dead for a day or more, but that didn't stop us from moving into position to get him down.

Mongo stretched above the man's head to cut the rope and asked, "You got him?"

"Yeah, we're ready," I said as Shawn and I positioned ourselves to catch the corpse when it fell.

"Freeze! Hands up! Do it now!"

We followed neither command. Instead, the four of us turned with our rifles raised, bearing directly on a six-man team dressed in black from head to toe, standing in a perfect spread formation near the bottom of the ladder. Each man held an MP5 submachine gun trained on us.

"Drop yours, or we drop you," Mongo ordered.

"Not a chance," one of the masked men said. "We've got you outnumbered and outgunned. Put your weapons on the dirt and get on your knees now."

The authority in his tone left little doubt that we were dealing with an absolute professional. The men behind the masks were warriors, and the man giving the orders was right—my team was the inferior force.

I said, "Do it, guys. Put 'em down, and we'll work this out nice and peaceful."

Hesitantly, my men followed the order and surrendered.

# Chapter 16
## *Spank Me*

Everything inside me wanted to fight, but the chances of us four surviving a gunfight against the six men in front of us were absolutely zero. We might take a few of them with us to the afterlife, but I promised Skipper I wouldn't make her a widow again. And I was certainly not interested in leaving Pogonya fatherless, as she'd been for the first fifteen years of her life.

Talking our way out of the situation was only slightly more likely than surviving the alternative gun battle, so I kept my mouth shut and listened for clues to the identities of the men behind the masks. The one voice I'd heard was distinctly American, so we weren't dealing with a foreign force. That gave me a small glimmer of hope, but the reason I wasn't terrified yet was that we were still alive. If their goal of holding us at gunpoint was for my team and me to be dead, they would've accomplished that objective before we knew they were in the pit with us. They wanted—or needed—us alive, and I've always been a huge fan of staying alive. Just as Clark taught me from day one as an operator, sometimes the most important thing in the world is to just keep breathing. And at least for the moment, all four of us had hearts still beating and lungs still pumping.

"On your faces, fingers laced behind your heads. Now!"

*Another very good sign*, I thought. *We're about to become prisoners, not corpses.*

As instructed, I lay on the floor and slipped my fingers together behind my head. I was certain our abductors would've preferred that we close our eyes, but they hadn't given that order, so I stared at six pairs of identical black Salomon boots. The sight brought a smile to my face. No independent team of operators wore identical boots. Somebody issued those Salomons to the six men who were about to cuff and search us. That meant they reported to somebody, and that somebody very likely reported to the president of the United States.

"Roll 'em up," the apparent leader of the team ordered.

Four of the six men stepped forward, flex-cuffed each of us, and started their gloved frisking. I chuckled silently when one of the men asked for a second pair of flex-cuffs. He was obviously dealing with Mongo.

My guy planted a knee just above my belt in the small of my back, but he wasn't overly aggressive. He applied enough pressure to assert his perceived dominance but made no effort to hurt me. His search was methodical and precise. Every item on my body found its way into a well-organized stack just far enough from my face to prevent me from reaching any of it if I miraculously broke free of the plastic cuffs. My pistol sat with its magazine extracted and the single round that had been inside the chamber lying only inches from the muzzle. My radio was next, followed by my knife. I lay in anxious anticipation of what was soon to come, but what happened next was nothing remotely like I expected.

I watched the team leader's boots leave the ground and heard an unmistakable voice cut through the silence. "You will drop weapons and lie on floor immediately, or I will cut off his head."

*Ah, my disobedient little Russian assassin.*

Her timing wasn't perfect, but she certainly knew how to make an entrance.

I raised my eyes to see Anya pressed against the ladder with the leader of the assault team drawn tightly against her body. The only parts of her that were exposed to potential gunfire were the backs of her hands, in which she gripped the man's chin in one hand and her favorite knife in the other. Any round fired through either of those exposed areas would ultimately penetrate the leader's face or neck. Russian training is a beautiful thing when applied in support of the good guys.

The pressure from the knee on my back vanished, and the man who'd been my captor suddenly became my deck mate as he lay down beside me.

The pop of breaking flex-cuffs came next, and Mongo hopped to his feet. Seconds later, roles were reversed, and six men lay hogtied in the bowels of a Kentucky tobacco barn.

We yanked masks from faces, and I jerked the leader to his knees. "This would be a very good time to tell me who you are."

We locked eyes, and he said, "We're SOG, and who the hell are you?"

I drew the one remaining item my previous captor hadn't lifted from my body and unfolded the credentials pack with a thumb over my name. "I'm Secret Service, and if you're really with the Special Operations Group, you're not authorized to operate on American soil."

He said, "That's Parker Kemper hanging there, isn't it?"

"Probably. If you hadn't interrupted us, we'd know by now."

He said, "Would you mind cutting us loose? It's obvious that we're all on the same team."

"I'm not convinced yet," I said. "And let me guess. None of you are carrying CIA credentials."

"We don't carry credentials, and you know that."

"Then you and your men are staying on the ground until I get confirmation on who you are from a source I trust."

He groaned, and I lifted my phone from the ground. When I stuck it in his face to get a picture, he ducked away, hiding from the lens, just as I expected him to do. With the press of a button, I sent the short video I'd shot while pretending to take a picture to Skipper.

With our radios back on our belts and operational again, Skipper said, "Stand by, Sierra One. I'll have confirmation of ID in ten seconds."

"Standing by."

A few seconds later, she said, "Oh, yeah. You've got a SOG team tied up in a basement."

"They started it," I said. "Thanks. I'll handle it."

She said, "Mr. Bossman is Valentine Cardone. At least that's what the database says. Who knows what his mother named him—if he had a mother. Are you sure you don't want me to call Langley?"

"I'm sure. I'm going to give Valentine and his boys a chance to avoid a lot of embarrassment back in Virginia."

At the mention of his name, the man spun back to me. "How did you—"

I pressed a finger to my lips. "Shh. I'm a ghost, and so are you. We don't exist, you and me, and we certainly never saw each other here, or anywhere else for that matter."

"What are you going to do?" he asked.

"I'm going to cut Mr. Kemper down using *your* knife, take his picture and fingerprints, and disappear. What you do after that doesn't interest me, and if you know what's good for you, you won't take any interest in what I'm doing either."

"I can live with that," he said. "So, cut us loose."

My finger went back to my lips. "Shh."

Mongo pulled on his gloves and opened Mr. Cardone's switchblade. Shawn and I caught the body and laid him gently on the floor.

After several rounds of electronic fingerprints and at least fifty photographs, I turned back to the CIA's choice to lead the unlawful operation inside the States. "He's all yours, Val. Do you want to share anything you may have learned about why Mr. Kemper ended up at the end of a rope?"

He didn't flinch, and I didn't expect him to.

"That's what I thought. Your knife is in one of the corners, and all of your bullets are in our pockets. Surely, six SOG operators can pool enough brain cells together to find that knife and cut yourselves free without slicing any arteries when we're gone. If you need adult supervision, I'll see if I can find you a kindergarten teacher on our way out. I do have to give you a little credit, though. Nice work finding that tunnel we missed. Without it, you never would've gotten the drop on us."

We sprinkled around six hundred nine-millimeter rounds across the landscape and waved to the Blackhawk pilots waiting a quarter mile away as we ran back to our Suburban.

Inside the rented SUV, I turned to Anya. "How did you get here?"

She smiled. "Uber, baby."

* * *

We were airborne and headed south at four hundred fifty miles per hour by the time I assumed the SOG team had cleaned up the mess and climbed back aboard their helo with Parker Kemper's body.

I listened to Clark's phone ring on speaker six times before he answered in a breathless tone. "Yeah?"

"Are you all right?" I asked.

"I'm naked and dripping wet."

"That's quite a visual. Thank you for that."

Anya said, "I think is very nice visual."

"That's enough out of you," I said. "You're already in enough trouble for disobeying an order."

She performed her well-practiced, most seductive smile. "Then perhaps you will have to spank me for being bad girl."

Clark almost yelled, "What on Earth is going on up there?"

"Anya saved our lives again. We were about to get shot in the head by a team of CIA SOG operators when she showed up with her pig sticker in hand."

"What? CIA SOG can't operate in the States."

"Maybe not," I said, "but according to Skipper, their boss was a cat named Valentine Cardone."

"That sounds made up."

I laughed. "He's CIA. What do you expect?"

"So, give me the scoop."

"We found Parker Kemper the Second hanging in the basement of his barn."

"He killed himself?"

"Not unless he jumped into the noose. There was no stool or chair anywhere near him, and he was at least three feet above the floor."

"This is getting serious, College Boy."

"You're telling me."

"What did you do with the SOG team?"

"I wanted to let Anya gut them like pig, but instead, we left them cuffed in the barn, with one knife, as far away as we could throw it."

"Good call," he said. "Do you have confirmation that the dead guy was Kemper?"

"Skipper's working on it. We took prints and pictures. How's your dad?"

"No change, as far as I know. I'm headed back to the hospital as soon as I dry off and get dressed. I'll let you know if there are any updates when I get there."

My phone clicked. "Skipper's calling. I'll hit you back." I thumbed the button. "Go, Skipper."

"It's him, one hundred percent."

"I didn't have any doubt," I said. "I need you to do the impossible now."

"The difficult I do immediately. The impossible takes only slightly longer."

"I need you to find out who else *didn't* work with Kemper and Dominic. Somebody's picking off a team of former spooks, and I need to know who's next on the list."

## Chapter 17
## *America*

I spent the remainder of the flight playing out possible scenarios in what remained of my mind. If Dominic knew immediately who'd taken a shot at him after hearing about Parker Kemper the Third's murder at Gettysburg, there had to be some tie between them. The only rational connection could be the congressman's father, who shared Dominic's profession during the Cold War. There had to be a way to untangle the silent and invisible cords of that mysterious period, and I needed to make that happen before the CIA screwed the whole thing up so badly that it could never be resolved.

We touched down on South Bimini and climbed aboard the waiting chopper for the short ride to the RV *Lori Danielle*. When I stepped from the Vertol on the helipad, I came face-to-face with a man I'd never met, and part of me considered drawing my sidearm in defense of my ship.

When he spoke, his accent was country British, and I checked off one item on my seemingly endless to-do list. I had acquired a more suitable staff of officers for Captain Sprayberry.

"Good day, sir. Welcome back aboard. Do you require a condition briefing, or do you have a report for the captain?"

"Condition briefing?" I asked.

"Of course, sir. We lay at hover at the same precise coordinates as the time of your departure, with only a slight alignment adjustment to meet the current wind . . ."

I waved him off. "No. I wasn't asking for a briefing. I've just never heard the term *condition briefing* when I've returned to the ship from a mission."

He appeared taken aback. "It's proper naval procedure for the commodore to be kept apprised of—"

"Commodore? You need to relax a little. I'm just Chase. And you are?"

He nodded almost perceptibly. "I am Winston Longmire, sir, the captain's new chief mate. Ah, forgive me. Old habits die hard. You Yanks call us first officers."

I offered a hand, and he accepted. "So, you're the new second-in-command. Welcome to the team, Mr. Longmire. If Captain Sprayberry chose you, you must have quite the résumé, and it's an honor to have you aboard."

"Thank you, sir. When the time is appropriate, the new staff and I should like an audience with you."

I chuckled. "I'm afraid it's going to take me a while to learn proper English, but we don't really have audiences with each other aboard the *Lori Danielle*. We get together and talk when we need or want to. I'm not quite as formal as the captain."

"In that case, sir, shall we, um, get together and talk later today?"

"That sounds fine. Now, if you'll excuse me, I'd like to get a proper briefing from Lady Skipper, if you please."

Mr. Longmire furrowed his brow and froze until I patted him on the shoulder and broke into laughter. "Relax, Winston. I'm just messing with you. Get used to it. But do me a favor, will you?"

"Of course, sir."

"First, stop calling me sir, and second, when a giant steps off the chopper, do all this stuff again with him. He's *my* chief mate on the tactical side. His name is Marvin Malloy, but he doesn't answer to anything besides Mongo."

"Will do, sir . . . uh, I mean, Chase."

I found Skipper exactly where I expected, and she huffed. "Remember when I said the impossible only takes a little longer? Well, that's not the case this time. I'm running into stone walls every direction I turn. I've even got Ginger trying to piece the old network together, and she's not doing any better than I am."

I pulled up a seat. "Take a breath. We'll figure this out. I think we may have to go old school, though. The answers we want aren't in any computers. Have you met the new officers?"

She frowned. "Of course the answers are in the computers. Everything's in a database somewhere."

"Not everything," I said, tapping my temple. "Some things live and die up here. So, the new officers . . . Have you met them?"

"Yeah, I met them. They're pretty stiff, but Barry *almost* smiled once. I think that's the happiest I've ever seen him."

"They'll loosen up. But don't tell anybody you saw the captain *almost* smile. They'll never believe you. Where are we on finding Billy Goddard?"

Skipper said, "About that. The officers aren't the only new additions to the crew. Captain James Millgood and Dingo showed up as well, and they brought two other mates, as they call them. I haven't learned their names yet, but they've got the look."

"What look?"

"The same look you and the whole team have—that thousand-yard stare and quiet confidence that comes from knowing you could kill everybody in the room without breaking a sweat."

"Oh, that look. So, I assume the Brits are out searching for Billy with Singer and Kodiak."

"They *were*, but the search is over. We found his body about half a mile from the last place his phone pinged. He was on the bottom in eight feet of water."

I closed my eyes, said a silent prayer for Chuck, Billy's brother, and asked, "How?"

She gripped her mouse. "You're not going to like it."

A second later, the screen filled with a close-up picture of shriveled flesh that had obviously been in salt water for days.

I leaned in. "What am I looking at?"

"Billy Goddard's neck and chin. Take a look at the tiny indentation just above his Adam's apple."

It took me a minute to spot the tiny speck. "What is that? A needle mark?"

"An ice pick, according to Dr. Shadrack."

"An ice pick?" I said in utter disbelief.

Skipper nodded. "Talk to your fiancée about it. She'll explain it to you."

"Anya? She's not my fiancée."

Skipper smiled. "Just because you haven't officially asked yet doesn't mean she isn't going to be your wife. Ask her. She'll say yes, *and* she'll explain the ice pick thing. I don't have the stomach to tell you about it."

"How's Chuck? And more importantly, *where* is Chuck?"

"His brother was murdered with an ice pick and thrown in the ocean, so he's not great. As far as *where* he is, you're not going to love that, either. He's with the Bahamian police. We didn't have any choice."

I said, "I figured. I assume they have the body as well?"

She nodded, and I asked, "Autopsy?"

"You will like this part. They don't have a medical examiner who can perform an autopsy on Bimini. They'd have to ship the body to Nassau."

"Why would I like that part?"

"Keep your shirt on, Shooter. I wasn't finished. Yours truly talked Chief Inspector Belafonte into holding the body in the morgue on Bimini until arrangements could be made to have the *American* shipped back to *America* for an *American* autopsy."

"I could kiss you!"

"Please don't," she said. "I've already had my shower today, and I don't have time to take another."

"So, when can we pick up Billy's body?"

She recoiled. "We?"

"Yes, we. We'll bring him on board, and Dr. Shadrack can perform the autopsy. This is an American-flagged vessel, so legally, this is America."

She waved a hand. "That's between you and Belafonte. I just kept Billy's body from being shipped to Nassau. The rest is up to you."

"I'll take care of it. What are they going to do with Chuck?"

She shrugged. "I don't know. That wasn't my task. I'm supposed to be finding a connection between Dominic, Kemper, and some other people I've never heard of, who probably never existed and never had anything to do with each other. Remember?"

"I remember. And I think I know just how to find at least some of those answers your computer is never going to tell you."

"Okay, Super Spy, how are you going to do that?"

"I'm going to phone a friend," I said.

"And who is this friend? I'm the analyst. I need to know what's going on."

I dialed the number from memory and pressed the speaker button.

Three rings later, a gentle voice whispered, "Chase? Is it really you?"

The years had forced a rasp into his tone, but it was still the same comforting voice I'd heard a thousand years before, when my beloved mentor and psych professor, Dr. Robert Richter, flew me to Jekyll Island in the P-51 Mustang that was now mine. He'd introduced me to the three other men who would recruit me into the world of covert operations in which I now lived, thrived, and loved. Ace, the de facto spokesman for the group of old guys, had been a World War II fighter pilot and one of the most decorated aviators of the era. He succumbed to the ravages of cancer before I finished my initial training. Beater had pummeled his way through the Naval Academy as their heavyweight boxing champion and eventually into a career as one of the most feared interrogators of the mid-twentieth century. The final member of the gang was the father of acoustic signature identification, learning his craft and honing his ear for sonar returns as an officer in America's silent service aboard diesel submarines that were state-of-the-art at the time but now considered dinosaurs. He was the man I had on the line.

"Hello, Tuner. It's great to hear your voice."

He laughed and cleared his throat. "At my age, son, it's great to *be* heard. How've you been?"

"I'm doing fine. Thank you for asking."

He said, "Still saving the world, I hear."

"Is that what you hear?"

He laughed again. "You know me. Hearing is all I really know how to do, and even that's becoming challenging these days. Something tells me this isn't a social call."

"No, sir, it's not. And I apologize for not checking in on you as often as I should."

"Ah, give that a rest, boy. You've got plenty to do without worrying about an old man. What can I do for you?"

"Dominic Fontana is in the hospital and fighting for his life."

"Oh, dear," Tuner said. "Is it his heart? He always had trouble with the ticker."

"Partially, but it was a sniper who put him there."

"A sniper, you say?"

"Yes, sir, but that's not the only reason I'm calling. Dominic isn't the only victim. Parker Kemper—"

Before I could finish, Tuner said, "Chase, this isn't a conversation we should have on the phone. Can you meet me at the same place we had our first important conversation?"

"Yes, sir, I can. When?"

"I'll be waiting when you get here. And Chase, the conversation we're going to have will change your life far more dramatically than our first one did—if you can imagine that being possible."

## Chapter 18
## *Obedience*

I knocked on Anya's cabin door, and she said, "Come inside, Chasechka."

I stepped inside. "How did you know it was me?"

She shrugged. "I know things. Also, you do not have to knock. You may come and go anytime you wish. Are you here to scold me for disobeying direct order from man I love?"

I parked myself on the edge of her bed. "No, that's not why I'm here, but we do need to lay some ground rules for how we operate in the field. Our relationship can't play a role in the chain of command out there."

She rubbed her hands together. "Oh, goodie. Tell to me these rules. I love rules because they are so much fun to break."

"I should've known this conversation wasn't going anywhere, so let's move on. Can you land on Jekyll Island?"

"How long is runway?"

"Thirty-seven hundred feet."

She closed one eye and studied the light in the ceiling. "If temperature is below thirty-seven degrees, yes."

"Are you serious? It's never below thirty-seven degrees on Jekyll Island."

She patted my face. "You are so cute when you cannot think clearly inside room with me. Temperature is Celsius, silly boy."

I ignored whatever that comment was supposed to mean. "Let's go for a ride. I've got an old friend I need to see."

She stood. "We are going now?"

"Yes, right now."

"For how many days? I will need nice LBD for dinner inside Jekyll Island Club."

"Zero days," I said. "And no little black dress. It's an up-and-back trip, just long enough for a conversation with Tuner."

She frowned. "Are you certain we cannot have this conversation while also having dinner?"

"I'm certain. Let's go."

"I am taking dress because you will change mind."

On our way down the corridor toward the navigation bridge, I discovered an old friend coming the opposite direction with an armload of linen. "Captain Millgood. I heard you were aboard. Welcome."

He dropped the sheets and towels and threw his arms around me. "Ah, Chase. I ain't captain no more. I report to you now."

"We're pretty informal around here," I said.

He laughed. "That ain't what I hear from the officers."

"Well, Captain Sprayberry looks at the world a little differently than I do."

He said, "I tend to agree with the captain on that one, mate."

"I thought you might. Listen, I hate to run, but we have to be four hundred miles away in an hour. We'll be back, and I want to sit down with you and your men as soon as I can carve out a couple of hours."

He gathered his linens. "I look forward to it. Can I offer you a ride ashore? I was just about to drop off these bedclothes and go muck about in the RHIB."

"That would be great. You'd save us from getting the chopper out again," I said. "We'll meet you on the weather deck."

"Boat's already afloat on the port quarter. I'll meet you on the water in a jiff."

I followed Anya—and her LBD—down the ladders to the deck just above the waterline, and we made our way astern. When I opened the hatch, Millgood was already aboard the RHIB with the engines running.

"How'd you beat us down here?"

He grinned through his decidedly British teeth. "Do you make a regular go of hiring commandos who are slower than you?"

We stepped aboard, and I said, "Drop us at the airport while I figure out how you pulled that off."

As we motored away from the *Lori Danielle*, Anya nudged me and pointed toward the rope ladder dangling over the ship's rail.

Millgood dropped us at the short dock beside the airport and pulled away almost before our feet hit the planks.

"I like him," Anya said, "but he is strange person."

"We're all strange."

She frowned. "Not British Special Boat Service kind of strange, though."

The walk to the plane took only a minute, and I conducted the exterior inspection while Anya set up the cockpit for our relatively short hop to Jekyll Island. Convinced the beautiful little jet would fly, I climbed aboard and twisted my way into the cockpit. "Walk-around complete. No squawks."

She said, "I will fly first leg, and you may fly back. This is okay with you, yes?"

"It's your airplane."

She turned the page to the engine-start checklist. "Yes, but we are in field, so I must obey your orders."

I laughed. "Yes, that's you, the obedient one. I've got the radios. Let's go."

The flight was perfect until we descended into the island through a layer of darkening clouds that somehow felt like foreshadowing. The world outside the windshield turned black, and the Citation shuddered as if being tossed about by some cosmic beast determined to shake us from the cockpit.

We broke out of the clouds at three thousand feet, and the majestic spire of the Jekyll Island Club stretched into the sky as if reaching for our hands. Anya's landing was flawless, and we rolled to a stop with plenty of runway left in front of us.

"Beautiful," I whispered.

She taxied toward the parking apron. "I love it when you say to me that I am beautiful."

"I was talking about the—"

She said, "Shh. Do not talk yourself out of compliment."

A young lady drove up in a golf cart as we came down the steps from the Citation. "Dr. Fulton?"

Anya pointed at me. "That is him. I am only his obedient nurse."

I tipped the young lady generously in a wasted effort to help her overcome her embarrassment, but I'm not sure I had enough money in the bank to pull that one off.

On the short drive to the club from the airport, I asked, "What was that all about?"

Anya slid her hand onto my thigh and smiled, but she didn't say a word.

I suppose some wild things can never be tamed.

As the exquisite nineteenth-century club came into view through the Spanish moss dripping from oaks that had watched the construction in the eighteen eighties, a flood of memories and emotion poured over me. It had been there, at that illustrious institution, where I stepped out of a world I knew and understood and into one I would come to know all too well but never truly understand. A twenty-one-year-old boy had gone to this place with the ink still wet on his college diploma and his promising career as a professional baseball player lying in ruin on the dusty earth behind him. That boy rode away from Jekyll Island as a man destined to preserve that which America could never let die, and to become a weapon of war unleashed only in the shadows, until the day those same dark shadows consumed him. No matter how hard I tried, I couldn't douse the flames dancing inside my head, telling me I was on the verge of stepping into what could be the darkest and final shadow of my life.

"Are you okay, Chasechka?"

I nodded, and she withdrew her hand. "Are you certain? I will make no more jokes of obedience. I am sorry."

"No, it's not that. It's just . . . I don't know. This case is really getting to me."

"I understand," she said. "Shall I remain out of sight for meeting with this person?"

"No, I want you with me. Whatever this thing is, it's too big for me to grasp alone. I need your insight and experience, but I also need you to be professional."

"I will be for you whatever you want, and especially what you need."

Although she'd been playful and even a bit out of bounds since our talk about ground rules, the sincerity in her voice reassured me that she was, and would always be, one of the greatest assets of the American intelligence community, and I was fortunate to have her not only by my side, but also in my chaotic life.

We rounded the end of the club and drove toward the stone patio at the rear. A weathered, worn man I barely recognized forced himself from his wrought-iron chair beside the same table I'd smoked my first cigar at a lifetime ago.

We embraced, and he took a step back. "Let me look at you, boy. I've heard so many great things about the work you're doing. It's good to see you, Chase, my old friend."

I studied the canyon of walls the club formed around us. "This place . . ."

He nodded. "Yes, this place, indeed."

A moment of silent understanding hung between us until he reached for Anya's hand. "Forgive me, Ms. Burinkova. I'm Tuner, and it's an enormous pleasure to finally meet you."

Anya shook his withering hand. "The honor is mine, sir. I hope you do not mind if I join you."

He glanced at the small, round table and three chairs placed evenly around it as if measured by a mathematician. In the center of the table rested three Cuban Cohibas, three glasses, and a bottle of bourbon that likely cost more than some cars. "I was expecting you."

Anya sat first, and Tuner and I joined her. He poured the whiskey and slid a glass toward each of us. I stared at the golden amber siren inside the ornate crystal tumbler. "Thank you, but we're flying, and I don't drink anymore after . . ."

Tuner lowered his head. "Yes, of course. My heart was broken when I heard of Penny's murder, but you avenged her, my boy."

"How do you know so much?" I asked.

He took his first sip, and the look on his face said he tasted and savored every detail inside the bourbon. "If you live as long as me, young man, you'll astonish even yourself at the things you know. But even more astonishing will be the things you realize you'll never know."

"You're starting to sound like Dr. Richter."

He raised his glass. "To Rocket Richter, the best of us in every way."

That was the moment I accepted the fact that I'd get to see Anya in the little black dress she'd insisted on bringing, and I lifted the glass in front of me to touch the rim of his. When the thirty-year-old bourbon crossed my tongue, it felt as though a chain I'd borne around my neck fell away, and the weight of regret I'd carried for more than two years turned to a wisp of wind. Dr. Richter was gone. Penny was gone. And before the passing of more than a few years, the brilliant man in front of me would join them. I was not yet among those who'd crossed the River Styx or the Jordan, and I owed it to myself, those who loved me, and those I loved to not only live, but thrive without the burdens of anguish and loss crushing the beauty of what remained for me.

I punched the waiting cigars, handed one to each of my companions, and pulled my well-worn Xikar from my pocket. The smoke smelled like five hundred years of craftsmanship, backbreaking labor, and the rich dark soil of the island ninety miles south of *Cayo Hueso*.

Anya toasted her Cohiba and watched it turn from earthy brown to cherry red before taking her first draw. When the smoke rose from her lips, forming a veil of white in front of her, I wondered for an instant whose face I'd see when it wafted away.

When the coastal breeze finally took the white cloud, I drank in the heart-stopping blue eyes and flawless skin of the woman I'd first seen behind a rifle on top of a water tower when we were little more than seedlings of the trees we would become—and I fell in love with her a thousand times before I drew another breath.

# Chapter 19
## *The Breath of a Fish*

Tuner snapped his fingers across the wrought-iron table and smiled. "I understand why you'd rather look at her than me, but I'm the one with the information you came to hear."

I twisted to face him. "I'm sorry. I was . . ."

"I know what you were doing, and every man on the island and beyond would be doing the same thing if he were sitting next to her. Never apologize for that."

I looked back at the woman who'd waited a lifetime for me, but until I'd met our perfect daughter, I never could've understood why she would do such a thing.

Tuner checked the courtyard for prying eyes and ears, but we were alone except for a pair of honeymooners a hundred feet away who couldn't care less that we were there. "You're trying to piece together a connection between Dominic and Parker Kemper, right?"

"Yes, sir. That's right. Somebody killed Congressman Kemper during—"

Tuner held up a hand. "Let's not waste time by telling me things I already know. Kemper the Third was murdered at Gettysburg, and when we finish this conversation, you'll know why."

I swallowed hard and drew another mouthful of the irresistible Cohiba smoke.

Tuner did the same and followed it with a sip of bourbon. "Not a bad pairing, huh?"

As much as I wanted to keep my eyes locked on his, there's something so powerfully alluring about a beautiful woman smoking a magnificent cigar. It was impossible to ignore.

Tuner chuckled. "Oh, how I miss those days. Enjoy each other, but don't distract each other when this thing turns into a war. And a war it shall become."

He suddenly had my undivided attention. "A war?"

He sighed. "Just because that wall of stone and concrete came down doesn't mean the Iron Curtain collapsed along with it. The stage master may have drawn back the curtain, but rest assured, they didn't burn it from its rod. Just ask Ms. Burinkova."

Anya met my gaze as if asking if she should speak. The look surprised me, but I nodded.

She said, "Inside heart, Putin is still officer of KGB. Tuner is correct. If we give to Russia opportunity, they will draw again Iron Curtain that is still waiting and hanging in wings of stage."

Tuner shrugged. "It's the sad and frightening truth of the Cold War. It'll never truly end in any of our lifetimes. In fact, it just claimed three more victims in Dominic and the Kempers."

"Fortunately," I said, "Dominic is still alive."

"That doesn't eliminate him from the list of victims. Often, Chase, the survivors are the victims who suffer most."

Sometimes, wisdom hits like a hammer, and I'd just been struck. "So, tell me what's going on. No matter how deep we dig, we can't find any connection between Dominic and the Kempers."

The old relic of a bygone era leaned back, drew on his cigar, and studied his bourbon. "That's because you're looking for the wind."

I wondered at what point in my life I would begin to speak in riddles. "I'm not following you."

He said, "You know the wind exists—you can feel it. But no matter how hard you look, you'll never see it."

Anya motioned toward the aged oaks and magnolias around us. "Wind is easy to see in trees."

Tuner smiled. "No, my dear. You're not seeing the wind. You're seeing evidence of the wind. That's the same thing you're seeing when you look for the tie that binds our friend Dominic to the Kempers."

"I'm listening," I said.

"It's obvious the wind exists because the trees are moving and your hair is waving on the breeze. Just the same, there's obviously a connection between Dominic and Parker Kemper. Of course, I'm talking about the father, not his son, the congressman. He's merely a collateral casualty, likely because he knew what I'm about to tell you."

I asked, "But you know the connection, right?"

Tuner closed his eyes and took a long, deep breath. "I spent the first twenty years of my adult life listening for the breath of a fish. Just like the wind, I knew it was there, and I was convinced that if I devoted enough time, energy, and patience to the pursuit, I would one day learn to hear it. And I did."

The idea wound its way through my mind, but I didn't have the capacity to understand where my old friend was leading me.

He smiled again. "It's okay, son. If you live long enough, you'll be on this side of the table someday. Here's what I know about Parker Kemper the Second and Dominic Fontana. You know that's not really his name, right?"

For the first time in my life, I lied to Tuner, but I did it wordlessly, with only a nod. I lacked the patience to follow him down a rabbit trail about how Dominic got his moniker.

He obviously knew I was lying, but in the interest of time, he let me get away with it. "In nineteen sixty-five, Americans were moving into the jungles of Vietnam. The French had given up, and the freedom of half of a country lay in our hands."

He paused for a sip, and my impatience bubbled. "Are you saying this thing is about Vietnam?"

Disappointment filled his eyes. "Ignore the noise, son, and listen for the breath of the fish."

I subconsciously checked my watch, and of course Tuner noticed.

"Patience, Chase. I have a beautiful room reserved for you two and dinner reservations at eight. We have plenty of time."

Anya squeezed my leg beneath the table, and I immediately wished I'd listened to her back aboard the *Lori Danielle*. We were going to need more than a dress.

Tuner asked, "What do you know about Hayastani Soc'ialistakan Xorhrdayin Hanrapetut'yun?"

I sat in dumbfounded silence, but Anya saved me. "This is first name for Socialist Soviet Republic of Armenia that later became Hayastani Hanrapetut'yun, Republic of Armenia in nineteen ninety."

Tuner pointed toward Anya. "See? Aren't you glad you brought her along?"

"In more ways than you could imagine."

He grinned. "Oh, I may be an old man, but I can still imagine. Let's not get sidetracked on the glories of beautiful Eastern European women. We have a lot to talk about."

Anya blushed, and I tried to picture the withered man across from me as a dashing, thirty-year-old naval officer. Ah, the stories he could tell.

Tuner stood and stretched. "Getting old is hard on the body, but it certainly beats the alternative."

"We can go someplace more comfortable," I said.

He nestled back onto the small, metal chair. "No, this is where we belong. How much Armenian history do you know?"

Anya started to speak, but Tuner held up a hand. "Not you. Chase."

I said, "I'm ashamed to admit that I don't know anything about Armenia."

"That's okay. The important thing to know is that a nation is not defined by its borders imposed by any regime. It's defined by its people, and the Armenian people are some of the strongest and most beautiful people who've ever lived. I'm not speaking of physical beauty—although they certainly are—I'm speaking of the beauty of their character and uncrushable spirit."

I settled in for what was clearly going to be a lengthy history lesson.

"I'll be as brief as I'm capable of being, but it's important that you understand the history. In April of nineteen fifteen, the Ottomans threw the Armenian scholars and leaders out of Constantinople, and over a million citizens were sent on death marches into the Syrian Desert. They were starved, robbed, raped, and murdered in mass. There's no way to know the actual number who died, but in nineteen sixteen, possibly as many as two hundred thousand Armenian women and children were forced to convert from Christianity to Islam and were integrated into Muslim families. Turkish nationalists continued the genocide throughout the Turkish War of Independence."

He hesitated before saying, "*Ethnic cleansing* is the term they like to use, but it was genocide of the highest order. In fact, before the Nazis, what happened to the Armenians was considered to be the 'apex of horrors conceivable.'"

He coughed, lost his breath, and took a few minutes to compose himself. Finally, he continued. "The genocide destroyed over two millennia of Armenian civilization in Eastern Anatolia."

With a glance at Anya, he asked, "How'd I do, Ms. Burinkova?"

Anya bowed her head. "This was terrible time and horrific thing. You are very good history teacher."

"I'm no teacher, my dear. I'm merely an observer and reporter. I listen, remember?"

She gave him a warm smile. "Yes, and please, I am just Anya."

He said, "I told you all of this so you could understand the soul of these people. Now, fast-forward to the nineteen sixties when Leonid Brezhnev took over the Soviet Union from Khrushchev. Even though the Kremlin didn't restrict the Armenians to the degree Stalin had, the leadership was still concerned about the probable resurgence of Armenian nationalism. It's impossible to crush a people whose hearts are so strong and thirsty for freedom."

"You love these people, don't you?" I asked.

He stared at Anya for a moment that was almost uncomfortably long. "I do, and I loved *one* of them more than I've ever loved anyone or anything else in my life. Her name was Anush. She, however, is a story for another day when madmen aren't shooting at our friends."

Anya pressed her lips into a tight line—her common expression when trying to stifle a coming tear. "Anush means *sweet* in English."

Tuner sighed. "She was exactly that, in every language."

He coughed again but kept talking. "Back to April of nineteen sixty-five. Tens of thousands of Armenians demonstrated in the streets of Yerevan at the fiftieth anniversary of the Armenian genocide. That's precisely the kind of thing the CIA loves to see and take full advantage of. And that, my friend, is the breath of the fish."

I furrowed my brow. "That was over fifty years ago. How could that possibly have anything to do with what's happening right now?"

His words were barely more than a whisper—barely more than the invisible wind in the trees. "Parker Kemper the Second, Dominic Fontana, David Bellingham, Benjamin Copel, and I were dispatched to Yerevan to demolish the economy of the Republic of Armenia, from the inside out, in hopes of driving the people into further revolt and ultimate succession from the Soviet Union."

My heart pounded as if driven by a raging storm. "We have to get you someplace safe, now! Are Bellingham and Copel still alive?"

He relit the cigar he'd ignored for fifteen minutes. "Ben Copel died in Cambodia in seventy-one, but Dave Bellingham is still alive."

I yanked my phone from my pocket, but Tuner caught my wrist. "Don't call your analyst. She won't find him. Just like Dominic, he's had a thousand names and lived ten thousand lives. More importantly, though, we're having dinner with him in half an hour."

## Chapter 20
# *Undefendable*

I stared at the phone in my white-knuckle grip and Tuner's gnarled fingers encircling my wrist. "Are you saying Dave Bellingham is here on Jekyll Island?"

He released my wrist. "He is, but not under that name, of course."

Ignoring his admonition not to call my analyst, I thumbed the button and pressed the phone to my ear.

"What are you doing?" Tuner asked.

Skipper answered. "CIC."

"Move everybody to my location, immediately."

"Everybody?"

"Everybody and everything. Put the team on the Herk for airborne insertion . . ."

Tuner leaned toward me. "Chase, my boy, what are you doing? Relax. We're perfectly safe here."

Skipper's tone hardened. "Assets are moving now. Go to secure sat-coms."

I ended the call and brought my satellite radio online. "CIC, Sierra One."

"CIC has you loud and clear, Sierra One. How me?"

"I have you the same. Advise ready for sitrep."

Before Skipper answered, I took Anya's hand. "Get Tuner inside the library for now and find Bellingham. I need to know if Jack Ford is on the property."

Anya moved immediately, taking Tuner by the arm and leading him from the table.

"Send sitrep," Skipper said.

I paused, gathering and organizing the information flooding my senses. "Tuner revealed the connection between Dominic and Kemper. He was also part of the network. There's a fourth man named David Bellingham. He's here on the property, but that's not his real name. I'll brief you on the details later. Right now, we have to get Tuner and Bellingham aboard the ship."

She said, "Understood. Do you want—"

The sound of a distant explosion rolled across the spired peaks of the resort.

I jumped to my feet and sprinted for the end of the massive building. "Stand by."

A decade before, Skipper would've asked a thousand questions, but her maturity and competence as the finest intelligence analyst in the game had peaked, giving her the ability to bury her curiosity beneath necessity and focus on details that mattered most instead of succumbing to the nearly irresistible need to know what was happening outside her lair.

When I rounded the end of the main resort building, a plume of black smoke rose from the north, and my gut tied itself into a knot.

"We're under attack," I said. "There was an explosion near the airport, and I suspect it was Anya's Citation. Do you have any satellite coverage of the island?"

"I'm on it," she said in the calm tone I'd come to expect from her.

"I've got two birds, but neither is a high-def camera platform, and the weather doesn't look great there."

I found myself lost in the darkening sky. "This is about to turn ugly, Skipper. Get my shooters on that Herk. We're in trouble."

"They're moving," she said just as a second explosion rumbled to the southwest. "What was that?"

"I don't know yet, but I'm going to open-channel comms with

you. I'm on foot. Record everything, and feed me what I need as you have it."

She said, "Roger."

Anya's confident tone filled my head through the bone-conduction device affixed to my jawbone and electronically linked to our satellite communication devices. "Sierra One, Sierra Three."

"Go for One."

She said, "Primary is secure, and Jack Ford is at desk, waiting for you."

"What about Bellingham?" I asked as I sprinted along the back of the resort.

"I am moving to secure him now. Tuner says he is inside wheelchair and using name of Tom Jones."

*Oh, great. That's exactly what I need—a lounge singer in a wheelchair.*

I darted between a young couple in matching tennis outfits coming out the back door of the resort, and they muttered some utterance of disgust at my undignified behavior, but my reception inside the aged manor was quite different.

Jack Ford, longtime manager of the Jekyll Island Club and a proven friend of the original organization I worked for, pointed from the end of the reception desk and into his office. I followed his finger, and he closed the door behind us.

"Give it to me," he said.

"You remember Anya, the Russian. It's just her and me. She just stuck Tuner in the library, and she's moving to secure David Bellingham. He's probably registered as Jones."

"Secure him from what?"

"I don't have time to explain it all, but your island is under attack, Mr. Ford. I think they just blew up our Citation at the airport, and they may have taken out the bridge."

"They *who*?" he demanded.

"I don't know yet, but help's on the way."

Jack lifted the receiver from his desk. A few seconds later, he said, "This is Jack Ford. Look out your window and tell me if the bridge is on fire."

More explosions rocked the air, rattling the more-than-century-old glass of the resort's windows.

Jack covered the mouthpiece. "The bridge isn't burning, according to the State Patrol."

"Good," I said. "Get them over here, and have them bring everybody and every weapon they own."

He spoke into the receiver, then hung up. "What's going on, Chase?"

I took a breath. "It's a convoluted situation, but Dominic Fontana was shot by a sniper, and a man named Parker Kemper was murdered in his barn. Somebody tried to make it look like a suicide."

"Parker Kemper the Second?"

"Yes."

Jack closed his eyes and blew out a long stream of air. "They killed his son, the congressman, too."

"I know," I said. "I was there."

"So, who is this Bellingham person?"

"I don't know his real name, but he's tied to an operation that Dominic, Kemper, and Tuner worked on in the sixties in the Soviet Union."

"Armenia . . ."

I asked, "How do you know about that?"

"Look around, Chase. Everything about this place is founded in money—most distinctly its misuse, abuse, and torture. From the establishment of the Federal Reserve down the hall to American aristocracy and robber barons planning more wars than we can count, it's all been done right here on this property."

The phone rang, and Jack yanked it from its cradle. "Ford . . . What? . . . How about a helicopter?"

More explosions shook the air around us, and I yanked the blinds away from the window behind Jack's desk. The sky threatened, and rain pelted the manicured lawn as a burst of thunder roared through me. I wondered how many of the explosions I'd heard had actually been the thunderstorm and not a sinister assault.

*Am I overreacting? Or panicking?*

While Jack was on the phone, I stuck my head back through his doorway and caught the clerk's attention. "Please call the airport and make sure everything's okay."

She hesitated. "O . . .okay. Does Mr. Ford—"

"Do it now!"

The young lady recoiled and fumbled for the phone.

I called Anya. "Three, One. Say status."

She said, "I have second primary, but I do not want to take him back to library."

I turned to Jack. "Do you have a bunker we can get a wheelchair into?"

"I've got a vault."

"Where?"

He motioned across his office and toward a door that looked like the entrance to a typical closet. I turned the knob and pulled it open, revealing a black steel wall six inches inside the opening.

"Is there ventilation in there?"

Jack said, "Some, but it's not like air-conditioning."

I said, "Bring Bellingham to Jack Ford's office."

Anya answered, "Sixty seconds."

The clerk tapped at the door and timidly stuck her head into the room. "Excuse me, sir, but there *has* been an incident at the airport."

"Do you still have them on the phone?" I asked.

She nodded, and I pushed past her to press the receiver to my ear. "Is the Citation jet damaged?"

"Who is this?" a man's voice demanded with authority.

"The owner of the Citation. Is it damaged?"

He said, "No, the jet isn't damaged, but there was a crash on the runway."

The whole world swirled inside my head.

*The bridge wasn't on fire. The Citation hadn't been blown up. A routine coastal Georgia thunderstorm produced sounds that felt and sounded like explosions.*

Remaining calm and thinking rationally under fire are the hallmarks of an effective warrior.

*Am I doing either?*

The front tires of an electric wheelchair penetrated the doorway into Jack Ford's office, and a man who could've been Methuselah appeared nestled in the seat. He said, "What the hell is this all about?"

Jack swung open the vault door just as I said, "Somebody hit Dominic Fontana and Parker Kemper. Now I think they're here for you and Tuner."

The old man's hazy eyes brightened. "I'm gonna need a gun."

I hoped I'd have the same reaction when my years on earth approached triple digits.

"I'll see what I can do. For now, let's get you in the vault while I figure all of this out."

Bellingham looked up. "Can I take her with me?"

Such levity in that moment was exactly what I needed. "I'm afraid I'll need her if this thing turns into a fight, but I'll bring her back when it's over."

"See that you do, sonny. And I'm sorry to hear about Dom and Parker."

"Dominic's still alive," I said, "but it's not looking good."

"Where's Tuner?" Bellingham asked.

Anya said, "He is inside library."

"Not a bad choice, but if you'll get him up here with me, we can look after each other while you two—whoever you are—sort things out."

"We're friends," I said. "And I think I like that idea. Hopefully it's nothing, but I'd rather err on the side of keeping you guys alive."

He chuckled. "That's my favorite side on which to err. But please tell me there are more than just the two of you."

"The cavalry is coming."

Anya asked with her eyes, and I said, "Go get him."

She left to retrieve Tuner, and Jack said, "That was the State Patrol on the phone. The bridge isn't on fire, but there's been a wreck, and all of the traffic lanes are blocked."

I drew a mental picture of our situation. "I wasn't just being paranoid. Something's going down. They, whoever they are, have cut off the island. The bridge is blocked, and the airport's closed. And the thunderstorm will keep the choppers out."

"So, you think they can control the weather?" Jack asked.

"No, but I think they're smart enough to take advantage of a gift from Mother Nature. We're gonna need some weapons and shooters if you've got 'em."

He motioned toward the vault. "What little I have is in there. Help yourself. I have three security officers on the property, but they're just window dressing."

"How about you?" I asked.

He bowed his head. "I'm just a resort manager. I've quietly been on your team for fifty years, but I'm just support."

Anya shuffled Tuner through the door, and I briefed the situation.

"Somebody wrecked a plane at the airport and simultaneously crashed some cars on the bridge. I suspect whoever's behind it moved up their timetable to make use of the storm. We're going to hold down the fort and keep you two alive until the rest of the team gets here. Have you got any input?"

Tuner stepped to the window and parted the blinds with a crooked finger. "How long will it take for the rest of your men to get here?"

I instinctively checked my watch, although nothing on my wrist had any bearing on the flight time from Bimini to Jekyll. "CIC, is the Herk airborne?"

Skipper said, "Affirmative. They've been airborne for nine minutes, but the weather—"

"Forget the weather," I said. "Have you weighed anchor?"

"Affirmative. We're underway, and the ship will be on the foils and making as much speed as the Gulf Stream will allow in ten minutes."

I sighed. "Roger. I'm afraid we're in an undefendable position. I can keep Tuner and Bellingham alive, but four hundred innocent guests at the Jekyll Island Club are about to become hostages."

# Chapter 21
## *Whispers of a Phantom*

"Hostages?" Jack Ford almost yelled. "I can't have guests becoming hostages."

"I understand," I said, "but it's too late to prevent that from happening. All we can do now is protect our two primaries and defend the resort the best we can with the limited resources at hand."

He eyed Tuner and Bellingham. "Chase, everybody here is a primary to me. I understand your desire to keep these two alive, but my responsibility is far greater than just two men."

I stepped beside him. "You're right, but being right doesn't always dictate priorities. Someone is killing people associated with an operation—"

He cut me off. "An operation that happened over half a century ago. I'm living in *today*, and I've got four hundred eighteen registered guests at this property, *today*!"

The situation was growing dire, and nothing in my head would form a solution. Whoever was coming was likely drawing nearer by the second, and all I had were two rifles, four pistols, three knives, and a former Russian assassin to defend over four hundred people from a completely unknown enemy.

Closing my eyes, I took a moment to turn to the one force who'd never let me down, but I kept the prayer brief, lasting no longer than one of the few breaths I might have had left on Earth.

Jack seemed to notice the direction I'd turned and said, "Here's hoping God's on our side in this thing."

To my surprise, Anya answered before I could. "No, this is wrong thing to hope. We should hope that we are on *His* side."

"Point taken," Jack said. "But do you have a plan?"

I wanted Anya to answer again, but she stood silent at my side, her eyes scanning every angle through the doorway and both windows.

"Take a breath and seize the high ground" was the phrase that wouldn't leave my head, but the high ground was a wasted position when it was impossible to identify the enemy.

A buzzer yanked me from my thoughts, and I drew my pistol.

Jack laid a hand on my arm. "It's just the desk." He stuck his head through the door and paused. "Oh, I'm sorry. Gloria must've stepped away. May I help you?"

I peered around the doorframe and saw a middle-aged couple, dripping wet and leaning against the high counter.

The man spoke in a British accent that didn't feel authentic. "Good evening. My wife and I are to join a friend for dinner, but I'm afraid we are a bit early. Tried to beat the storm, you know. Just failed, it would appear, but I wonder if you might direct us to his room. As I said, we are a bit early."

"Of course," Jack said. "What's your friend's room number? I'll be happy to point the way."

The man patted his pockets. "Oh, dear. I must've left the slip in the taxi. Forgive me. His name is Sidney Throckmorton. Perhaps you could look him up."

Jack turned ever so subtly, allowing his eyes to meet mine before saying, "I don't recall a Mr. Throckmorton, but let me see what I can find. Give me just a moment, if you will. I don't know the system out here, so I'll need to check in the office."

Jack stepped from the reception desk and back through the doorway, where he met Tuner's gaze and froze. "He's asking for your room number."

I mouthed, "Sidney Throckmorton? Really?"

Anya said, "Give to him room number."

Tuner produced a key from his pocket and whispered, "Give him this, too."

Jack frowned, but I loved everything about the plan that had fallen into my lap.

Giving an Oscar-worthy performance, Jack stepped back to the desk. "You'll have to forgive me. I'm just the auditor, so I don't know anything about this. The young lady who manages the desk has stepped away, but I did find Mr. Throckmorton's room number. It's two twenty-seven, just down that hallway there, but I have a request if you wouldn't mind."

The man took a step back. "A request?"

Jack cleared his throat. "I'm a little ashamed to admit it, but there was a note saying that Mr. Throckmorton had requested a new key because his was sticking. As you can see, I've been left alone up here." He held out the key on its green plastic paddle. "Would you mind?"

The man pretending to be British laughed. "Of course not. Sid will be happy to see us and doubly happy to get his fresh key. I'm sure he'll return the original sticky one after dinner."

The couple left, pressed through the doorway leading down the second-floor hallway, and Anya motioned toward the vault. "Get in and lock door. We will be back."

She brushed past me, and I followed one step behind until we reached the hallway door. She pushed it open just enough to see the couple still approaching room two twenty-seven.

She whispered. "I count eight doors on left. Be ready."

I laid a hand on her shoulder as she continued peering through the tiny slit.

She whispered, "Key is in door. Get ready."

Anya gave no further command as she watched. I felt the muscles in her back tighten and detected the slightest lean forward before she burst through the door and accelerated into a sprint. I followed two strides behind with my pistol ready and my mind full of everything I thought could possibly wait for us inside Tuner's previously empty room.

If everything went perfectly, we'd pin the couple to the floor, disarm them, and wait for our ambitious young interrogator to arrive. By my calculation, he and the rest of the team were halfway between Bimini and Jekyll Island, somewhere high above the Atlantic. My focus, though, needed to be a few feet ahead and inside an elegant guest room that could become a cauldron of chaos if things went sideways.

Anya's well-earned reputation for aggression showed itself again as she planted her right foot and exploded through the open door of room two twenty-seven, a pistol in her left hand and a glistening blade in her right.

When clearing a room, the first gunner through the door is never wrong. Regardless of the turn she takes, number two must turn the opposite direction to cover the rest of the room. In a four-man clearing operation, the stack pours through the door like liquid and consumes the space with overwhelming force. A two-person op isn't quite the same. With the force being only Anya and me, each of us had twice the space to secure, and a single well-placed shot from a bad guy could cut our team in half in an instant. Two lucky shots could send the fat lady into an aria that might bring down the house.

Anya went right, so I went left, expecting to see surprise on the face of either the man or woman who'd used Tuner's key to step inside seconds before. Instead, I saw an empty room.

Anya threw herself to the floor and shone her pistol-mounted light beneath the bed. She called out, "*Nichego,*" and my English-thinking brain struggled to translate the Russian word into *nothing*.

I raised my boot to freight-train my way through the bathroom door, but I changed my tack at the last possible second to take full advantage of the oversized mirror and the partially open door to survey the small space. I made the step inside to claim the angle around the door. *Nichengo*.

"Clear!"

I double-checked the hallway and stepped back into the room.

Anya asked, "Where could they have gone? Is very strange . . ."

Almost before she ended the assessment of our situation, two figures materialized as if from another dimension, and the chaos I thought possible suddenly became reality.

The man swung a blackjack with blinding speed toward my head, and I raised a shoulder to slow the assault, but the strike came hard. He trapped my pistol against my body with one hand and plowed me backward until I collided with the room's open door. The crash slammed the door into its jamb, and stars circled my head.

Fighting with everything I had to raise my pistol proved to be wasted effort. Whoever the fake Brit was, he was stronger than me, and he had the advantage of leverage from his position. I pressed my back against the door and raised a knee at full force. He seemed to anticipate the coming strike and turned to absorb the blow with his thigh instead of letting it hit my intended target.

I was in a fight for my life, but every thought was of Anya and what she was facing a few feet away. So far, there had been no gunfire, but there had also been no sickening sounds of blades piercing flesh and bodies collapsing to the floor. Until either of those occurred, I had to believe the woman I loved—the mother of my child—was waging a war of her own against an opponent we may have badly underestimated.

The blackjack came again, but I ducked, allowing it to swing past my head and into the oak door, splintering the heavy lumber. I threw an arm into the air, desperately attempting to trap the weapon that would do the same damage to my skull if I couldn't get it under control.

Taking full advantage of my compromised position, the man dropped the weapon and drove a seasoned fist into my exposed ribs in a rapid succession of punches as the breath exploded from my lungs.

It took an eternity, but I finally lowered my arm to defend the continued flurry of body blows. I didn't have the breath to counter his assault, but I had the fortitude.

Just as I'd done a thousand times behind home plate, I tucked my chin against my chest, rolled my shoulders inward, and leaned into the charging bull. He wasn't a base runner on that day. He was my would-be executioner, but the rules were the same. When the dust settled, both of us might be in the dirt, but I'd still have the ball, and he'd be out.

The blows kept coming, but most of them landed on my arm instead of my ribs. The Glock in my right hand was still solidly on my mind, so every time he threw a punch, I twisted a little harder, desperately trying to bring the weapon to bear on any part of him. If I could make him bleed, I would be one step closer to hearing the umpire call him out.

*God, this guy is strong. Come on, Chase. Think!*

A thundering fist made it past my elbow and landed like a rifle shot, centered on a rib that immediately turned to dust. I prayed it hadn't pierced my lung, but the pain was excruciating.

Had I thrown the punch, I would've believed I had won the battle, but my opponent offered no indication of letting up. To him, we were obviously in a fight with only one possible outcome. As I gagged and fought in vain to fill my lungs with the air I desperately needed, the relentless blows continued until my head fell in exhaustion.

The golden designs in the blue carpet beneath my feet came alive, swirling and dissolving and drawing nearer with every tick of the endless clock, until a break in the pattern caught my attention. Unconsciousness crept closer as I slid down the face of the door under the man's ravaging attack, and darkness clouded the limits of my vision.

The focus I'd devoted to my pistol and defending my rib cage morphed into a singular drive toward the darkened form lying in contrast against the carpet.

Whether I feigned withering or if it happened by nature's course, I'll never truly know, but my knees folded, and I came to rest with my butt on my boots at the man's feet. The pistol slipped from my hand and into his, but the shape on the ground still beckoned.

With my battered left arm, I reached for the carpet and gripped the leather handle of the man's blackjack. The world stopped turning for a moment, and perfect focus claimed my senses. The tendons in his hand tightened as the trigger beneath his index finger receded.

He would fire twice. Somehow, I knew him in that frozen blink in time. I understood him. At moments in my life, I had been him. His training and instinct would subconsciously put two rounds into my head before turning the weapon on Anya somewhere behind him.

He would've done all of those unthinkable things if my prayer hadn't been answered and the strength I demanded hadn't risen in me to swing the leaded weapon he'd launched at my head. Like David with his sling, I whipped the blackjack, catching the butt of my own pistol with the weighted load at the end of the weapon.

The two shots came, but they went high, penetrating the wooden door that had been my backstop throughout the battle.

Allowing the energy of the swinging blackjack to carry it high above my head, I summoned another wave of strength, drawing it back downward with even greater force until it collided with the man's knee. The sound of bone, cartilage, and the will-to-fight giving way beneath his skin filled me with renewed vigor.

The pistol was still in play, but agony had sunk her chilling claws into my opponent's flesh, giving me the first advantage I'd known in the skirmish.

I forced myself forward, driving all my weight against the demolished joint and folding the man's leg backward while thrusting my right hand upward to reclaim the pistol I'd carried into the fight.

He was heavy, but he didn't carry the soft weight of the man he'd pretended to be at Jack Ford's reception desk. He wore the armor of muscle over sinew and bone that he'd clearly spent a lifetime perfecting. His strength and bulk betrayed him in that moment, though, as the unimaginable pain from his leg, separated at the knee, overwhelmed his senses.

When the familiar metal and polymer of my Glock refilled my

hand, I continued my progress until I was on top of him and still moving. Just as he'd done out of ingrained instinct, I pressed the trigger twice, my muzzle trained on the center of his chest.

Without another thought of the man behind me, I slid onto a knee and raised my weapon toward the two women entangled in a fight even more fierce than what I'd just survived. A shot would likely enter, exit, and reenter one or both women if I were to press the trigger again, so I lowered the weapon, stumbled to my feet, and staggered my way forward, determined to force myself between Anya and the woman trying to end her.

Darkening edges continued to claim my vision, but I kept moving forward while daggers of fire stabbed my tortured ribs.

"Anya! Step back! Give me a shot!" I begged for a clean angle at the woman entangled with her, but the words drifted from my lips like whispers of a phantom, silent to everyone except what tiny consciousness remained within me. The darkness kept coming until it won, and I melted to the floor beneath a veil of terror of what would come without me.

# Chapter 22
## *Postponed*

The collision with the floor following my blackout brought some part of my brain back from silent slumber, but it left my body little more than two hundred pounds of worthless mass. Through lenses barely capable of focusing on any single, motionless object, I fought to take in the scene before me. Two gladiatrixes tore at each other with unimaginable force and speed, each filled with ardent determination to destroy the other.

One of Anya's blades lay silent and beyond my reach, not a single drop of blood showing from its glistening surface. The blur of motion beyond the blade writhed in a torrent of bodies thrashing at each other, mortal survival itself lying in the balance.

*Why isn't she bleeding? Why hasn't Anya cut her down?*

The answers came in the form of another hazy image of Anya's second knife protruding from the wall. She was fighting unarmed and making no effort to reclaim the blades that defined her lethality.

*Come on, Chase. Gut it out. Get your gun in the air. You've got to end this.*

My futile attempt to raise my arm and fire my weapon felt like pulling the whole world through an ocean of mud, and no matter how forcefully I commanded my arms to obey, they lay helpless, leaving me a mere witness to a spectacle beyond description.

Both women bellowed cries of animals in the throes of battle as my soul ached to intervene. At one moment, Anya would clearly have the engagement won, only to falter and succumb to the speed and agility of her foe. The tide of war wasn't ebbing and flowing before me—it was crashing on a rocky shore shaped more by chaos and fury than timeless predictability.

Before that moment, I'd never seen two opponents of such equal skill, strength, and determination locked in combat. Perhaps I watched for a thousand years, or maybe the fight lasted only a breath, but every strike was countered, and every defense was reattacked until all that remained inside either warrior was sheer will.

Exhaustion slowed their motion and weakened their cries, but each fought on until Anya faltered and crossed her ankles, giving the other woman the tiniest advantage. She drove Anya backward, off-balance and desperately fighting for purchase. Her heels struck the floor, sending echoes of thunder through my head, matching the still-raging storm outside the windows.

Anya's hip collided with a chair, crushing the antique into shards of wood and shreds of delicate fabric. The crash rolled the women to the left and sent both pounding against the wall.

When they hit the wall, my heart leapt, and the anticipation of what would follow in a flash of time made me forget the raging fire burning in my side.

A stream of blood flew high through the air like a crimson streak of light, and a piercing screech rose from deep inside the defeated fighter.

The crossed ankles hadn't been a mistake. They'd been Anya's perfectly orchestrated maneuver to make her way back to the fighting knife she left protruding from the plaster earlier in the fight.

With the sweep of a heel, my Russian goddess threw her bleeding opponent from her feet and onto her back. Anya landed astride her conquered foe, the bloody point of her blade pressed against the woman's throat.

Nearly breathless, Anya hissed in her native language. "You are very good fighter, but you stopped thinking when you became tired."

She raised the blade and drew downward with such force and speed that I expected the slash to decapitate her victim, but Anya rotated her hand, bringing the pommel of the blade to bear, and struck her in the temple. The blow rendered the woman unconscious instantly, and Anya collapsed to the floor beside her.

"My Chasechka. You are alive, yes?"

I mouthed the words, but I have no idea if the sound left my tongue. "I am."

She crawled toward me until her palm rested against my face. "Is he dead?"

"Yes. Is she dying?"

Her chest rose and fell as she heaved, reclaiming her breath. "No, is only small cut. They are Russian-trained."

Her breathing gradually slowed. "It felt like I was fighting myself. I was, for first time, afraid for my life in fight."

I tried to nod. "How badly are you hurt?"

Although I couldn't hear my own words, they must have reached her ears.

"I do not know yet, but I think maybe not as bad as you."

"Broken ribs," I mouthed.

"I have maybe also broken ribs and fingers. Shoulder is also painful. We need doctor."

"Help me up," I said.

She drew her knees beneath her and worked to sit me up until I was leaning against the edge of the bed.

After groaning, I said, "Ah, that's a little better. I can actually breathe."

She ran her hand down my side, feeling each rib. When she touched the spot where a rib should've been but was not, I flinched and let out a sound I'd never be proud of.

"Is badly broken. You are maybe bleeding inside. Is very serious."

I raised a hand to her face. "You were incredible."

She laughed. "No, my Chasechka. I was only more determined. This is all. We must now get you to hospital."

"There's no hospital on the island, and these two aren't alone."

Anya glanced at the body by the door and then back at her unconscious victim. "There are more, but so far, we are winning."

I wanted to chuckle, but the thought of the subsequent pain halted my ridiculous notion. "I need to get to my feet."

"I will steady you."

I pulled myself up until I was sitting on the bed, blazing pain coursing through my torso. "Okay, just a little further." I leaned forward and pressed my feet into the floor. The pain didn't worsen, but it certainly didn't surrender. Once on my feet, my balance was decent, and my vision slowly returned to some semblance of normalcy.

Anya lifted my pistol from the carpet and slid it into the holster beneath my shirt. "We must get her someplace quiet."

The implication sent chills down my spine. When the woman regained consciousness, the interrogation that followed would leave her begging for the merciful relief a blow to the temple would offer.

Anya dragged the man far enough away from the door for us to step over him and into the hallway. The short walk back to Jack Ford's office felt like a marathon, but we made it without encountering anyone else.

Jack was pacing in front of his desk with his cell phone gripped tightly in his hand. He said, "Phone lines are down, power is out, and we're on emergency generators. I can't get my cell to work."

"It's okay, Jack," I said. "They're either jamming cell phones or the power outage has the towers inoperative."

The realization of our appearance seemed to overtake him. "My God! Are you two all right?"

I shook my head. "No, but we're better than the other two."

Anya said, "They are Russian, most likely SVR. Man is dead, and woman is unconscious. We need place to move her that is very quiet and isolated from guests."

Jack swallowed hard. "There's the wine cellar or the freezer in the kitchen."

She said, "Do you have wheelchair?"

"Yes, there are two in the storage room to the right of the reception desk."

I asked, "Are Tuner and Bellingham okay?"

"Yes. They're locked in the vault."

"Good," I said. "Let them know we're okay and that we took out the first two."

"First two?" he bellowed. "Are there more?"

"There will be. Get your security guards up here while we move the woman to the wine cellar."

The wheelchairs were precisely where Jack said they'd be, and it only took a few minutes to move the unconscious woman from Tuner's room to the wine cellar.

The space was old, damp, and rugged, just as such places should be. The stone floor was uneven and worn smooth from decades of foot traffic and millions of dollars' worth of vintage wines destined for some of the most discerning palates in the country.

"Drink something," Anya said as she rolled the woman into the cellar. "It will maybe help with pain and give fluid for body if you are bleeding inside."

I didn't fully agree with her medical assessment, but I couldn't argue with the pain management plan, so I pulled a bottle of something from a rack and found a corkscrew in a cabinet near the back of the cellar. At the same moment I pulled the cork from the bottle, Anya dumped the woman from the chair, depositing her on the cold stone floor.

"You'd make a terrible nurse."

She said, "This is why I chose opposite profession. Kindness is not for me strong suit."

I was right. Laughter hurt, but it was worth it.

There were no glasses to be found, so I drank from the bottle and offered it to Anya. She waved me off and began opening every drawer and cabinet in the room.

After an exhaustive search, she'd collected enough material to securely bind the woman, preventing, or at least delaying, escape. When she finished, our prisoner looked like a cartoon character tied to a railroad track with a locomotive on the horizon.

Anya scanned the space and then reached for my bottle.

"Change our mind?" I asked.

She said, "Is not for me. Is rude to have guest and not offer wine, yes?" Anya emptied the bottle over the woman's head and slapped her face several times until the faintest flicker of light returned to formerly darkened eyes.

"Welcome back," Anya said in Russian. "You lost fight. I will give to you details later, but for now, you must know that you are prisoner."

The woman squinted and spewed, trying to clear the red wine from her face. "*Kto ty*?"

Anya glanced over her shoulder at me. "See? I told you they are Russian. She wants to know who we are."

I groaned. "You were right again, and in case you've forgotten, I speak Russian, comrade."

She ignored me and turned back to her prey. "Who we are is not important. You failed, and your partner is dead. He is lucky one. For you, I feel sorry, but not much. How is your English?"

The woman licked her lips and answered with a strong accent. "I speak perfect English."

Anya chuckled. "No, you do not. So far, you do nothing perfectly. We will see how good you are at resisting interrogation."

The woman grinned. "You will die before storm is gone, and I will be person who kills you."

It was Anya's turn to grin. "This is going to be very good night for me. It has been long time since I have done this, but it is like—as they say in America—riding bicycle." She reached above her head, pulled another bottle from the rack, and handed it to me. "Open, please."

I pulled the cork and handed the bottle back. She emptied the bottle over the rope and twine that bound the woman to the wine rack bolted to the floor.

I watched with curious amusement as Anya pulled a plastic bag from a drawer and dropped both empty bottles inside, then tied the top of the bag and dropped it to the stone floor. With repeated stomps, she pulverized the bottles inside the bag, and my interest was piqued.

With the bag untied, she poured tiny shards of glass over every inch of the soaked cord she'd used to constrain the woman.

*Brilliant*, I thought.

Every time the woman offered any effort to pull against her restraints, the glass would slice deeper into her flesh. Before that moment, I had a million reasons to be afraid of Anya Burinkova. Now I had a million and one.

She knelt in front of the woman and drew her knife. With motion too fast for my blurry vision to follow, she cut the sleeve from the prisoner's shirt and used it as a gag, tying it around her mouth and head.

Anya tapped the point of her blade against the woman's nose in a gesture that would've appeared playful in another setting. "Wait here for me. I will be back."

After we walked from the cellar and pushed the heavy doors closed behind us, Anya laced her hand inside my elbow. "I am now very sad."

"Sad? Why?"

She smiled up at me. "I would have looked beautiful for you in dress at dinner tonight, but is too bad we must now postpone."

# Chapter 23
## *Never Better*

The storm raged outside the walls of the resort, and guests hurried to their rooms in absolute ignorance of the potential terror building around them, although it had nothing to do with the streaks of lightning or reverberating thunder from the coal-black sky.

Jack Ford wasn't at the reception desk where I expected to find him, and his office door was almost closed.

Anya motioned to a spattering of crimson on the wall behind the desk. "I do not like this," she whispered as she took half a stride in front of me.

I caught her arm. "Wait. Let me take point."

"This is terrible idea. You are badly hurt."

"Exactly. If this is an ambush, it would be better for me to get hit rather than you. If you go down, there's no chance I can hold our ground until the rest of the team gets here. We need you on your feet."

She scowled. "I do not like this, but you are right. I will cover from left side, yes?"

I nodded and crossed the open expanse of the lobby toward the desk where Jack, or his clerk, Gloria, should've been standing. Tropical plants filled the corners of the room, and perfectly woven wicker furniture lined the walls, making the space feel like a subtropical escape from whatever reality waited beyond the island. The screaming pain in my side made me want to hack the palms into slivers and reduce the wicker to splinters, but what looked like blood on the wall screamed louder than the jagged remains of my ribs tearing at God-knows-what inside my body.

Approaching the desk, I rose onto my toes to see as far behind the counter as possible, but nothing caught my eye. Moving closer to Jack's door with every slow stride, I listened for the sound of anything or anyone moving ahead. I leaned as far to the right as my wounds would allow, giving myself as much view into Jack's office as the slit in the door would give me.

Nothing. If someone were behind that door, they obviously didn't want to be seen.

I rounded the end of the desk and spun on a heel, raising my pistol at the last thing I wanted to see. Anya immediately turned, covering my next few strides toward my target, which had suddenly changed. When I took a knee beside Gloria's body, her pallor and the amount of blood on the floor told me that reaching for a pulse was a waste of time, but the humanity in me overrode the logic, and I pressed two fingers to cold, still flesh.

When Anya shot a quick look at me, I shook my head, and her face hardened. As much as I wanted us to be wrong, we weren't. The dead guy in Tuner's room and the captured woman weren't the limit of the force sent to the island. There was at least one more, and my two decades of dancing with devils no one wants to know told me we were outnumbered far beyond our initial fear.

I took a long breath, fighting the urge to vomit from the pain, and I stepped toward Jack's door. When Anya moved into position behind and slightly to my left, we didn't need words. Her knee against the back of my leg told me she was ready, but my crushed ribs told me I was not.

But it didn't matter how badly I hurt. Going through the door wasn't optional, so I positioned the toe of my boot against the bottom of the door and gave a brief nod to announce my move.

Pushing with enough force to fully open the door into the room, I started through, but something abruptly stopped the wooden door just over a foot inside the space. My momentum drove me against the door, sending electric ice ripping through my side.

Few positions are deadlier than stairwells and doorways. They are fatal funnels where far too many operators have fallen, never to stand again. I was determined to avoid being trapped in that space, so I drove my shoulder against the stationary slab of oak and raised my pistol. Part of me expected to see Jack Ford's body lying on the carpet, just like Gloria's, but instead, I came face-to-face with a man with cobalt eyes.

The man held a glistening blade tight against Jack's neck, tiny rivulets of blood already trickling across the steel. He said, "You will drop your gun, or I will cut off his head."

Regardless of the dangers of being trapped in the doorway, I froze, leaving Anya still beyond the jamb and dancing to get around me.

"Go ahead," I said. "The second you move that blade, I'll put fifteen rounds through both of you. What good is a hostage if you cut his head off?"

My position was strong, and my point was valid. If the man killed Jack, I'd waste no time ending him, but I suddenly realized I'd stepped on a proverbial landmine. The door exploded toward me as if driven by the Devil himself.

The collision with the door left me staggering backward, reaching for the wall with one hand while desperately trying to hold on to my Glock. I was off-balance, badly injured, and on the verge of becoming a one-man show.

Whoever forced the door against me finished the job by closing it and shouldering a bookcase onto its side in front of it. The situation had just become two on one as the necessity of protecting the hostage flooded my mind and I braced for another collision with the wall.

The crash came, and my body tried to surrender. I wanted to sink to the floor and take the bullet or the blade, but a flash of the vault door reminded me why I was in the fight, why I had to stay on my feet, and why I had to finish what somebody else started.

Anya kicked the door from the outside, rattling the overturned bookcase with every blow, but made no progress. I was alone in the fight, and the reality that my position was likely unsurvivable poured over me.

I raised my gun to get at least a pair of rounds into the man who'd shoved the door before I succumbed to the pain, but the front sight of my pistol never appeared. In horrified disbelief, I watched as my empty hand aligned itself with the oncoming man's chest and I tried to pull a nonexistent trigger.

The man thundered toward me, and his grip on the knife told me he wasn't an average street fighter. Someone had taught him to wield a knife, and I was on the verge of learning just how good his training had been.

I'd brought a gun to a knife fight, but neither my brain nor my hand knew where that gun was as the distance between me and death closed in the blink of an eye.

Whether it was some trained reaction in me or a dead man's last grasp at survival, I drew the switchblade from my pocket and forced the pad of my thumb against what I hoped was the button. With my back against the wall, I continued the rising arc with a fistful of steel springing into place. My heel bit against the carpet as I forced myself to the right to avoid the coming strike, but I continued my assault of desperation.

The two blades landed simultaneously, mine burying itself to the hilt beneath the man's chin, and his striking the hundred-year-old plaster of the wall just beneath my arm.

He wasn't a big man, but when the full weight of his corpse fell against me, it pinned me against the wall with a waterfall of blood pouring over my body. I was still alive but unable to take the fight to the man holding Jack Ford hostage a few paces away.

Tactics were failing. I was pinned beneath a dead man without the strength to move him. My partner was trapped outside the door with a couple hundred pounds of books and lumber keeping her at bay.

The hurdle hadn't diminished Anya's attempts at entry—she continued assaulting the door with everything in her, and I had no doubt she would make entry at some point. The question was, how long would it take her?

Out of ideas and covered in another man's blood, I replayed the words of my mentor, Dr. Robert Richter. "Things are rarely as they appear, my boy. And when they are, we likely perceived them incorrectly from the start."

Perception was fact to most eyes, at least temporarily, and I had fallen into the perfect arena to paint a picture of deception so believable that even I might be fooled.

With the man's warm blood covering my chest, I let the light leave my eyes, and I allowed my body to slide down the wall beneath the soulless figure pressed against me. From across the room, it would be impossible for Jack's captor to know whose blood was staining the floor. If I could paint a picture of two dead men, maybe I could buy enough time for Anya to finally breach the doorway, but I could only pull it off for a few seconds at most. Sooner or later, I would have to breathe, and doing so with a corpse on top of me would inevitably hurt badly enough to make me exhale noises I didn't want to make.

With my eyes open only enough to see a horizontal sliver cutting through the center of the room, I lay motionless with my lungs empty.

The knife-wielding man across the room was little more than a blurry silhouette, but he was moving and getting bigger with every stride. When the situation eventually became a fight, I had a shield, but it weighed at least one eighty, and I barely had the strength to lift my blade.

*Come on, Anya. Tear the top of that door from its hinges. I could really use some help in here.*

One mighty crash hit the door from the outside, and I felt a wave of relief. That had to have done it. There was no way the door could withstand a force so great without giving way.

Fighting the urge to open my eyes, I screamed inside my head to keep holding my breath, no matter how badly my body begged for air, because with a breath would come an attack I probably lacked the strength to fend off.

As I waited for Anya to climb through what had to be a demolished door, the world turned silent.

*Am I unconscious again? Am I about to be unconscious again? Why isn't Anya shooting? Where is she?*

The gig was up, and it was time to continue the fight for my life. Throwing open my eyes, I drew in every bit of air I could force into my lungs and tightened my grip on the knife. Assessing my situation, I realized things were far worse than I'd imagined when my eyes were closed.

The door and bookcase were still solidly in place. Anya was no longer attacking the barricaded door. Jack was gone. And the man who'd been holding him was within striking distance in front of me.

Slithering like the cornered lizard I'd become, I dragged the dead man's body higher to provide any measure of protection I could get, but the approaching man showed no surprise. My act obviously hadn't fooled him, and he was inches away from making me pay the ultimate price for a terrible plan gone terribly wrong.

His first blow came high and hard. I dodged the strike and shoved the body toward the coming blade. The corpse took the brunt of the slash and gave me a fraction of a second to counter, so I hooked my blade behind the man's heel and drew it toward me as hard as I could pull.

He bellowed in pain and leapt backward, staggering as he went. I forced another deep breath and shoved the corpse toward my wounded opponent. As I thrust the bulk from my chest, I caught a glimpse of black polymer four feet away, and I'd never been happier to see the grip of a pistol. I'd never be able to throw the body hard enough to make contact with my foe, but maybe I could turn his small frame into enough of a hurdle to give me time to scramble to my gun.

My attacker recovered, glanced at the blood pouring from his ankle, and lunged forward with his blade extended like a spear at the end of his arm. He was a wounded beast driven by a motivation I didn't yet understand, but I had gained a powerful advantage. Although he was dangerous and unpredictable because of the wound I'd inflicted, he was also growing weaker with every beat of his heart, and desperate, bleeding men make mistakes. I was counting on him doing just that as I kicked as hard as I could, propelling myself across the floor and stretching for my pistol.

Just as my fingers wrapped around the familiar grip, the air above me filled with flying glass. Nothing about the scene made sense, but I didn't have time to analyze the new situation. I was on my side, pistol in hand, with a lunging knifeman only inches away. Flying glass was the least of my concerns.

I don't know how many times I pulled the trigger, but I know without question that my muzzle was directed at the center of his chest. To my confused disbelief, the man's face collapsed into his head, and bits of brain and blood splattered behind him.

When he came to rest on the floor in front of me, I looked up to see Anya's upper body protruding through the shattered window above my head. "You are okay, yes, Chasechka?"

Rainwater poured from her drenched hair, and her pistol rested in her outstretched hand.

"I'm sure you would've looked incredible in that LBD at dinner, but from where I sit, you've never looked more irresistible than you do right now."

## Chapter 24
## *Lie of Omission*

I climbed to my feet, groaning with every movement, and Anya pulled herself through the shattered window.

She dusted herself off and froze, mouth agape. "Oh, my Chasechka. Is so much blood. Sit down now!"

"Take it easy. It's not mine. You're not the only knife fighter in the family."

A smile I never expected came across her face. "You think we are family?"

"We've got a pretty terrific daughter, so that makes us family in my book."

"I like this book of yours. Maybe we can make more pages inside when all of this is over."

"I'm sure we can," I said. "So, how many more fighters do you think there are?"

She shrugged. "I do not know, but I know someone who does. We should give to her visit and politely ask her to tell us how many people she brought to party."

"I'm sure she'll be quite forthcoming," I said. "Let's check on our charges before we go."

I stepped around Jack Ford's desk, and for the second time in less than fifteen minutes, I discovered a body lying on the floor.

Just as I'd done when I discovered Gloria, I took a knee beside my old friend and thrust two fingers against his neck. He stirred, and his eyes fluttered open, but I pressed a gentle hand against him. "Just stay there. You're okay."

He placed his palm against the side of his head and grimaced. "I thought he was stabbing me, but it must've been the butt of his knife. How long have I been out?"

Before I could answer, his eyes reclaimed their ability to focus, and he grabbed my blood-drenched shirt. "My God, Chase. You're—"

"I'm okay," I said. "It's the other guy's blood. Let's get you into your chair."

"No!" Anya said. "I will help him. You are injured, and pulling him up will only make it worse."

I surrendered, and she helped Jack onto his plush office chair.

"I could sure use a scotch."

Anya said, "Is funny you would mention this. We are on our way to wine cellar, so we will bring back for you drink."

He tried to smile. "I'll be sure to leave a nice tip."

Anya motioned toward the pair of bodies on the office floor. "Maybe instead of tip, you could have somebody clean this up."

"I'll get right on that," Jack said. "This is about to turn really nasty, isn't it?"

"It already has, but it's likely to get worse before we shut them down. We need to know how many of them there are. In the meantime, I suggest you join Tuner and Bellingham in that vault of yours."

"I'd love to, but I've got a houseful of guests who are my responsibility. I can't run and hide."

"I know that feeling well, my friend. In less than half an hour, I should have an airplane full of commandos armed to the teeth and ready to eliminate any threat to your guests."

He turned sharply to the demolished window. "Just how do you propose getting those commandos onto the island with the airport closed and this storm beating down?"

"Neither rain nor snow nor dark of night . . ."

He rolled his eyes. "Yeah, that's you, a mailman."

"That's Herodotus's from *The Persian Wars*, three thousand years ago," I said. "The post office stole it. Open the vault if you would."

Jack entered the code and swung the heavy door aside. Tuner and Bellingham sat with their feet propped up as if enjoying a summer afternoon.

"Are you guys all right?" I asked.

"We're just fine," Tuner said. "What's going on out there?"

I glanced at the bodies. "We had a couple more unwanted guests, but we asked them nicely to leave."

Tuner leaned, peering around the door. "I see that their souls left, even if their bodies didn't. Are you two okay? You look like you've been baptized in blood."

"It's not my blood," I said. "Stay in there and keep your heads down. We'll keep you posted as things progress out here."

We raked away the pile of books and muscled the bookcase far enough away from the door to make our exit. Through the windows of the lobby, Mother Nature continued shaking her fist.

Anya said, "Jack has point. How will rest of team get from airplane onto island?"

"That's up to Mongo and Gordo. I've got enough to worry about."

She said, "Gordo knows how to land airplane on water. We have seen him do this."

As we continued our anxious pace toward the wine cellar, I said, "Yeah, but our bank account can't survive replacing another Herk that Gordo puts in the Atlantic."

As soon as we stepped into the cellar, Anya morphed into a persona few have survived. She grabbed the closest bottle of wine and swung it like a hammer, shattering it until all that remained were the neck of the bottle in her hand and a jagged ring of razor-sharp glass.

With one swift move, she planted one knee between her prisoner's legs and the broken bottle against her forehead. "You and I went to same school to learn how to resist interrogation. Do you remember this school?"

The woman didn't make a sound, and Anya twisted the bottle, tearing arcing cuts of skin across her forehead.

"Yes, I remember."

Anya withdrew. "Good. This means you understand rules. I have only one more rule you must remember."

The woman glared up, and Anya said, "If you lie to me, you will receive either bullet or blade first in legs, then arms, where wounds will not kill you. Tell to me that you understand this."

The woman growled in angry Russian. "I will tell you what the rules are. First rule is that I am going to kill you tonight."

"Stop it," Anya ordered. "And speak only English."

"Why? So your wounded lover over there can understand?"

I answered before Anya could, and I did it in nearly flawless Russian. "I know your language better than you. She wants you to answer in English for an entirely different reason. And I suspect you know precisely what that reason is."

She narrowed her eyes as if burning holes through my skin.

Anya said, "Tell to me how many of your team are on island."

The woman set her gaze and didn't say a word, so Anya drew a pistol and put a round through the woman's left ankle.

The woman let out a guttural groan but maintained her composure. "I did not lie."

Anya hissed. "Was lie of omission. This is worst kind. Next time will be knife, and will be much more painful than bullet."

She let a moment pass before repeating her question. "How many are there?"

"You know I cannot tell you this number."

The first inch of Anya's blade sank into the woman's leg, just behind her kneecap.

The groan that followed became a growl, and Anya said, "I told you it would hurt worse. Lie to me again, and you may choose bullet or blade."

"I did not lie," she yelled. "You know I cannot tell you."

Anya didn't change her expression. "This is refusal to answer and is same as lie. How many?"

The woman closed her eyes, took a deep breath, and spoke through gritted teeth. "Bullet."

Former SVR Captain Anastasia Burinkova granted her former countrywoman the wish and sent a nine-millimeter round through her thigh, tearing muscle from bone, but creating no immediate mortal wound.

The woman's chin fell, and Anya smacked her, the blow echoing through the cellar like the thunder still pounding outside. "No, no. You will not pass out. This is too easy. You must stay conscious while I put on tourniquet."

She wrapped a piece of line around the woman's thigh above the most recent gunshot wound. The barrel of an ink pen became the handle, and Anya tightened the cord, twist after twist, as her victim writhed in pain.

Anya smiled. "This hurts too, yes? Tourniquet is no good if it is loose. You should know this because we went to same school."

"Enough!" the woman yelled.

"No, this is not part of rules. Only I can say when is enough. How many fighters are there?"

The woman held her breath, and Anya pressed her knife against the other thigh. "This one will be very slow and most painful of all."

"Twelve," the woman barely whispered.

Anya's interrogation technique was one of the most effective in existence. Rather than celebrating every minor concession, she watched for any sign of surrender and turned a tiny morsel of truthful admission into a mountain of usable intelligence. I doubt she learned that skill in any of the shared schools she and her victim had on their résumés. I believe she developed it from getting men to melt into her waiting hands, and I knew exactly how it felt to be the one melting.

"Why are you doing this?"

The woman frowned. "I do not understand question."

Sixty seconds earlier, the response would've cost the woman a great deal of pain, but Anya's redirected focus left her speaking softly, just a few inches from the woman's face. "Why is SVR assassinating Americans from operation from fifty years ago?"

The bound woman with far too many excess holes in her body laughed.

Anya recoiled. "Why are you laughing?"

She said, "We are not SVR, you simple-minded traitor. We are *naymnik*, same as you."

"I am not mercenary," Anya said.

"Sure, you are. You are being paid to do terrible things for those who are not capable of doing them for themselves."

The woman's English was improving, and she'd just landed a verbal left hook that Anya never saw coming.

"Who is paying you?" Anya asked.

The woman shrugged. "I never know, and I do not want to know who is paying for service. It does not matter, does it? People like us are prostitutes. Money is just as green from one hand as it is from any other."

"We are not same," Anya said. "This is not what I do."

The woman looked between Anya and me several times and then forced a smile. "Is like James Bond story of spy who loved me, no? Is not love, comrade. He is paying you, so this makes you only one thing."

The punch Anya threw landed like a falling boulder, knocking the woman's lights out in an instant.

I stepped in. "Easy. Don't kill her. We need her."

She jerked away. "I am not mercenary, and I am not prostitute."

I ushered her outside the cellar. "Stay focused. You're letting her get in your head because she knows all the same tricks you know."

"Of course, you are right," she said. "I am sorry. Tell to me what you think is truth."

"The twelve?"

"Yes, this, and also that she is not SVR."

"I don't know," I said. "I just know they're trying to kill Tuner and Bellingham, so we've got eight more to catch before they get it done."

"I am certain she was trained to fight by same person as me. Is personal style of fighting like fingerprint. No one else teaches technique like this."

"Okay, so maybe she was trained by the SVR and is now a mercenary for hire."

She said, "This is maybe true, but she does not have mental strength of SVR. She gave in to questions too easily. Officer of SVR would have spit in my face and asked to have tourniquet tightened one more time."

I said, "So, we know they can fight, and we now know they're mercenaries and probably former Russian operators."

Anya put on an expression I couldn't identify. "Were you talking to me or to yourself? If yourself, this is very bad sign."

I tugged the stiffening shirt stuck to my skin from the drying blood. "Look at me. Anyone can see that I'm perfectly sane."

My phone pinged and vibrated in my pocket. I'd forgotten I even had it after the last hour I'd lived through.

"Hello. This is Chase."

"Chase," Mongo said through the poor excuse for a speaker on my phone. "Why aren't you answering the sat-com? We've been calling for half an hour."

I patted my pocket where my satellite transceiver should be. "Uh, about that. I've had an exciting last few minutes. It would appear I lost my radio somewhere along the way."

"Are you okay?" he asked.

I ran a gentle hand across my ribs. "Not so much. We're both hurt pretty badly, and we're definitely going to need a doc when we get out of this thing."

"Give me the goods," Mongo said.

"Three dead, all Eastern European. We suspect they're former Russian Intelligence or military, but we think they're mercenaries now.

One captured operator. Anya interrogated her. She claimed there were twelve of them, and she doesn't know who's writing the check."

"Believe her?"

"No. Where are you?"

"Ten minutes out, but that storm dug in its heels, and the ATIS says the airport's closed. How long can you hold on without us?"

Attempting to steady my voice instead of expressing what I was truly feeling, I said, "We're not going to survive the next contact with these guys, and if I were betting man, I'd say they're going to hit us hard within the next ten minutes."

# Chapter 25
## *My Second Time*

"We're working on a plan," Mongo said. "Well, we're working on an idea that might *turn* into a plan."

"Let's hear it."

"We can get on the ground at St. Simons Island, but we can't get to Jekyll from there."

"What about the boats?"

"I'm getting there," he said. "We don't have a vehicle that can pull the boats to the water, so here's what I'm thinking. St. Simons is reporting three hundred overcast. Gordo says he can get us below the cloud deck over open water so we can deploy the inflatables and let the wind and current beach them at the south end of the island."

A wave of nausea washed over me, and the world dimmed. "Whatever you do, hurry, and bring a couple bags of A positive. I'm going to need it."

He said, "Try to find your sat-com, and we'll be there as soon as possible. Is Anya hurt as badly as you?"

"Probably, but she won't admit it."

"Hang on, brother. We're coming."

I hadn't realized I was leaning against the wall, but Anya clearly had.

"We have to get you back to office and inside vault. You are going to pass out, and I cannot carry you."

"No. I'm good. I just need some water."

"You need doctor," she demanded. "I know you are in command, but you must listen to me. We must get you to safe place before you go down."

I motioned toward the cellar door. "What about back in there? I don't think I have it in me to climb those stairs again."

She pulled up my shirt and pressed four fingertips against my swollen, discolored abdomen. "You are bleeding inside, and you will die if we do not get you to doctor. Does island have hospital?"

Wishing I hadn't seen the extent of my injuries, I said, "The team will be here soon. We just have to—"

A howling wind of dizziness blew me back against the wall that had been my bulkhead—and was once again.

Slipping her shoulder beneath my arm, Anya helped me back into the cellar, where she deposited me on a wooden chair that appeared to be as old as the island itself. She uncorked another bottle of wine and sprinted from the room.

When she returned, she stuck the bottle in my hand. "Is full of only water now. You must drink, and do not move."

The woman tied to the racks at the end of the room let out a satisfied breath. "We will die together."

As if transporting herself through time, Anya covered the space between them in a heartbeat and crushed the woman's left knee with her heel.

I spent years destroying my knees behind home plate, but I never had anybody stand on my kneecap. The pain the woman must've have experienced in that moment was beyond my comprehension, and the howl that left her throat confirmed my suspicion.

Anya reverted to the first language both of them learned as children. "You will not die today, but you will beg me to kill you. I promise you this."

She returned to my side and laid a pistol on my lap. "I am going to find satellite radios. Do not move, and if she tries to talk to you, you must shoot her in foot until she stops. You understand, yes?"

The psychological warfare both women had learned to wage in their time under the iron fist of their Russian tutors made their words almost as deadly as their blades. Anya was right. I didn't need that woman's voice in my head, especially in my diminished state.

"Yeah, I get it, but I've got a pistol. I don't need yours."

"Is not mine," she said. "Is hers. Use only her pistol. You will understand later."

Even though my body and mind were falling apart, Anya's tactical brilliance needed no explanation.

The door had been closed for less than a minute before the woman said, "Polya."

I swallowed a fourth of the water from the wine bottle. "What?"

"Is my name, Polya. Woman with you is Captain Anastasia Burinkova, no?"

I studied the pistol still lying on my thigh. "Don't make me shoot you."

"I cannot make you do anything. I am tied to wall and bleeding to death. Apparently, you take orders only from Captain Burinkova."

The water helped clear my head, and the psychologist in me begged to come out and play.

"We thought she was maybe dead."

Lifting the pistol, I slowly shook my head. "Don't."

Unfazed, Polya said, "She is legend and also disgrace to Russia. You are foolish enough to believe she loves you, no?"

"Why would you care what the Kremlin thinks of her or anyone else? You're not their soldier anymore. You're a privateer . . . a capitalist, like me."

"I can stop them," she whispered.

Even in the most physically vulnerable situation of her life, she was still strong and fighting with the only weapon she had left.

I let a silent stare be my reply, and the sharp features of Polya's face spoke of a shared Slavic lineage with Anya . . . and my daughter.

"They will listen to me. Give to me telephone, and I will make this stop. Many people will die tonight, but you have power to save them."

Silence, just as Dr. Richter taught, was often louder than any word could ever be, so that's all I gave her.

She licked her lips, cast a dismissive look at her wounds, and softened her eyes. "Please give to me water. I will not drink much, but I have lost a lot of blood."

I took another long swallow and appraised the bottle without acknowledging her plea.

Her eyes followed the bottle's every move. "Please."

When I raised the pistol, taking careful aim, she closed her eyes but made no attempt to pull either foot from my sights.

After several seconds, she opened one eye. "You are compassionate man. I understand how easy it must be for Captain Burinkova to pretend to love you."

I tried not to be impressed, but it was getting more difficult by the minute. Polya had to know I would pull the trigger if she kept talking, but that didn't stop her from working her mind just as skillfully as she'd worked her body during the fight with Anya. She was a dangerous woman, but I was far from a soft target.

"We are not capable of love. You understand this, yes? We are sparrows, Captain Burinkova and me. The part of us we once used to love was cut from our bodies at State School Four, on banks of Volga River, when we were still girls and not yet women."

Her technique was flawless. If she could lay the groundwork for me to doubt Anya, her training and experience told her that she could break my will to resist. She was beautiful, but that wasn't the sword she drew. Instead, she stabbed at my confidence with pinpricks so sharp that few men could resist their piercing.

"I will surrender to you," she said, her tone now carrying an air of attempted seduction. "I will give to you exactly what you want."

That was a brilliant tactic. Rather than defining what she believed I wanted, she let the idea form in my mind while implying that she already knew every detail of my desire.

My silence reached its limit. "Give me the number."

She frowned. "Number?"

"Yes. Give me the telephone number of the person you can order to stop the attack."

She hesitated, exposing the first chink in her armor. "No. You must give to me telephone. I will make call."

"I'll make the call on speaker, and you'll order the assault team to surrender."

"This is not how it is done," she said.

"It's exactly how it's done under my command, Polya, or whatever your name is. You see, I know enough about operations like this to know that anyone with the power to call off the assault wouldn't be one of the first two people through the door. You came in with a man—a man who's dead now, by the way—with the intention of putting a bullet in another man's head. You failed. You're not in command of anything, and you have absolutely no power to give me anything I want."

Her eyes brightened, and she caught her breath. "If Captain Burinkova were capable of love, it would be you. I see this. You have strength of great Russian man."

"Yeah, that tack isn't going to work either, but nice try."

She stared into my soul. "Two zero two, five five five, one seven six seven."

*D.C. area code. Interesting.*

I dialed the number, and a man answered on the second ring. "Barev. Vov es?"

The language might as well have been Martian. I didn't understand a single word, but the second half was definitely a question. I took a guess that whoever the man on the other end of the line was, and whatever language he was speaking, he wanted to know who I was and what I wanted.

I said, "I killed three already, and the one man who's still alive won't be for long."

Polya opened her mouth to yell something, and for the second time in my life, I shot off the toe of a beautiful Russian operative.

I thumbed the mute button while Polya growled in pain.

When she gathered her composure and sat gasping, her chin resting on her chest, I said, "Tell me who I'm on the phone with."

She panted like a dog, and I unmuted the call. "Tell me your name."

The man spoke in practiced English with a definitive Eastern European accent. "Congratulations. You just murdered three innocent people. Give us Sidney Throckmorton, and those will be the only three innocent people who will have to die tonight."

The line went dead, and seconds later, three gunshots pierced the ceiling overhead.

I glared at Polya. "What just happened?"

She watched blood trickle from the gaping wound where toes had been only moments before. "You threatened wrong person, and he ordered hostages to be killed."

Anya burst through the door of the cellar. "What is happening?"

I said, "She gave me the phone number of the person who could stop the attack, and I called him."

Anya shoved my sat-com toward me and scowled. "She better have hole in foot."

I pressed the two buttons to re-pair the radio to my bone-conduction device and shoved the sat-com into my pocket.

When the tone confirmed the connection, I said, "Sierra Two, Sierra One."

Mongo's voice reverberated inside my head. "Go for Two."

"Comms restored. Sitrep."

He said, "The boat idea was a bust. We're jumping in. We'll be out the door in thirty seconds and on the ground in two minutes. Can you give me some idea what we're jumping into?"

"What? You can't jump in this storm! You'll never survive it."

He said, "Either tell me what I'm going to find on the ground, or I'll figure it out with the muzzle of my rifle. Either way, we're coming."

## Chapter 26
## *The Devil's Own Heart*

I closed my eyes and tried to imagine the next four minutes of my team's life. They'd soon step through the door of the Herk and into the thundering heart of a massive coastal storm no sane person would want to endure with both feet solidly on the ground, let alone hanging beneath a nylon canopy designed to carry its passenger through smooth, clear air to the placid earth below. Aside from the physical danger of lightning and punishing winds strong enough to toss them through the sky like rag dolls, they'd spend most of the insertion jump completely blind, enveloped in clouds darker than the devil's own heart.

I said, "Based on the unconfirmed intel we have, you'll face a force of eight, but again, that's unconfirmed. It's only the result of an extremely brief interrogation."

Mongo asked, "Who was the interrogator? You or Anya?"

"Not me."

"Is the prisoner still alive?"

"She is, but she's got a few extra holes in her. We just heard gunfire overhead, and we believe they executed three hostages."

Mongo's tone changed in an instant. "Go to open-channel comms. We're out the door in ninety seconds."

The push of a button gave every team member the ability to hear each other, based on voice activation, without any of us having to key up.

Anya didn't switch her sat-com immediately. Instead, she took a step toward me. "They are jumping into storm? This is terrible idea."

I thumbed my sat-com to avoid transmitting. "Do you have a better plan?"

Her eyes told a story her lips weren't willing to say out loud. "How do you feel?"

"Better. Let's work our way to the front, if we can."

She shot a look toward my side. "Do not leave our daughter without father, please."

She double-checked Polya's bindings and said, "Do not go away. I have more questions for when we come back."

"Wait," Polya said in Russian. "What if I want to—"

Anya glared down at her and answered in English. "If you lied to me about number of fighters with you, I will kill you slowly and take from you everything you have inside. If you told truth, I will give to you opportunity to do what you are thinking."

Polya bit her lip as if weighing her loyalty against her life. "Twelve more . . ."

"Twelve more what?" Anya demanded.

"Twelve *more* fighters in addition to Volodya and me."

While Anya continued her renewed interrogation, I called Skipper. "I need you to run the last number I dialed from my sat-phone and give me everything you can find."

"I'm already on it. The phone number is owned by the Russian diplomatic corps."

"Russian?" I asked.

"Yes. That number is part of a bank of numbers the Russians bought, in addition to the thousand or so numbers they were given by the U.S. State Department. There's no way to tie that particular number to any one person, but I've narrowed the voice analysis down to four distinct possibilities. The most likely is a guy named Hayk Gasparyan. Ever heard of him?"

"No, not that I remember."

She said, "The team's out the door. Do you want to continue with me or listen to them?"

"We'll continue this later. I'm going back to open-channel comms."

Mongo's voice was first. "Sierra Two is open and normal. Report by the numbers."

Kodiak was next. "Sierra Four is open and under a good canopy."

Gator said, "Five is good."

Singer's calm tone followed. "Six is open and good."

Shawn, our SEAL, should've been next, but his report didn't come. My mind screamed for me to call him, but it wasn't my operation. Mongo was in charge, so I clenched my teeth, waiting for Shawn's voice.

"Sierra Seven, Sierra Two. Report."

The sound that followed was one I'd heard and made on several occasions, and although it was painful, it was music to my ears.

The groan associated with enduring a fast-opening canopy came, and Shawn said, "Seven is under a good reserve. Main was a streamer. Had to cut it away. Some jackass needs to learn to pack a chute. I'm through forty-four."

Relief washed over both my face and Anya's, and she silently mouthed, "He packs his own parachutes."

Mongo said, "Roger, Seven. We're well above and passing fifty-five hundred. Continue reporting."

The next two reports weren't voices I expected, but I recognized them immediately.

Former British SBS Captain James Millgood said, "Sierra Alpha One is beneath a proper canopy and on course for the objective."

Dingo yelled, "Whatever me call sign is, this is bloody awesome, mates!"

I hadn't anticipated the Brits joining the team, but I did tell Skipper I needed everybody she could send. I liked the improved odds of my nine hard-charging trigger-pullers against the ten remaining Russian mercenaries. For the first time since the ordeal kicked off, things were looking up.

Mongo grunted. "Sierra One, this is Two. We're getting beat to death up here, but we're on our way. Are you up?"

I said, "One is up."

"We're on GPS, and I've got maybe a hundred feet of visibility right now. Dingo and Gator are in sight, but we'll be in the black in another ten seconds. Expect us on deck in less than a minute. Where do you want us?"

The precision GPS devices the team was carrying could pinpoint their positions within three feet, but maneuvering a parachute in the wind and rain the sky was throwing at them would be an overwhelming task.

I said, "If Six can hit the roof, that would be optimal. I want Gator on the ground. We'll need his muscle and speed."

Singer said, "Are you calling me weak and slow, boss?"

"Negative, but if somebody's going to get punched in the face, I'd rather it be Gator than you. He needs a good battle scar."

Skipper weighed in. "No more scars for anybody."

The moment lightened the mood, but only for a moment as Anya and I moved down the wide corridor outside the main dining room, scanning the environment with our pistols at the ready. Muffled sounds of despair filtered from the room, and I dared to peer through the first doorway into the massive space. Two bodies lay across a table, and a third lay on his side in a pool of crimson near the center of the room.

Someone inside yelled "Door!" in Russian, and I instantly regretted insisting on taking a look.

"Retreat to cover," I ordered, and turned to run for the most substantial piece of the building I could find in the next two seconds.

Every stride felt like being hit by a freight train, but a bullet in my back would be far worse. I felt like I was running through mud when Anya shot a look my way and then raised her pistol toward me.

At well over six feet, I made an enormous target, so I dived for the deck, giving Anya a clear lane of fire and reducing my silhouette.

Her pistol belched four times before I landed on my uninjured side and rolled onto my back with my Glock aimed between my feet. One man lay slumped against a cabinet with at least one of Anya's bullets in his brain.

"Come, Chase. You must keep moving!"

I forced myself back to my feet and scampered to her side, taking cover at the end of a curved mahogany bar with a gleaming brass rail six inches above the floor.

The sounds of my men grunting and groaning under Mother Nature's battering pulsed in my ears, and my breath came hard.

"Are you okay?" Anya asked.

"No worse," I said. "How many did you hit?"

"One dead, and one wounded in shoulder."

Shawn said, "Sierra Seven is down and safe in the rear courtyard. Say position, One. I'll get you out of there."

A quick check gave me a view of Shawn shucking off his parachute and sprinting toward the building. I said, "Keep coming. We're at your twelve o'clock, just inside the double doors on the left and taking fire."

"Keep your head down. I'm coming." Shawn burst through the doors, and his eyes darted in all directions, taking in every detail. "Are either of you hit?"

I said, "No. One down in the corridor, and one wounded inside the third set of doors on the right."

"What's behind those doors?"

I replayed what I'd seen in the few seconds I'd spent peering into the space. "Approximately twenty-five to thirty hostages and three gunmen."

"Including the dead guy?" he asked.

"Yes. They're down to one solid shooter and one wounded inside."

"Are you sure that's it?"

I said, "No. I only got a glance, but that's what I saw."

"What kind of comms do they have?"

Anya said, "Cell phones with earpieces is all we found on three we killed and one we captured."

I watched the wheels turn in the SEAL's head as he pieced together the battlefield picture. "And they're after Tuner, right?"

"Yes, and a second man named David Bellingham, who's in a wheelchair. They're both in the vault inside the manager's office."

The bar above our heads splintered as a flurry of gunfire cut into the mahogany and sent glass raining down on us.

Sane people run from gunfire, but SEALs are drawn to it like moths to a flame. Shawn set his jaw, leaned into the corridor, and sent a controlled pair of rounds down the barrel of his suppressed rifle.

He slid back toward me. "Add one more to the coroner's list. He was the one you winged. By my count, we've got 'em outnumbered now."

Mongo said, "Sierra Two is down and safe on the front lawn." His bulk brought him to the ground a little faster than the rest of the team, each at least a hundred pounds less than the giant.

"Take cover, and hold the front," I said. "Six of fourteen are down, and we have at least one pinned inside the dining room."

"Where are the rest?" he asked.

"Unknown."

Skipper said, "Sierra One, I'm on the line with the state police incident commander and Glynn County Sheriff's Office. State police just deployed a pair of boats with two six-man SWAT teams. Do you want direct comms with them?"

"Not yet," I said. "Continue coordinating, and let me know when they're ashore. Make sure they know the guys under the parachutes are ours."

"Six is on the roof. Where do you want me, One?"

Hearing Singer's voice and knowing he would be on overwatch behind his heavy rifle gave me a sense of security I hadn't felt in what seemed like a lifetime. "I recommend covering the front, Six."

His unhurried, confident tone filled my ears. "Moving forward. I've got three chutes in sight."

Gator's voice came next, "Oh, crap! This is gonna suck."

The comfort I'd felt in the previous seconds came crashing down around me. "Sierra Five, sitrep."

The next collection of sounds was impossible to interpret. It was garbled chaos followed by several seconds of silence.

I said, "Does anybody have Gator in sight?"

I ran through a list of a thousand things that could've gone wrong. My greatest fear was Gator taking a round from one of the aggressors, but only slightly behind that was the fear of him colliding with a building or tree after a blasting gust of wind.

My fear subsided when Singer laughed on the radio. "We've got a hundred thousand acres of island out here, and Boy Wonder just landed in the swimming pool."

I held back my chuckle. "Are you good, Sierra Five?"

"Yeah, I'm fine. Just soaked."

I said, "Sierra Two, it's your operation outside."

Mongo said, "Five, clear your gear, and move to the north to cover the rest of the landings."

The unmistakable sound of heavy gunfire rumbled, and I said, "Six, is that you?"

"Negative," Singer said. "It sounds like it's on the water. I'm looking, but nothing yet."

Millgood said, "This is Sierra Alpha One. I'm on deck near the boat landing. The fire was a heavy machine gun. He cut down the crew of a police vessel. I'm moving to silence the gun now."

Dingo said, "Don't waste your time, Cap'n. I'm in the bloody river, and I just put two rounds frough what used to be that heavy gunner's eye holes. He won't be makin' no more troubles for us 'round 'ere tonight."

## Chapter 27
### *My Quota*

With the full team safely on the ground, it was time to go to work, and my immediate priority was securing the dining room.

I turned to Anya. "How do you feel?"

"Good enough to clear dining room, if this is what you are asking."

"It's exactly what I'm asking. Can you and Shawn handle it?"

The SEAL said, "Not with just one rifle. Let's get a long gun in her hands before we kick down those doors."

She said, "Chase believes there is only one gunman left inside."

Shawn huffed. "Yeah, Chase doesn't believe dinosaurs ever existed, either, so his judgment's a little questionable."

I said, "Define *dinosaur*."

Someone tapped the glass behind me, and I rolled, raising my pistol as pain from my side exploded through my body. Relieved to see Kodiak through the glass, I lowered the weapon and motioned for him to come through the door.

"You should've had somebody covering your six, boss. I could've capped you."

Shawn went to bat for me. "He didn't need to know you were there because I knew. We're clearing that room in front of us. It's a couple hundred feet long and maybe eighty feet wide. One likely gunner with something warm dripping down his leg. He just watched two of his buddies eat it, so he's going to be a little jumpy."

Kodiak eyed the multiple sets of doors into the dining room. "Got it. I'll take door number two and go on your signal."

The two commandos moved into position, Shawn on the first door and Kodiak ready outside the second set, fifteen feet down the corridor.

Shawn looked up. "Ready?"

Kodiak nodded, and Shawn said, "On three . . . Three!"

Their boots hit their doors simultaneously, and Kodiak's rifle burped twice.

Shawn spoke in a firm, but somehow soothing tone. "Everybody, stay calm. We're the good guys. Are there any more gunmen left in this room?"

A trembling woman to his right said, "There were only three of them. What's happening?"

Anya and I moved into position on the doors they'd just cleared, and Shawn said, "I want everybody to move into the kitchen. We're going to post a guard and clear the rest of the hotel. Is anyone hurt?"

"They are," a man said near the center of the room, motioning toward the bodies of the three innocents who were my responsibility.

The crowd followed Shawn's direction and moved toward the kitchen.

As the procession passed, Anya asked, "If anyone is doctor, we need you."

A man who appeared to be in his seventies paused. "I'm a dentist."

Anya shot a look at me, and I said, "My teeth are in good shape. We need someone who can stop some internal bleeding."

I pulled up my shirt, revealing my bloated and bruised abdomen.

The dentist said, "I'm sorry, but I don't know—"

"It's okay," I said. "I'm not dead yet. Keep moving into the kitchen."

When the room was empty, I said. "I'll guard them. I'm not good for much else at this point."

Shawn leaned in and pressed his hand against my side. "Yeah, brother, we'll have to take care of that. Get on the table on your back."

He slung his weapon and said, "Mongo, we need you in the dining room with that blood."

I shook my head. "We're not doing this here. We're too exposed. I agree we've gotta do something, but let's get to a smaller room."

An Asian lady, who'd been on the planet a very long time, slipped her head through the doorway from the kitchen and said softly, "My husband is a physician. I can take you to him."

"Can you bring him here?" Anya asked. "I will go with you and protect you."

The woman seemed to withdraw into herself. "He can't walk. Our room is not far away, though."

"He can't walk?" I asked.

The lady stepped close to me. "No. He had a stroke. I was his nurse for fifty years, and now I'm his personal nurse."

Shawn eyed Anya and said, "We have to do something. What's your call?"

I snapped my fingers. "I'm right here, guys. It's not her call. It's mine."

Anya said, "Tell to me room number. We will meet you there."

Before I realized what was happening, I was lying on the floor of a room nearly identical to the one where I'd received the injury that brought me there. I looked up into the eyes of man who could've been Mr. Miyagi's twin, and for some reason, that made me feel better. What didn't help my mood was that, just like David Bellingham, Mr. Miyagi was buckled snugly into an electric wheelchair.

"I am Dr. Itsuki Yoshida. What is your name?"

"Chase. I'm Chase."

"Okay, Chase. You need to be in a real hospital, but under the circumstances, this will have to do. I don't have any tools, and—"

Mongo dropped an enormous med pack beside me. "He's type A positive. Everything you need should be in there."

Dr. Yoshida looked between Mongo and the pack and held up his trembling hands. "I was about to say, even if I had tools, I can't . . ."

Shawn said, "I'll do it. Just tell me what to do. He's going to die if we don't stop his bleeding."

Mongo took a long breath. "I've got this, Chase. Just let them take care of you. We'll handle what's going on outside."

Anya squeezed my hand, and I said, "Go. They need you out there. Take Kodiak, and leave Shawn here with me and the doctor."

Seeing fear in Anya's eyes sent a shiver through my body that was cold enough to make me forget I was knocking on death's door.

"I love you, my Chasechka."

The chill was replaced by a bolt of electricity that could've been a million volts. I bucked against the pain and grabbed my side.

The doctor said, "Start IV and administer blood."

In seconds, the softspoken woman in the dining room became a trauma nurse of the highest order. Shawn spread open the med pack, and Mrs. Yoshida slipped a needle into my arm before I felt the sting.

The doctor said, "Palpate the upper left quadrant of his abdomen."

Shawn followed his instructions, and I growled in pain.

Dr. Yoshida asked, "Does your shoulder hurt?"

"No. It's my ribs."

The doctor said, "That is very good news. I was looking for what is called Kehr's sign. If your shoulder felt like it was on fire when we palpated, you would likely have a ruptured spleen. If that were the case, there is nothing we could do for you here. It would require an operating room and a qualified surgeon. Let's listen to your lungs now."

Shawn pulled a stethoscope from the bag and held it toward the doctor.

He said, "Give it to my wife."

The woman listened to each of my lungs and put me through the agony of several deep breaths.

Although their English was perfect, she spoke to her husband in what I could only assume was rapid-fire Japanese.

Dr. Yoshida's eyes brightened. "Although it may not sound like good news, it is. You have a hemothorax. This means that your chest is filling with blood, most likely from a punctured lung. That is why you are having trouble breathing."

"And that's supposed to be good news?" I asked in disbelief.

The old man smiled. "Yes, we can temporarily solve the problem with a simple chest tube. You will still require surgery later if the wound is severe, but the tube will drain the blood and relieve the pressure."

Shawn exhaled what I took as a sigh of relief and said, "I've done this before."

The doctor said, "You are going to do it again, my friend. I don't want to know how the first one worked out yet. You can tell us later."

Shawn chuckled. "It was a bloody mess. That's how it worked out."

The doctor said, "This one will be as well. Someone will have to pay for new carpet, but based on what I understand is happening outside, carpet is not the hotel's biggest concern at the moment."

I liked Dr. Yoshida, and I trusted Shawn. What I didn't like was the thought of him cutting me open while I was awake.

"Do you have a clotting agent in that bag?" Yoshida asked.

"We've got QuikClot by the sackful, Doc."

"Have you ever done sutures?"

Shawn said, "Yes, sir. I'm a SEAL. I've stuck my hands in lots of bloody bodies. My stitches aren't pretty, but they're better than bleeding out."

Yoshida cleared his throat. "Chase, are you also a SEAL?"

"No, sir."

"Then this is going to hurt almost as badly as the injury itself."

Mrs. Yoshida pulled vials from the kit and read off the names of the drugs to her husband. When she read "bupivacaine," the doctor said, "Yes, that will do. Start IV morphine and anesthetize the area with bupivacaine."

The nurse followed her husband's instructions to the letter as he guided her to the spot where Shawn would soon pierce my side. I expected some pain from the local anesthetic injection, but the pain I was already feeling overwhelmed anything Mrs. Yoshida did.

The doctor said, "The morphine should make you feel much better soon, and the site where we will insert the tube will be completely numb in a few minutes. Do you want to know what we are going to do?"

I asked, "Am I going to die?"

He said, "Probably not, unless your friend has some reason to kill you."

"Then I don't want to know. Just do it."

Shawn scrubbed his hands in the sink and pulled on a pair of surgical gloves while Mrs. Yoshida cleaned the skin that would soon be the site of my next scar.

Dr. Yoshida closed his eyes and whispered almost silently for several seconds, and I noticed.

"Who were you praying to?"

He smiled. "What makes you think I was praying? Perhaps I was talking through the procedure."

"Medical procedures don't end with the word 'amen,' Doctor."

"I was praying for you and for the SEAL, and I suspect I was talking to the same God you talk with."

"I've been talking to Him myself. Here's hoping He's in a listening mood today."

"Let me see the scalpel," Yoshida said, and Shawn held it up for his inspection.

"That will do. Imagine slicing into a perfectly prepared filet with the sharpest knife there is."

He guided Shawn's hand with his voice until the blade was positioned perfectly. "Good. Now, begin the incision and draw toward yourself without hesitation. Two inches long, and no more."

I expected to see fear on Shawn's face, but I found quite the opposite. He wore a look of complete concentration, but I caught his eye and said, "Don't you let me die, SEAL."

He didn't change expressions. "Don't worry. I've already killed somebody today, so I've met my quota."

I felt the pressure of his hands against my body, but there was no pain—at least no more than I'd felt for the past hour.

"Excellent," the doctor said. "Now, firmly grip the Kelly clamp and insert the tip across the rib. Press aggressively until you feel the tip of the clamp pierce the parietal pleura."

*There it is*, I thought as an entirely new pain made its entrance.

Shawn said, "We found the blood."

Dr. Yoshida talked Shawn through the process of inserting the chest tube as the morphine dug its claws into my brain and softened the edges of everything, including my consciousness. I fought to stay awake, but the doctor's words and Shawn's work faded in and out. In their place, Pogonya's beautiful face and infectious laughter consumed my mind. I wondered what she was doing, which book she was reading, if she was in the CIC with Skipper, or standing on deck with the wind in her hair as Captain Sprayberry plowed through the Atlantic.

The crack of distant gunfire pulled me from my haze, and I reached for my pistol.

"Easy, Chase. We're safe, and I've got your sidearm."

It took several seconds for the voice to register, and I fought to focus on his face. "Tuner?"

"Yep, it's me. You've been banished to the drunk tank with the two old men. How are you feeling?"

"They're shooting out there. I need to—"

Tuner said, "I know how you feel, cowboy. I want to be out there, too, but I'm under strict orders to shoot you if you try to get off that cot."

As my head cleared, I took in my surroundings. "I guess I survived, huh?"

He said, "That Japanese nurse told me to tell you that Shawn did well and that you're going to live."

"That's good news," I said. "Please tell me you've got my radio."

He bounced the small, rugged device in his palm. "I'm only supposed to give it to you when you've got your faculties about you again."

"I'll take it now. Otherwise, I'll never get it back. I have no idea where my faculties are. In fact, I don't remember the last time I saw them."

He chuckled and slid the radio into my hand.

I powered it up, paired it with my bone-conduction device, and slid it into my pocket. When the voices came alive inside my head, the relief I felt from surviving the surgery vanished.

It was Millgood's British tone. "Sierra Six, we're taking heavy fire from the south. Put some lead on them, if you please, or we're done for."

## Chapter 28
*Ticktock*

Singer's tone was the same whether he was eating a fresh slice of baked apple pie or sending super-sonic lead downrange into the unsuspecting bodies of assailants. "Sierra Six is moving to engage. Sierra Five, say position."

Gator was developing the confidence and skill to remain calm under fire, but he was still years away from possessing Singer's well-earned confidence and ease. He said, "I'm at ten o'clock to your original position and gaining elevation."

"I see you in the tree. Fire as you bear," Singer ordered, and within seconds, the sound of .308 rounds leaving Gator's SR-25 echoed through the hotel walls and even into the hardened vault, where I'd become an apparent prisoner.

"I've got a squirter," Gator called. "He's moving north along the riverbank, and I can't make the shot from here."

Singer said, "Put a few on his heels to encourage him to keep coming."

"Roger."

Gator squeezed off four more rounds, and one roar reverberated from overhead.

Singer said, "Splash one. Sierra Alpha One, sitrep."

Millgood's relief was apparent on the radio. "Nice shooting, mates. Two and I are in the clear and moving to the northwest corner."

Mongo, who'd assumed command in my absence, said, "All Sierra elements, we've got a situation. The remaining aggressors appear to be collapsing into the front of the main building. The heavy fire was obviously a diversion to cover their movement, and we fell for it."

The world seemed to stop turning in the silence following Mongo's transmission until he said, "Sierra One, are you up?"

I pressed my left arm tightly against the bandage taped to my side, the clear plastic tube protruding from underneath. "Sierra One is up."

"Have you been listening?" Mongo asked.

"Only for a few seconds," I said. "I caught the gunfire along the river and Gator's and Singer's suppression."

He said, "I intend to—"

"Don't intend. Do it. You're in command. I'm out of the fight and watching from the cheap seats."

My phone chirped and vibrated. The number on the screen was the same D.C. number I'd called from the wine cellar, so I hit the button connecting my phone to the sat-com network, giving the whole team the ability to hear the conversation.

When the line clicked, I said, "You're running out of men. Call this thing off before you lose them all."

The man laughed. "They're expendable, just like you, but you are quite wrong about the situation at hand. You may have killed a few of our operators, but we now have twenty-six hostages under our complete control. I will have one hostage killed every ninety seconds until you give me what I want. By my calculations, that gives me thirty-nine minutes to gather more hostages. There were four hundred eighteen guests registered in the hotel tonight. You killed three of them with your reckless foolishness earlier."

I said, "Listen to me—"

"I will not. You will listen to me, and you will give me exactly what I want. Otherwise, the four hundred fifteen remaining guests and sixty-one employees of the hotel will pay for your arrogant stupidity."

As the man spoke, I texted Skipper.

*Voice ID?*

Her text came back almost immediately.

*Confirmed. Hayk Gasparyan, special envoy with the Armenian embassy.*

I texted, *Location?*

*Working on it.*

I wanted to call the man by name to assert the small degree of strength we had by knowing his identity, but discretion won me over. "Okay, tell me what you want."

Gasparyan said, "You know *who* we want. Tell me where Sidney Throckmorton is in the next ninety seconds, and no one else has to die."

The morphine I'd absorbed still lingered, but I could hear the clock ticking a little louder with every tick of the second hand.

"I don't have Throckmorton, and I don't know where he is, but—"

Gasparyan spoke away from the phone. "*Spanek' arrajinin.*"

When he came back on the line, he said, "Well done. You just killed the fourth hostage of the night. You now have ninety seconds before number five dies."

Silence consumed the moment, so I asked. "Are you still there? Are you still on the line?"

Nothing.

My phone screen showed the call had ended, so I said, "Skipper, location?"

"I'm still working on it. I need another minute or two."

Tuner said, "They want me, don't they?"

I nodded. "Yes, but I'm not giving you up."

"They'll start killing hostages," he said.

I wanted to withhold what I knew, but I couldn't lie to him. "They already have."

He stood and reached for the latch on the vault door.

"No!" I ordered. "We can stop them. Does anyone have visual confirmation of the aggressors' location?"

Anya said, "They are inside first conference room, and I heard one gunshot."

I begged my brain to work faster, and Skipper said, "Got him! He's in Georgetown. Who do you want me to roll?"

"Valentine Cardone," I said.

Skipper asked, "Who?"

"The SOG team leader from Parker Kemper's farm in Kentucky."

She said, "How about local PD while I'm looking for Cardone?"

"No. They'll screw it up, and Gasparyan will claim diplomatic immunity. Find Cardone. Get Clark on it if you have to."

Mongo said, "We're in position outside the conference room. I know you said it's my call, Chase, but I can tell you've got something working in that head of yours."

"Hold your position," I said. "You're right. I've got an idea. Give me Kodiak and Anya. We're moving Tuner and Bellingham back to the library."

A few seconds later, Kodiak opened the vault door while I dialed the phone. Before Gasparyan answered, Tuner and Bellingham were on their way out of the space.

Gasparyan said, "Fifteen seconds."

I didn't waste any time. "I don't have him, but I know where he is."

"Ten seconds."

"Listen to me. I'm giving you what you want. Please don't kill anyone else. You've won. I surrender."

He paused and then said, "If you are lying to me, you just killed a dozen hostages."

I said, "Sidney Throckmorton is inside the vault in the hotel manager's office."

Gasparyan laughed again. "You take me for a fool, and that just cost you two more hostages."

"No! I'm giving you exactly what you want."

"No, you are setting a trap and expecting me to walk into it."

"That's not what I'm doing," I said. "I'm trying to end this thing without anyone else getting hurt."

He said, "We will see. Have Throckmorton stand on the croquet field, alone, within the next three minutes. If you do this, we take what we came for, retreat, and you will never hear from us again. If you fail to obey, well . . . I think you know what will happen if you fail."

"I need at least six or seven minutes. I can't do it in three."

"You have five before we kill all twenty-five innocent guests under our control."

The line went dead again, and I asked, "Skipper, have you found Cardone?"

"Affirmative. He's rolling."

"ETA?"

"Fifteen minutes. You've got to do something to stall them."

"I'm working on it."

Kodiak said, "Sierra One, Sierra Four. Tuner wants to talk with your man on the phone."

I let the idea roll around for a few seconds before saying, "I'm on my way."

When my feet hit the floor, it felt like my head was inside a washing machine on the spin cycle. I grabbed the wall. "Uh, I'm going to need a hand. Is anyone available to help me down to the library?"

Anya answered immediately. "I will be there in thirty seconds. Do not move without me."

She appeared before the clock in my head ticked off the thirty seconds she asked for. "You should not be standing, Chasechka."

"Take me to Tuner. Just keep me from bouncing off the walls or going down. And don't argue with me."

Taking my arm, Anya led me in what may have been a straight line, but it felt like a winding pathway through a Salvador Dali painting—the world around me melting and dripping down its own sides.

As we walked, a plan took shape amid my fog. When we reached the library, I pulled out my phone, reconnected it to the sat-com, and fell into a chair beside Tuner. "Here's what I want you to do. He wants you on the croquet field in two minutes. I need you to buy me at least five more minutes and tell him you're in a wheelchair."

Tuner reached for the phone, and I placed it in his palm. He pressed the button and stuck the device to his ear. "This is Sidney Throckmorton. Call off your goons. I'm coming out, but I'm in a wheelchair."

An air of satisfaction rang in Gasparyan's tone. "Hello, Sidney. Or should I call you Tuner?"

"Call me whatever you want. Just stop killing people. I'm an old, decrepit man. I don't know what you want from me."

"Oh, that's simple, Sidney. We want your silence, and there's only one way to ensure we get exactly that."

*We*, I thought. *That's the first time Gasparyan has used the plural.*

It must've struck Tuner as well. "Who is *we*, sir?"

The man's laughter stoked a fire in my gut. "*We* are the people who need *you* to disappear."

Tuner said, "I don't think that's a long-term concern. If I live another year, it'll be a miracle."

The laughter continued. "If you live another half hour, it will be a miracle."

"Death doesn't frighten me," Tuner said in a slow, measured voice, obviously trying to keep Gasparyan on the phone as long as possible.

"How about the death of innocents? Does that frighten you?"

"There's no reason to make threats. I told you I'll surrender, but I can't do it on the croquet field."

"And why not?"

"I told you I'm in a wheelchair. Have you looked outside lately? It's been raining like mad for well over an hour. I wouldn't make it six feet onto the grass. If you'll just tell me what you don't want me to reveal, I'll give you my word—"

The laughter came again. "Your word? Oh, Sidney, you're quite the comedian, aren't you? What is the word of a dying spy worth?"

"What do I have to gain by talking about anything? No one takes an old man like me seriously anymore. I'm a senile fool who rambles on about nothing. I can't even remember what I had for breakfast."

Gasparyan said, "That may be, but there is far too much at stake for us to risk leaving any more loose ends."

"Your accent," Tuner said. "I know that accent. Tell me your name."

"My name isn't important, but perhaps I'll whisper it in your ear just before you die."

I checked my watch and gave the hand signal for Tuner to keep Gasparyan talking.

"I'm coming out," he said, "but I'll stay on the driveway. I will get as close to the croquet field as I can. That will have to be enough to satisfy you."

"You have three minutes."

"I'll do my best, but it won't be three minutes. That's impossible. But if I hear you kill any more hostages, you'll have to come find me."

I said, "Kodiak, get Mr. Bellingham out of his wheelchair."

He hefted the old man from the chair and placed him gently on the sofa inside the library.

I motioned for Tuner to stand, and he did so while keeping Gasparyan on the phone. Studying Anya beside my old friend, I loved the plan that was coming together beautifully inside my skull.

We'd apparently reached the limit of Gasparyan's patience. "Enough! If you are not outside in three minutes, we will kill everybody in our way until we find you. Do you understand me?"

## Chapter 29
### *No Greater Love*

"Are you sure?" I asked.

Anya nodded slowly. "I am certain. Is perfect plan."

"No!" Tuner roared. "Absolutely not. I will not have it."

Anya took his arm. "But they will kill you if we do not do this."

He laid a hand on top of hers. "I should've died a thousand times already. I should've died when all of this began half a century ago on the streets of Yerevan."

He paused, seemingly reliving a moment half a lifetime ago and half a world away. When he looked up again, he smiled at Anya. "We're the same size, yes, but they would never believe that you're an old man . . . not even in my clothes. You're an angel far braver than anyone should have to be—just like Anush, the only woman I ever truly loved."

I wanted nothing more than to hear every word of the story brewing in Tuner's mind, but inside my mind, the clock ticked like the blows of a blacksmith's hammer. "We don't have time for this. Give her your clothes. We can make this work."

Tuner cocked his head, and his hooded eyes glowed behind the lines of age, experience, and a lifetime spent in sacrifice. "If anyone could, it would be you and that team of yours, my boy, but I won't watch you lose Anya the way I lost Anush. She stepped between me and a Soviet gunman on a storm-filled, night just like this one, and she died in my arms while I emptied my pistol into that communist bastard in front of us. I can't be the reason you spend the rest of your life with only the memory of a love like that. The men who are doing this will kill everyone in the hotel if I don't surrender. My time has come, and one day, yours will as well."

Leaving the wheelchair empty, he turned from the library and stepped toward the storm on what would likely be the final night of his life.

The pain of my wounds vanished beneath the torture of the scene unfolding in front of me. I swallowed hard to free my voice of the tears welling inside me. "All Sierra elements, this is Sierra One. Tuner is coming out on foot. Keep him alive at all costs."

A chorus of "Roger" returned, and I followed my old friend through the door.

I shoved my pistol into his hand. "You don't have to do this."

He gripped the weapon and threw an aged arm around my neck. "Men like us understand why I have no other choice. Love that woman, Chase, and remember me well. When your sun finally sets, never forget that no greater love does any man have than this—that he lay down his life for his friends."

Tuner walked away into the darkness, and several seconds later, Singer said, "Sierra Six has eyes on our man."

"I need a head count," I demanded. "Where are the shooters?"

Gator said, "Two are moving from the conference room toward the portico."

"Rifles?"

"One has a rifle, and the other one's hands are empty. If he's carrying, it's concealed."

"Somebody give me the count," I said. "I've been out of it for . . . I don't know how long."

Mongo said, "With Singer's last shot, they're down to six."

"Are all of them accounted for?"

He said, "Gator's got two, and we've got three still in the conference room."

"Where's number six?" I asked.

Silence.

Anya stepped beside me and whispered, "I will find him."

Stopping a train with a push broom would be easier than stopping Anya Burinkova when she's determined to accomplish a mission. I was living proof of that determination. Although I would never understand why, she spent half of her life waiting to be the woman I loved. And if I were the hidden sixth man on the team of Russian mercenaries, she would be the last person I'd want hunting me down. So, I made no effort to stop her.

With Anya gone, I turned to see David Bellingham perched on the couch in the corner of the library. The sight of him sent klaxons ringing in my head. I said, "Why aren't they after you?"

He stared somberly. "I don't know, but you're not really going to give Tuner to them, are you?"

"Answer my question. Why haven't they come for you?"

"What are you suggesting?" he asked.

I drew my knife, and he recoiled. "Wait a minute! What are you doing?"

I leaned down and sliced the bundle of wires connecting the body of his wheelchair to the controls. "I'm closing holes."

With the knife still firmly in my right hand, I searched him thoroughly with my left, dropping an ink pen, a cigar lighter, and a small pocketknife on the floor before palming his cell phone. Twisting the knife between my fingers, I said, "Code?"

He closed his eyes and breathed the six-digit number that unlocked his phone.

"What am I going to find on your phone, Bellingham?"

He scowled. "You're going to find that you're a fool who's wasting time and my friend's life."

He was likely right about part of his declaration, so I shoved his phone into my pocket. "Stick around. We'll finish this conversation when I get back."

He let out a bellowing protest, but I was already several steps down the corridor, having forgotten about the plastic tube protruding from my side.

I called, "Mongo, can you clear the conference room with the two men gone?"

His answer came without the slightest hint of reservation. "Affirmative."

I said, "Singer, verify you still have two aggressors in sight."

"Affirmative. I have Tuner and the two men approaching him."

I gave the orders with more confidence than I'd ever felt before. "Mongo, hit the room. Singer, take them down."

Singer's response came in the form of two thunderous rounds fired from the rooftop, and Mongo said, "Execute, execute, execute!"

If my count was accurate, nine rounds were fired, and I waited impatiently for reports.

In Singer's trademark silky tone, he said, "Splash two."

Mongo was next. "Three down. No friendly losses."

"Get Tuner back inside!" I ordered.

Before my words stopped echoing, Gator said, "I've got him, and we're moving to the office unless you've got other directions."

I said, "Get him in the vault and cover him until I get there. Sierra Three, report."

The next sound reinforced the confidence I had in Anya's prowess as a hunter/killer. She clicked her tongue against her teeth twice, producing a noise just loud enough to transmit through her bone-conduction device.

"Do you need support?" I asked.

One click.

"CIC, Sierra One."

Skipper said, "Go for CIC."

"We have thirteen of fourteen, and Anya has the last one in her sights. What's the status of the SOG team on Gasparyan?"

She said, "No contact yet, but they're on-site."

"Roger. How does this storm look on radar?"

"It's almost over. You should expect to be dry in fifteen minutes or less."

In icy Russian, Anya's voice rang over the sat-com network. "Get on your knees or die."

I asked, "CIC, do you have a location on Sierra Three?"

"Affirmative. She's in the hallway leading to the library."

"Gator, let Jack Ford know the hotel is his again. All other Sierra elements, close on the library."

I couldn't move quickly, but I pushed myself as hard as my body would permit. When I stepped into the corridor leading to the library, Anay's back was toward me, and her foe stood a dozen feet away, frozen in the middle of the hallway. Unarmed except for my knife, I continued down the hall, waiting to hear the boots of my men approaching from behind.

I spoke softly. "I'm on your six, Anya, and the team is coming."

She took a step toward her opponent but halted when a door popped open between them.

A man weighing over three hundred pounds and wearing a massive cowboy hat stepped from behind the door and faced Anya. "Well, howdy, little lady. Ain't you something? When God was handing out good looks, you must've jumped in line twice."

"Move!" she demanded, shoving the huge man aside and kicking his door closed as she ran.

"What in blazes?" the man said as he watched Anya run toward the fleeing man in the corridor.

I pushed by him and tried in vain to keep up with the pursuit. The runner burst through an exterior door, and Anya raced behind him.

I called, "Everyone, redirect to the rear courtyard. Anya is in pursuit of a solo white male on foot."

When I cleared the doorway, I watched my team explode through the glass doors at the north end of the courtyard and race down the stairs.

As I succumbed to the realization that I couldn't add anything of value to the chase, a question ricocheted in my thoughts.

*Why was the man Anya was chasing headed for the library?*

That turned me on a heel and sent me back inside the hotel with David Bellingham in my sights. I needed the whole situation to make sense, and getting answers from him was the surest way of making that happen. But when I stepped through the door, any hope I had of learning the truth from Bellingham crumbled before my eyes.

His body hung suspended over the back of the couch, a torn section of the curtain wound tightly around his neck, and his legs twisted uselessly beneath him.

With a powerful shove, I knocked the couch onto its back and dug at the strands of curtain cutting into the man's neck. There was no breath leaving his body and no pulse beneath my fingertips.

Skipper's voice filled my ears. "Sierra Team, CIC. The SWAT team is back en route, and four choppers are inbound. Do not engage them. They know your positions and descriptions."

Mongo answered in a breathless, pounding tone, obviously still sprinting. "Roger. We're still in pursuit and moving toward the turtle sanctuary."

I cut Bellingham free of the strips of cloth that had been his noose and left the room with only one destination in mind.

For dramatic effect, I kicked open the wine cellar door and plowed inside without an ounce of compassion left inside me. A well-placed heel kick to Polya's already broken knee completed the task of capturing her full attention. The knife I pressed beneath her eye was merely punctuation.

"Why didn't you want David Bellingham?"

She winced against the pain but almost smiled. "We didn't want him because we've already had him for months. How do you think we convinced Sidney Throckmorton to come to the island?"

That confirmation of my suspicion felt like another body blow to my already splintered ribs.

"You've got one chance to answer. Otherwise, I'll drive this knife through your eye and straight into your brain."

She bit her lip. "What do you want to know?"

"Who does Hayk Gasparyan work for?"

"I will tell everything I know to your Central Intelligence Agency . . . in return for my life."

"The CIA isn't here," I said. "So, I'll have to do."

# Chapter 30
## *Enjoy Cuba*

"If you are not CIA, then who are you?" Polya asked.

"I'm the last person in the world you want to piss off right now. That's who I am. The police will be here in five minutes, and you'll be handcuffed to a hospital bed half an hour after that. Once that happens, you're a captured terrorist. Ever heard of a nice little tropical paradise called Guantanamo Bay?"

She grunted, and I said, "That's where you'll die on the dirt floor of a cage if you don't start talking."

"You cannot make to me any promises. You won't even say who you are."

I yanked my Secret Service credentials from my pocket, spread open the pack, and shoved the badge and ID against her nose with far more force than necessary.

Reading a single word on the ID or making out the badge's markings would've been impossible at that distance, but all I needed was to make an impression.

After three seconds of pressing my creds against her face, I shoved the pack back into my pocket. "That's who I am, and we don't make promises until we've corroborated every word. So, here are your options. Tell me everything about your little operation that just fell apart under your nose, or enjoy Cuba."

She moaned. "I need doctor."

I pocketed my knife and stood. "Okay. I'm sure the SWAT team will get you one. Good luck."

She let me take four steps before saying, "May I please talk with Captain Burinkova? She will understand."

I paused, turned, and said, "No such person exists anymore, and the person you're talking about will be far less sympathetic than I am."

Polya said, "Perhaps, but she will understand. Please, if you will let me talk with her, I will tell to her everything I know. Is easier in Russian."

I said, "*Russkiy yazyk menya vpolne ustraivayet.*"

She bowed her head. "Speaking language is not same as understanding. Captain Burinkova will understand."

I retraced three of the four steps I'd taken. "Here's what you need to understand. If she comes back in here and you don't give her absolutely everything she wants, you'll *beg* for a cage at Guantanamo."

In her native Russian, she said, "Yes, I completely understand."

I left her alone in the cellar once again, reset my sat-com back to open-channel operations, and listened for several seconds. When I didn't hear anyone, I said, "This is Sierra One. Has anyone located the subject?"

I expected to hear Mongo's voice, but Singer said, "This is Six. We believe the subject is barricaded inside a storage building near the turtle sanctuary. I repositioned to provide overwatch."

"Has the SWAT team arrived?"

"Affirmative. That's why we haven't blown the building into north Canada yet. Sierra Two surrendered command to the SWAT team. I'm backing up their sniper while they come up with a plan to get the subject out of the building."

Skipper said, "Chase, I can connect you to the SWAT network if you want to talk with the commander."

"Do it."

After a few clicks, a deep voice with a low-country Georgia drawl said, "This is Lieutenant Brown. Who am I talking to?"

"My name is Fulton. I assume you're working with my man, Mr. Malloy."

Brown said, "The great big guy?"

"That's right."

"Yeah, I took over the scene from him, and we've been waiting for you. I understand you're with the Secret Service. Is that right?"

I considered his question. "Do you have someone you can send to pick me up under the portico at the hotel? I'd rather do this face-to-face."

"You betcha. I'll have a man over there in three minutes. There's cops everywhere, so don't come blastin' outta there with a rifle on your shoulder."

"Thanks. I'll meet your man out front."

Descending the steps of the hotel, I checked for a blood trail from my chest tube and discovered it to be dry. I hoped that meant the bleeding had stopped, not that the tube had slipped or clogged.

From behind the wheel of one of the club's golf carts, a man in full tactical gear asked, "Agent Fulton?"

I slid onto the seat and shook his hand. "I'm Fulton."

With no further conversation, we raced away and came to a stop two hundred feet from a stone building the size of a garage.

I stepped from the cart and approached the only man with the same look of responsibility I wore in the field. "You must be Lieutenant Brown."

"Special Agent Fulton? Nice to meet you. How 'bout tellin' me what's goin' on here?"

I said, "I'll keep it simple. A group of Russian mercenaries came to assassinate a former U.S. intelligence operative who's a guest at the hotel. We stopped them, and the man inside that building is the only one left."

Brown scratched his head beneath the edge of his helmet. "And what's the Secret Service doing on Jekyll Island?"

"I just told you. We were saving the life of a former intelligence operative from potential assassins."

"Huh. Ain't that somethin'? And if I were to call Washington, they'd tell me this was a fully sanctioned Secret Service mission. Is that what you're telling me?"

I pulled a business card from my cred pack and pressed it into his hand. "The number is on the card. You can use my phone if you want."

He slipped the card into his vest without looking at it. "Let's get that ol' boy outta that shed first. What do you say?"

"I'm sure he's already rigged that building to blow when you kick down the door. If not, he'll pump all the lead he has toward anything that moves when it opens."

He spat a long stream of tobacco juice onto the muddy ground. "Sounds to me like you think we can't handle one man in a rock building."

"I didn't say that. I'm sure you and your men are more than capable. I just want you to know what you're up against. He's a highly trained operator who's likely willing to die to avoid being captured."

Brown wiped his mouth. "Then I guess we'll have to let him do just that, won't we?"

I took half a step toward him. "How much drama does a dead body full of SWAT team bullets bring down on your head, Lieutenant?"

He closed one eye and stared at me with the other. "Are you offering to eat this one, Agent?"

"Supervisory Special Agent," I said. "And yes, I'll eat it, and you can keep your hands clean if that's how you want to play it."

"We've got a robot," he said.

I gave him a Clark Johnson crooked grin. "Where's your sniper?"

He motioned with his head. "On top of that barn over there. Where's yours?"

"Sierra Six, say position."

A Lapua Magnum cartridge landed in the mud between the lieutenant and me. The SWAT commander looked up, but I did not.

I said, "Have your robot knock on the door, and we'll take care of the rest."

Brown asked, "Gas?"

I nodded. "If you've got it."

Seconds later, a robot with rubber bulldozer tracks was headed toward the door, a tear gas grenade in one mechanical hand and what looked like the short barrel of a shotgun in the other. The operator drove the machine to the door and skillfully manipulated its arm into place, just beneath the door latch.

He pressed a pair of buttons on the remote control, and the robot fired a breaching round into the door. A small blast sounded, and the door flew open.

The operator directed the robot through the doorway with a stream of white smoke pouring from the tear gas grenade in its grasp. Just as the robot disappeared inside the building, an explosion rocked, and orange fire billowed from the opening. A few SWAT team members covered their faces and turned away, but Brown stood like a stone pillar.

When the roar of the explosion finally subsided, he said, "He wasn't in there, was he?"

I turned to the one person on the island who knew more about Russian mercenaries than everyone else combined, and she grimaced before saying, "Probably not, but it is not safe for you to go inside. If I were being chased by you, I would have first small explosion and then second device to blow when you came inside to search for remains."

I asked, "Have you got another robot?"

Brown said, "Not one I'm sending in there to get blown up. What's the Secret Service doing hiring Russians these days?"

Anya produced her credentials. "Secret Service is part of Homeland Security. I am with Department of Justice."

Brown scowled. "Who are you people?"

Kodiak stepped beside me and pointed toward a piece of machinery reflecting the flickering light from the burning building. "That looks a lot like a backhoe to me, boss. I bet I could push what's left of a burnt airplane off the runway with that thing."

"Make it happen," I said.

Brown protested immediately. "Wait a minute. You can't move a crashed airplane. The FAA and NTSB—"

I pointed toward his vest. "You've got my card. Have them give me a call if they want somebody to blame. I've got a plane to catch. Nice work tonight, Lieutenant. Jack Ford is the hotel manager. He'll be able to answer your questions."

Brown said, "What about the guy?"

Anya fielded that one. "You will not find him, but someone will. It will take time, but he is lone survivor from failed mission. Person like this is dead man, even if he does not know this yet."

Kodiak vanished into the night aboard the backhoe, and I called the real boss. "Hey, Skipper. Let Gordo know the runway will be usable in fifteen minutes."

She said, "Aye, aye. Where do you want the ship?"

"Cumberland Sound," I said. "We're going home tonight, but this thing is a long way from over."

Gator and Anya collected Polya, while Mongo and Shawn pulled Tuner from the vault.

Singer climbed down from his perch and asked, "Where are the Brits?"

"Good question," I said. "Sierra Alpha One or Two, this is Sierra One. Say position."

"Oi there, boss. You ain't never gonna believe what I found hidin' in the bushes."

I couldn't suppress my grin as I turned to see Dingo dragging a man by one leg toward us through the darkness.

He said, "He put up a bit of a fight, this one, but he ain't in no shape to do no more fightin', I'd say."

"Is he alive?" I asked.

Dingo said, "I reckon so, for now, but he ain't lookin' so good. He stuck a gun in me face, and I nearly broke one of me pretty teef. You know how much the ladies like me smile, so I gave him a good walloping for his trouble." He dropped the unconscious Russian at the SWAT commander's feet, just as Captain Millgood caught up.

I said, "There you go, Lieutenant. It looks to me like you made an apprehension tonight. When he's conscious again, I suspect he'll have quite a story to tell. Although, you may need a Russian interpreter."

"Just where am I going to find one of those on Jekyll Island?" he asked.

I said, "I've discovered that captured Russians and cue balls have one thing in common." Brown looked confused, so I said, "The harder you hit 'em, the more English you get out of 'em. Have fun, Lieutenant. Call me if you need me."

* * *

Gordo made the landing look easy, and we climbed the Herk's ramp, Tuner walking beside us as if he were twenty-five again. Polya was cradled in Mongo's arms, her ankles and wrists still bound so she'd understand that her ordeal had just begun.

## Chapter 31
## *There's No Place Like Home*

The flight to Bonaventure took less time than it did getting everyone on the airplane. Dr. Mankiller's lab was the cleanest space we owned, so that became our temporary field hospital until we could get aboard the *Lori Danielle* and into Dr. Shadrack's hands.

"Take care of Polya first," I said when Mongo gloved up and stepped toward me.

"Are you sure?" the big man asked.

"I'm sure. She's had a tough night, and I don't want to risk losing her."

"How about you?" Mongo asked Anya.

"Do as Chase says. He is boss. I am okay for now."

Mongo shrugged and stepped beside the woman claiming to be Polya. "If we untie you, are you going to behave?"

Anya perked up. "Absolutely not. Do not release her. She is very dangerous."

"Fair enough," Mongo said. "Somebody get me restraints that won't cut her wrists open."

Shawn delivered and applied the padded leather restraints that would hold the Russian to her bed while Mongo determined the extent of her injuries.

Polya examined the straps. "Why are you doing this if you are simply going to have Captain Burinkova interrogate and torture me again?"

Anya said, "This is not what I will do. Fight is finished, and we are no longer enemies."

Polya's face wore the stress of prolonged physical agony, but a new expression overshadowed her previous one. It could've been curiosity, or perhaps it was her inability to comprehend the Western concept that had slowly become Anya's nature.

Our former Russian killing machine approached Polya's bedside. "Kindness made no sense to me, either, but things you and I were trained to believe are now unthinkable for me. I do not wish to hurt you. You are no longer threat to any of us. I will ask questions, and you will give to me answers. If you refuse, you will become prisoner of United States, and you will be considered terrorist. If you cooperate, perhaps there are concessions that can be made."

"Concessions?"

Anya said, "Perhaps, but first, you must allow us to care for your injuries. We will have real doctor and hospital here soon. For now, Mongo is very good medic. What is type of blood?"

Our gentle giant started a pair of IVs, one with fluid and antibiotics slowly dripping in, the second lying empty, awaiting Polya's answer.

"O positive."

Mongo hung a bag of blood and began his triage. The bullet hole through Polya's thigh muscle made the top of his list, so he cleaned the wound and asked, "Have you been shot before?"

The woman sighed. "Two times tonight, but never before."

The biggest, gentlest man I know pulled off his shirt and stood on display in front of his patient. He said, "You can count them because I can't remember how many there are. None of them killed me, obviously. You'll have a couple of nice scars, but dying isn't in your immediate future."

"Why are you doing this?" she asked.

Mongo pulled his shirt back over his head and stuck his massive arms through the holes. "Doing what?"

"Caring for me."

"It's what we do. You're hurt, and it doesn't matter how you got hurt. I'm capable of taking care of you, so that's my responsibility."

"I have things to tell you," she said.

He didn't change his pace. "We'll have time for that later, and somebody else will listen. I've got my hands full at the moment."

With the wound in her thigh clean and dressed, Mongo said, "There you go. Gunshot wounds are self-cleaning when they're through and through like yours. This one was up close and personal, wasn't it?"

Polya gave Anya an icy stare. "You might say that."

He nodded. "Yeah, there were some powder burns and GSR, but I got it as clean as I could. The doc will open it back up."

She said, "I do not understand something you said earlier. You said hospital will be here soon. What does this mean?"

The big man gave her a grin. "You'll see."

A few minutes spent cleaning and bandaging the wound to Polya's foot, where her toe had been, was followed by a stabilizing brace on the knee Anya had used as a step stool. "This is the one that'll take some time."

"What do you mean?" Polya asked.

"Everything else is relatively superficial. The knee is going to take some orthopedic work. Don't worry, though. We've got you covered."

I watched the exchange from a distance and waited for news from Georgetown until I couldn't wait any longer. "CIC, Sierra One. Any news from Cardone?"

Skipper said, "Funny you should ask. I was just about to give you a call. He'd like to talk with you."

"Make it happen," I said. "And what's your ETA?"

"Just over two hours if we don't have to slow down for any reason."

"All right. Can you connect Cardone and me?"

"Here's his number," she said, and read off the digits.

"Thanks. If the weather's good enough, I'd like you to launch the helo."

"Already done," Skipper said. "It's almost like we're sharing a brain, isn't it?"

"If we're sharing one, it must be yours. Mine's not big enough for one person, let alone for both of us."

She said, "Barbie should be on the ground in half an hour."

"Well done. If you're in comms with her, have her land in front of Dr. Mankiller's lab."

"Will do. Oh, and Chase . . ."

"Yeah?"

"Don't antagonize Cardone. We're on the same team."

"Are we?"

She sighed. "Be nice."

I dialed the CIA Special Operations Group team leader and listened to the ringing line until a voice I'd heard only once before said, "Cardone."

Without preamble, I asked, "Was it Kemper in the basement of the barn?"

"It was, but he was dead before they strung him up."

"No surprises there," I said. "My analyst told me you wanted to talk with me."

"She's sharp."

"You're right about that, but you can't have her."

He almost laughed. "I get the feeling the feds couldn't afford her. I don't know what kind of operation you're running, Fulton, but you ain't Secret Service."

"As my analyst reminded me, we're on the same team, regardless of who pays our salaries."

"Something tells me you're not on salary, but who or whatever you are doesn't really matter right now. I've got eyes on your boy, Gasparyan, and I'll roll him up if you want, but he doesn't look like he's running. He's making a lot of phone calls. And before you ask, yes, we're recording them, but they're speaking in a language I don't know."

"It's Armenian," I said.

"That explains it. I'll work on getting it translated."

"Can you forward the audio to Skipper?"

"Who?"

"My analyst."

Cardone said, "Her name's Skipper?"

"That's her call sign. Her name is—"

He cut me off. "I don't want to know. Just tell me what's going on, will you?"

"I'll tell you what I think, but a few of the pieces are still missing. Gasparyan is likely a mid-level handler for the team that hit Jekyll Island tonight. We took down the team, by the way."

"Did you lose anybody?"

I said, "Negative, but we brought home a pet."

"Oh, really? Are you getting anything from him?"

"He's a she, and she's anxious to play ball."

"Don't overplay it," he said. "If it looks like you're excited to get her information, she'll feed you a crock of garbage."

"We're not amateurs. Our doc is patching her up and blowing her off every time she tries to talk."

"Nice play," he said. "Does she know you put down the rest of her team?"

"She does."

"Good. So she understands that you're serious players."

I said, "She's getting the picture. From all indications, she's Russian-trained, most likely SVR, and we just happen to have a former SVR officer on our team. I think you met her when she put a blade to your neck in the basement of that barn."

"We got the drop on you first."

"Yes, you did, and that one will sting for a while, but like a friend of mine says, there's no need to beat a sleeping dog while he's lying."

"What?"

I said, "Never mind. Inside joke. So, here's what I think. Gasparyan was running the team that I turned into stacked bodies tonight, and he's doing it for somebody who speaks Armenian. There aren't many of those outside the country of Armenia, so we need to know who he's working for."

"But what's Kemper's connection?" he asked.

"That part is a long story, but here's the short version. Gasparyan's team was picking off former U.S. operatives who were involved in a Cold War mission inside Armenia in the mid-sixties. Kemper was part of that mission."

"Wait a minute," Cardone said. "I can buy that the senior Kemper was involved, but why kill his son, the congressman? He wasn't even alive in the sixties."

"How connected are you on the Hill?"

He huffed. "I'm the opposite of connected on Capitol Hill. I'm a door-kicker, not a politician."

"I know the feeling. We need to know what was on Congressman Kemper's radar. My gut's telling me his father told him some Cold War stories that somebody wants suppressed. If he was planning to make some public statement about a mission that happened before he was born, it would be nice to know that little tidbit."

"I'll put out some feelers," Cardone said. "The Agency is pretty good at—"

I said, "There's no need to finish that sentence."

"I thought you'd understand. So, do you want me to roll this guy up or just keep him under our thumb for now?"

"Let's listen to your audio and see where it leads. Gasparyan may be more valuable on the loose than in cuffs. Just don't lose him."

Cardone paused. "You know I'm going to check you out, right?"

"I'm surprised you haven't already. Just get that audio to my analyst on the double, and I'll make sure you get the credit when we blow this thing wide open."

I stuffed the phone into my pocket, and Mongo said, "Your turn, big boy. Get over here."

He gave my chest tube a thorough inspection and retaped it to my side. "Dr. Shadrack will yank that out of there when we get on the ship, but I'm not doing it. How do the ribs feel?"

"Like they've been run through a car crusher—twice."

"Do you need something for the pain?"

"Not now," I said. "I need a clear head. Check on Anya. She took a pretty good thumping, too."

When Anya pulled off her shirt, her ribs looked a lot like mine. Her flawless skin shone purple and black, and she winced at Mongo's touch.

He said, "I don't think they're broken, but Chase was right—somebody put it on you."

Anya glanced at Polya. "She is very good fighter, but she made one small mistake."

"Sometimes, that's all it takes," he said. "Anything other than the ribs?"

"No, I will be fine. Thank you."

"Morphine?"

"No, thank you. I must now have conversation with your other patient."

The unmistakable sound of the twin-rotor Vertol reverberated through the lab as Gun Bunny touched down on the tarmac in front of the hangar.

"Sounds like our ride's here," Shawn said. "We're taking her, right?"

"We are," I said, so he and Gator rolled our guest on a gurney out of the lab and up the ramp of the waiting chopper. The rest of us followed them into the belly of the helo and settled in for the flight to meet our home away from home. In an hour, we'd be back aboard the RV *Lori Danielle*, and the real mission would begin.

## Chapter 32
## *Stacking Lies*

It shouldn't have surprised me that my daughter would be standing on the helipad when we touched down, but seeing her there reminded me how important our task truly was. If fifty-year-old grudges were still fatal in the world we lived in, nothing could have more meaning than protecting my little girl from everything that might ever threaten her. The impossibility of that pursuit only made it more crucial.

"Father! You're back! I was so afraid for you."

I winced beneath her embrace. "We're back, but this thing is far from over. We've still got a lot of work ahead of us."

"I know. I've been listening to the audio with Skipper. You're not going to believe what's really happening."

"You've been listening to the Armenian audio? Do you speak the language?"

She wiggled a hand between us. "A little, but not like Mama. She's fluent."

"She's just full of surprises, huh?"

The beautiful girl who'd somehow become a woman overnight smiled up at me. "I'd like to think I'll always be your biggest surprise from her."

I laughed. "You'll always be the best surprise anybody could hope for."

She touched my side. "How badly are you hurt?"

"I'm okay, but I need Dr. Shadrack to take a look, just to make sure. Your mom's a little bruised up, too. Don't let her avoid the doctor. Promise me that."

"I'll make sure she goes," Pogo said. "What about the Russian woman?"

I looked back as Shawn and Gator rolled Polya from the chopper. "She's been through a lot, but she's going to live."

"Mama did it to her, didn't she?"

"Some of it. I'll never lie to you, but there will be things you don't need to know about when your mother and I—"

"Just stop there," she said. "No matter how that sentence ends, it's going to sound dirty. So, I'll tell you that I understand, and we'll leave it there."

Anya, Polya, and I arrived in Dr. Shadrack's sick bay, and he stood in the center of the room, shaking his head. "I'm starting to feel like a surgeon on an eighteenth-century man-o'-war. I'll be pulling wood splinters and musket balls out of you soon."

I motioned toward the gurney. "She says her name is Polya. I don't believe her, but she's got a gunshot wound to the left thigh and one to her right foot. We'll call both of them 'self-inflicted.' Her wrists and ankles are likely a little raw, but her biggest problem is the knee that's twice as big as it was before she had her . . . accident."

The doctor stepped beside the gurney. "Accident, you say? What a shame."

He motioned for a nurse, and she appeared at his side.

"Get her in exam two, and clean up those wounds. I'll be there in a bit."

The nurse rolled Polya away, and the doctor turned to me.

I shook him off. "Nope. Ladies first. Take a look at Anya and then Polya. I'm alive and breathing, so I can wait."

"Fair enough," he said. "Show me where it hurts, Princess."

Anya smiled. "Princess? I like that. Chasechka, perhaps you should call me this name."

"I'll call you something, but it won't be princess. Show him your ribs."

She pulled off her shirt, revealing bruising even worse than the last time I saw it.

Dr. Shadrack flinched. "Ouch. Let's start with some X-rays. You too, Chase."

We held still while a tech shot pictures of what lay beneath our bruised flesh.

A few minutes later, the doctor said, "I've got bad news and worse news. We'll start with the worse. Chase, I get to cut you open."

I said, "I'd agree that sounds like worse news, so what's the bad?"

"The bad news is for Anya. You don't have any broken ribs, but you will be sore for a couple of weeks. The only thing we can do for you is a padded compression band and some painkillers. The bruising will heal, but slowly."

"This is what I thought. I have been through this before, many times. I have never had compression band, though. Only tape."

Dr. Shadrack said, "The compression band is a little better than tape, but not much. Since you're not hairy like the rest of the Neanderthals around here, tape is fine if you prefer it."

She said, "I would maybe like to try band first."

He directed a nurse to fit a compression band for Anya, then turned to me. "You're a mess, boy. Find a place to sit down while I look over the woman. What did you say her name was?"

"Polya is what she told us, but I have no reason to believe she's telling the truth."

He nodded. "We'll have a DNA sample in a few minutes, so if she's in the database, we'll find her."

He disappeared behind the curtain in exam two, and I took a seat beside the mother of my child. "He's going to cut me open."

"Are you frightened? I could hold your hand."

I sighed. "I'm not afraid, but I wouldn't turn down a chance to hold your hand."

She laced her fingers into mine and squeezed. "Is always offer, anytime you want."

"I'm sorry I got you hurt."

She laughed. "This is not hurt. This is only small bruise. You are the one who is injured. You have two broken ribs. I am sorry I did not stop man from hurting you."

"You had your hands full with that woman. Speaking of Polya, when do you plan to question her?"

"While you are having surgery," she said. "I will get more from her if I am only person inside room with her."

Dr. Shadrack appeared. "All right, Chase. Let's get in there and see how bad it really is."

"How's the woman?" I asked.

He said, "Next time you have a detainee shoot herself in the thigh, try to have her hold the muzzle a little farther away. The wound was full of gunshot residue and burnt powder. She did a nice job shooting herself in the foot, though. It was clean. The one thing I can't figure out, though, is how she could do it from the bottom. She must've been a contortionist in a Russian circus or something."

"You must be right," I said. "What about her knee?"

"Believe it or not, there are no broken bones, but there's massive soft-tissue damage. I'll have to get the swelling under control before I can do anything about that. In the meantime, let's get that tube out of you and clean up the leftovers."

* * *

Thankfully, I slept through my procedure, and Dr. Shadrack woke me as gently as his crass bedside manner would allow. "Welcome back, Sleeping Not So Beauty."

I blinked awake and studied the bandage around my torso. "It looks like the garden hose is gone."

The doctor scoffed. "Yeah, whoever put it in did a nice job, but it was a mess in there. I had to surgically stabilize the two broken ribs. They were too badly fractured to heal on their own. That means you've got a few more screws, plates, and some extra wire in there now. The metal detectors will smell you coming from a mile away."

"I'm slowly turning into a machine."

He said, "If you don't quit playing this young man's game, you're going to end up as coffin contents."

"I can't stop now, Doc. I'm just starting to get good at it."

He pointed toward the bandage. "It looks like you're good at it."

"You should see the other guy."

"I suspect he either escaped or didn't survive. Otherwise, he'd be here, too."

I gave him a wink. "What does a guy have to do to get a glass of water in this joint?"

He ignored the question. "Pain meds, extremely light duty, and deep breathing exercises for six weeks, old man."

"Six weeks? You can't be serious."

"When you were twenty-one, it would've taken half that time to heal, but guess what? You're not twenty-one anymore, so do as you're told for once in your life. Oh, and just in case you're planning to blow me off, I told Anya what you're supposed to do for six weeks. She promised to keep you straight."

"That really wasn't necessary," I said.

"Oh, it really was. Now, lie there and relax for a while. You don't need to be moving around right now."

"I don't have time to relax."

"Fine, do whatever you want, but every time you ignore what I told you, it adds another week to your recovery."

"How 'bout that water?"

His nurse showed up with two pills and a plastic bottle of water. "Let me know if you need anything else, Dr. Fulton."

* * *

When the pills and the sleep they produced reached their end, I eased off the bed and took my first tentative post-surgery steps. Surprisingly, I didn't scream like a wounded animal. The pain was there, but it wasn't crippling. Perhaps the pills hadn't completely worn off after all.

Dr. Shadrack met me two steps outside the door of the recovery room. "Well, if it isn't Muhammad Ali. How are you feeling?"

"Stiff and sore, but not as bad as I expected."

"Two pills every six hours. No flying, no fighting, no acrobatics. Sleep in a recliner if you can. If not, sleep on the other side, and don't do anything quickly."

"No acrobatics? Just when I was thinking about taking up the trapeze."

"Your fiancée and Skipper are waiting for you in the CIC."

"She's not my fiancée," I said.

He laughed. "Yeah, right. I'm keeping Polya here, so you may want to put a guard on her."

"I'll make it happen. Thanks for taking care of us."

He shrugged. "Thanks for writing me a big check every month and never threatening to sue for malpractice."

"Is that an option?" I asked.

"Blood from a turnip."

The walk to the CIC wasn't particularly pleasant, but I only winced half a dozen times. When I felt a sneeze coming on, I almost panicked, but thankfully, I willed it away.

"Hello, ladies. I hear you're waiting for me. Please tell me it's good news."

Anya stood, crossed the room, and pulled up my shirt. "You have tape. You should try compression band. Is much better."

"Maybe I will if Dr. Attitude down there will let me. He told me he recruited you to make sure I behave."

She said, "Is important to care for people we love, no?"

"Tell me what you learned from Polya."

"Sit down, and I will tell to you everything."

I followed her instructions, and she said, "First, she did not lie about name. Polya is short version of Apollinariya Kozlova, and she wants to defect to United States."

"Of course she does. I wouldn't want to go back to Russia after the failure she had tonight, either."

Anya said, "She did lie to us about one thing. She is SVR officer. She was once captain but is now only lieutenant. Apparently, this is not first time she has failed to complete mission."

"But this wasn't an SVR mission, right? She's working as a mercenary, a *nayomnik*, isn't she?"

"That is second lie she told to us," Anya said. "This was sanctioned mission of SVR and was ordered by Kremlin."

## Chapter 33

## *Do Better*

The conversation immediately turned from a standing chat to a sitting discussion, so I parked myself on the most comfortable of the twenty identical chairs in the combat information center. "Tell me everything you know. Go."

Skipper took the floor. "We'll start with an overview and fill in the details if you want them along the way. On the surface, Hayk Gasparyan appears to be a mid-level diplomat, but just like our attachés in embassies all over the world, he's obviously an intelligence operative."

"For whom?" I asked.

"Right now, he wants everyone to believe he's working for the Armenians, but his true alliance appears to lead straight up the Moskva River, through Red Square, and right through the front door of the Kremlin."

"Polya told you that?" I asked.

Skipper said, "Not in so many words. I pieced it together based on his history I dug up, combined with what Anya got out of her."

I said, "I want to know who he called."

"He made four calls that the SOG operators were able to record. The first call went to a guy named Levon Grigoryan."

"Never heard of him," I said.

"Patience," Skipper said. "I'll put it all together for you. Levon is what we'd call a power broker if he were in D.C. He makes things happen behind the scenes without a lot of questions asked and exactly zero questions answered."

"I'm intrigued. Keep talking."

She said, "Levon works for whoever pays the best or has the most to offer in political favors. In this case, he's working on behalf of a guy named Ashot Vardanyan. Ever heard of him?"

I shook my head, and she said, "I didn't think so. He's the guy who plans to be the next prime minister of Armenia, but there's a problem. His father, Gurgen Vardanyan, was one of the leaders of the resistance in the sixties, when Armenian people fought so hard for their national identity, the precursor to them ultimately leaving the Soviet Union when the wall came down."

I held up a finger. "Wait. Let's get Tuner in here."

It took ten minutes to find him and get the old man into the CIC.

He took a seat beside me and gave me the once-over. "You look better."

"I feel better. Thanks. Tell me about a guy named Gurgen Vardanyan."

Tuner sighed. "He was a remarkable man. Without him, Armenia never would've become the great country it is today. He not only led the revival, but he also had the political clout and popular support to become the first PM after we worked so hard to tear that country away from Leonid Brezhnev."

He paused, coughed, and finally caught his breath. "It didn't work, of course, but along with Gurgen Vardanyan, the American CIA laid the groundwork for the nation Armenia would become when Reagan won the Cold War."

"So this Vardanyan guy wanted independence from the Soviet Union back in the sixties?"

Tuner nodded. "More than anything. Man yearns for freedom, son, but freedom's a luxury. And like all luxuries, it comes at an enormous cost. Gurgen Vardanyan was willing to pay that price . . . and he did. He was assassinated and replaced by a pro-Soviet PM not long after taking office."

I said, "Let me guess. The KGB had a trigger finger in that operation."

"You're getting pretty good at this espionage thing, my boy."

Skipper asked, "Have you heard of Gurgen Vardanyan's son, Ashot?"

Tuner frowned. "You've got your generations wrong. Ashot is Gurgen's grandson, not his son. Ashot's father died in Vietnam, and Gurgen took the boy to raise as his own. After his assassination, Gurgen's widow raised the boy, so yes, of course I've heard of him. He has ambitions to be the next prime minister."

The old man froze and stared off into space for a long moment before saying, "Oh, my God. We have to talk with Parker Kemper's chief of staff. Please tell me you have a way to find him."

I asked, "The former congressman, Parker Kemper the Third, right?"

Tuner seemed to deflate in his chair. "That's what all of this is about, isn't it?"

Skipper said, "We think so. Ashot Vardanyan needed to bury everything his father—excuse me—his grandfather did in the sixties and early seventies to spark the flame of independence in the Armenians."

Tuner slowly nodded. "Find Kemper's chief of staff. He's the only person left on Earth who'll know exactly why Vardanyan needs all of us dead."

Skipper spun to her keyboard, and seconds later, she said, "Found her. She's on Ocracoke Island on the Outer Banks."

Tuner cocked his head. "Her? Who?"

Skipper said, "Kemper's chief of staff. Her name is Scarlett Varner."

I lifted the hotline to the bridge and expected Captain Sprayberry to answer, but instead, a definitively British voice came on the line. "Navigation bridge, officer of the watch."

"This is Chase. Set a new course for Ocracoke Island and make all possible speed."

"I'm afraid I'll have to wake the captain," the man said.

I rose to my feet. "Make the course change now! *I'll* inform the captain."

Laying a hand on Anya's shoulder, I said, "Assemble the team, and get Gun Bunny and Gordo out of bed."

I thought she would protest, but to my surprise, she bolted from the CIC without another word.

On my way to the bridge, I called the SOG team leader.

He answered quickly. "Cardone."

"It's Fulton. Do you guys have anyone on Scarlett Varner?"

"Not that I know of. Who is she?"

"She's Congressman Kemper's former chief of staff. How quickly can you get somebody to Ocracoke Island?"

"Why?"

"We're piecing this thing together, and all roads lead to Moscow. We need to protect Scarlett Varner."

He said, "Ocracoke is a tiny island. They've got maybe three or four cops. We could probably get a team down there inside five or six hours."

"Do better," I said. "We'll be there in four hours. I don't have time to explain it to you, but trust me when I tell you we've got a mess on our hands."

"What do you want me to do with Gasparyan?"

I thought for a second and said, "Spook him and see where he runs."

Cardone said, "I'll have to send that one up the chain. I don't have the authority to—"

I had neither the patience nor the time to listen to any more bureaucratic CYA, so I cut the call and picked up my pace for the bridge. When I got there, I didn't ask permission to step through the hatch. After all, the LD was my ship, but the officer of the watch didn't know that yet.

"Sir! Halt!"

I jabbed a finger through the air. "No, you halt. I'm in command. You just point this thing toward the Outer Banks."

With a hammer fist, I pounded on Captain Sprayberry's door twice before turning the knob and stepping into his cabin. I flipped on the overhead lights and said, "Wake up, Barry."

The captain shook his head and shielded his eyes against the assaulting light. "What do you want? Something better be on fire."

"It is, but I don't have time to explain it. Just give that Brit out there the authorization to make for Ocracoke Island."

The relationship Barry and I had built over the years gave me the latitude to be direct, and it gave him confidence knowing my orders were never frivolous.

He tossed back the cover, stepped from the bed in his T-shirt and boxers, and stuck his head through the hatchway onto the navigation bridge. "Mr. Markum, follow Dr. Fulton's instructions to the letter. His commands carry the same weight as mine in every circumstance."

Markum said, "Aye, sir. Helm, steer zero-three-five degrees and stand by for a new course for Ocracoke Island with all haste."

The helmsman said, "Aye, sir, zero-three-five degrees, maintaining all speed."

Markum bowed ever so slightly. "My apologies, sir. I wasn't aware . . ."

"It's okay," I said. "We're all learning tonight. We'll depart aboard the Vertol in less than twenty minutes, but I want you to leave the ship on her foils. Every inch closer to Ocracoke means one less inch we'll have to fly."

He made several entries into the chart plotter and said, "Helm, make your course zero-three-one degrees and engage autopilot."

"Zero-three-one and autopilot, aye, sir."

I glanced over the console. "Nice work, Mr. Markum. Your initial heading of zero-three-five was close."

He nodded. "Thank you, sir, but it wasn't a heading. It was a course. You see—"

Barry said, "Don't. Now's not the time for a navigation lesson. Besides, Chase knows more about courses and headings than anybody on this ship, me included. Now, there better be a fresh pot of coffee."

* * *

I changed clothes, and Anya met me in the corridor outside my cabin. "I know you will disobey, but I made promise to doctor. You should not come with us. You should stay on ship. We can pick up Ms. Varner without you."

"You're right," I said. "I'm going to disobey. I'll take the extra week of convalescing, but I'm not sitting this one out. Let's go get her before the Russians get there first."

"You are stubborn man, Chase Fulton, but I will love you forever."

I gave her a playful shove. "I wouldn't expect a woman like you to love a man who'd stay behind just because it hurts."

"This is only one of many reasons I love you, but if there is fight, you need to—"

"Need?" I said. "You know how well I respond to that word, but I'll make this promise to you. If there's a fight, I'll stay out of it until the rest of you look like you can't win without me. Deal?"

She furrowed her brow. "You did not say to me that you love me also."

I knelt on my good knee, or perhaps my less bad knee, and Anya froze. "No, my Chasechka! You must not do this here. Not now. Is not right time or place for this. I will, of course, say yes a thousand times, but we are in middle of mission."

I looked up with my best confused puppy face. "What? I'm just retying my boot. What did you think I was doing?"

She scowled. "I cannot wait for you to be healed again so I can break ribs on other side."

I stood and stepped beside her. "Come on. We've got a former chief of staff to add to the ship's manifest."

She took my hand in hers. "You *are* going to ask, yes?"

I squeezed her hand. "You already said *yes* a thousand times, so why would I ask? Let's go to work, *nevesta*."

## Chapter 34
# *I'm Bubba*

The flight to the Outer Banks of North Carolina began as a team exercise in attempting to boss the boss. Only Singer and Gator stayed out of the fray, and I ended it with, "The ship and the doctor are only two hours behind us. Thank you for your concern, but if I destroy everything Dr. Shadrack did, he can simply do it again."

Skipper's inhuman ability to work for hours on end with little or no sleep never failed to astonish me, and she delivered once again.

I said, "CIC, Sierra One. Have you made contact with Scarlett Varner yet?"

She said, "Negative, but I'm still on it."

"How about the police?"

"I'm on hold with the Hyde County Sheriff's Department now. They're patching me through to the deputy on Ocracoke."

I asked, "Did you say 'deputy,' in the singular?"

"I did, but my next call is to the North Carolina Marine Patrol. Apparently, Ocracoke is a sleepy little place."

I said, "You can call me back if they pick up, but in the meantime, can you send us aerials of Scarlett Varner's house?"

"I don't have any live satellite imagery, but I can get you the latest available shots. Will that do?"

"It'll have to," I said. "We just need to plan the approach and egress."

All of our phones and tablets lit up simultaneously.

"There you go," Skipper said.

I tapped the screen and zoomed in on a beachfront house on the western side of the long strip of sand jutting out of the North Atlantic, accessible only by air or ferry. The house appeared to be one of the largest on the island, and the Ocracoke Lighthouse standing due east made it impossible to miss.

"Well done. Keep working the locals. If possible, we need to get Varner in protective custody before we get there."

Skipper said, "Gotta go. I'll call you back."

Her voice through my sat-com went dead, and my phone chirped right after.

I recognized the number immediately. "Go ahead, Cardone."

The CIA Special Operations Group team leader said, "We intercepted some more audio from your boy, Gasparyan, and this time, he wasn't speaking Armenian. He was speaking a language I know well . . . Russian."

"Who was he talking to, and what did he have to say?"

Cardone said, "That's the part you're not going to like. He was talking with SVR operations in Moscow, and they're on the same manhunt—well, womanhunt—as you. They're going after the chief of staff."

"Do they know her location?"

He said, "They seem to know she's on the Outer Banks, but not specifically where. Have you been hitting her cell phone?"

"We've been trying, but Skipper can't get an answer."

"Good, because the phone is compromised. With any luck, Varner was smart enough to throw it in the ocean. I'm rolling teams out of Virginia Beach and Fort Bragg, but they're two and a half hours out, best case."

"We'll have boots on the ground in ninety minutes," I said. "Tell your boys not to shoot the good guys."

"How are they supposed to know who the good guys are?"

"That's the same question I ask myself every morning."

He chuckled. "Me too, brother. Me too. Hopefully, you'll be in and out before either of my teams gets there, but we'll stay in comms to avoid a friendly fire incident if they happen to hit the deck while you're still working."

"I like your thinking. Coordinate that with Skipper. We have open-channel comms, so she'll be in constant communication with the whole team."

"Will do," he said. "Do you still want me to spook Gasparyan and watch him run?"

I gave the question a moment's thought. "No. Just stay on him as long as he's stationary. If he moves, roll him up and shut down any electronics he has."

He said, "One more thing, Fulton. I did a little digging and got my nose slapped for sticking it where it didn't belong. Apparently, you've got a lot of friends in high places."

"I prefer the ones in low places, like you, Cardone. They actually get things done."

"I agree. I'll be in touch."

I said, "Route your comms through Skipper, unless it's a dire emergency and you need to talk with me directly."

"You got it."

* * *

"Ocracoke in sight," Gordo said through the intercom from the cockpit.

I said, "Roger," and called Skipper.

She said, "Marine patrol will be on scene in two minutes, and we finally found the deputy. He apparently didn't realize he was on the clock."

"Gotta love small-town cops," I said. "Any luck reaching Varner?"

"No, but I found the last ping her cell phone made, and it was in the middle of Pamlico Sound on one of the ferry routes."

"That's probably good news," I said. "According to Cardone—"

She cut me off. "Yeah, I know. I've been on the line with him, too."

"We're just minutes out, so let the marine patrol know the big grey helicopter is on their side."

"Wilco. Be careful, Chase."

"I'm always careful."

Gordo said, "Action on deck! It looks like a police boat's taking fire from the south side of the house, and a police car's approaching from the north."

I turned to Singer. "When was the last time you took a shot from a helo?"

He lifted his rifle and stepped toward the crew chief's window. "Doesn't matter. I still know how."

I stuck my head into the cockpit to get a look at the action unfolding ahead. The marine patrol boat broke off to the west and accelerated into the sound, but the police car kept coming.

I yelled to our sniper, "Put some lead on that shooter!"

He opened fire with his .338 Lapua, sending shock waves through the cabin of the Vertol.

"Skipper, get that deputy stopped until we silence that gun."

"I'm on it," she said.

I thought our marine patrol contingent had chickened out, but when they turned back for a second approach to the house, I had a moment of silent celebration.

Singer said, "The boat is back inbound."

"I see it. Keep putting rounds on that gunner. We need his attention on us long enough for the marine patrol to flank him."

Singer kept shooting as Kodiak lowered the ramp at the rear of the helo.

I pointed toward the long boardwalk jutting from the house into the water. "Put us on that pier, stern to."

Gun Bunny lowered the nose and dived for the end of the pier. Halfway to the ground, she brought the big machine's nose around to the right, bringing Singer to bear on the shooter again and pointing the ramp toward the dock.

The sniper said, "There's a pair of shooters, not just a single."

Gun Bunny said, "I can't stay on the pier with lead in the air. I'll break off to the southwest and hold for egress."

I turned to see every member of my team on their feet with rifles at the ready. There was no doubt they were aching to get into the fight.

Gun Bunny flew the chopper backward just as flawlessly as she drove it forward, then brought it to a hover with the ramp only inches above the rail of the pier.

I'd made it a practice for my boots to be the first on the ground in any engagement, but my team was down the ramp and sprinting up the boardwalk before I had time to point myself toward the back of the bird. My foot had barely touched the pier when Gun Bunny climbed and banked to the west with bullets still flying.

Skipper's voice filled my head. "Marine patrol is moving to the east to flank from the left."

As if by pure instinct, my team split into two squads. Singer led the frontal assault on the riflemen attempting to hold what little high ground they had, while Mongo brought Kodiak and Shawn to the right.

I raised my rifle alongside Gator, Singer, and Anya, and we opened up. Singer and Gator poured pounds of three-oh-eight into the gunners' nest, while the rest of us spat three-hundred Blackout at them.

Blue and red flashing lights caught my attention, and I turned to see the deputy's car racing toward us at breakneck speed.

"What's he doing?" I asked nobody and everybody.

Singer yelled, "Hit the deck! He's winning this gunfight for us."

I landed facedown on the sand, and it felt like a bomb went off in my gut. I didn't know if I'd been shot or if I'd torn the brand-new plates and screws out of my ribs. In that moment, it didn't matter. Either was just as bad as the other.

The deputy bounced his car over the curb and across the yard, still making at least fifty miles per hour. The pain I was enduring was bad, but not bad enough to keep me from watching every second of the circus unfolding in front of me.

The car's front bumper crashed into the stack of landscape timbers and driftwood the shooters were using for cover, plowing through it as if it were matchsticks. The first gunner leapt to his feet just in time to meet the hood of the car, but the second shooter never stood as the front tire pinned him to the ground.

The deputy locked the brakes and cut the wheel to the left, bringing the car to a sliding stop twenty feet in front of us. He threw open the door and stepped out with a pistol in one hand and a rifle in the other, towering over the roof of the patrol car and making Mongo look like a child.

I yelled, "U.S. Secret Service! Hold your fire!"

The enormous man yelled back, "I'm Bubba! *You* hold your fire."

The comedy of the moment temporarily relieved the pain I was feeling, and we moved into position beside the car that was only slightly smaller than its previous occupant.

Bubba asked, "What the heck is going on, and who's the dead guy on my hood?"

"We're trying to get Scarlett Varner safely out of that house, and the dead guy was trying to kill us. Needless to say, we're glad you showed up."

He blew off my gratitude and said, "Well, let's get in there and get her out."

Gunfire erupted from a second-story window, and I slid behind the rear bumper of the car to see the two marine patrol officers pinned down behind a rusty Jeep across the yard.

I raised my rifle to my shoulder, but the pain blurred my vision. "Somebody kill that guy."

Gator rolled to my right, using a low-slung tree for cover, and sent two perfectly aimed rounds into the second story of the house. A rifle fell from the window, but the gunman didn't follow.

I caught my breath and said, "Hey, Bubba. You and the marine patrol hold the perimeter. We're going in."

Every stride hurt a little less than the one before as I led the charge toward the front door, still standing ajar. Maybe it was the adrenaline, or maybe I wasn't as badly hurt as I thought, but I welcomed the relief.

Kodiak accelerated around me and kicked the door inward, knocking it from its hinges. Singer was second through the door, and I followed Anya into the foyer.

I took a long, deep breath and yelled, "Scarlett Varner! Secret Service. We're here to get you out."

A woman's voice rang from upstairs. "There are two left! Please hurry!"

"We're coming up," I called back, but Anya stuck out an arm to stop me.

She yelled, first in Russian, and then in what I assumed was Armenian, "If you surrender now, we will not kill you."

A pair of poorly placed rounds ricocheted off the floor a few inches left of my boot, and Singer answered with one round, silencing the gun immediately.

We climbed the stairs with Singer and Gator on point and Anya and me in the rear.

Anya growled, "No more warnings. You will die now."

When we reached the landing at the top of the stairs, Singer and Gator turned left to cover our approach toward Scarlett Varner's voice.

Anya called, "Scarlett, are you still there?"

A weak voice returned, "Help me . . ."

The pain was gone, and I sprinted with the stride of a much younger man, driven by my refusal to lose Scarlett Varner. I cleared the doorway and looked onto a scene I never could've prepared myself to see.

A man stood on trembling legs, his right arm drawn tightly against his body, and blood dripping from what remained of his hand tucked beneath his left armpit. In his one remaining usable hand, he held a fighting knife that could've been the twin to Anya's favorite blade. Across the bed from the looming man, a woman cowered with a revolver extended in a white-knuckle grip and her finger repeatedly pressing the trigger. The hammer rose and fell with every pull, but the weapon produced nothing more than the deafening click of empty chambers.

"Are you Scarlett Varner?"

"Yes, yes, yes. Please stop him!"

I raised my rifle and ordered the man to stop in both English and Russian. He never acknowledged my presence and kept sliding his feet toward Scarlet, his blood still draining from his demolished hand.

"Don't make me kill you. Drop the knife, and get on your knees."

As if he were aware of nothing more than the woman in his world, the man took one more shuffling step toward his intended victim, and I pressed the trigger twice.

## Chapter 35
### *Diplomatic Immunity*

Anya stepped around me and over the corpse I created. As only a woman can, she extended both arms, wrapping Scarlett Varner in an embrace meant to both comfort and control her. "You are now safe, Scarlett. Is okay."

At the sound of Anya's Russian accent, the woman bucked like a wild animal, shoving her away and backing farther into the corner.

I drew my credentials and held the pack open, exposing both my badge and identification. "It's okay, Ms. Varner. She may sound like them, but I assure you she's with us."

Anya backed away and drew her cred pack, but instead of displaying its contents, she handed the wallet to the trembling woman. Varner took it cautiously and opened the leather pack.

She studied the contents closely, and her eyes darted back and forth between Anya and her credentials. "What's this all about? What's happening to me?"

Anya cleared her throat. "It is very long story, but you are safe now. Police are outside. We can call them in, or you can come downstairs with us. Is up to you."

Varner's eyes bounced between the two of us. "Why do you sound like them?"

Anya smiled. "I was born inside Soviet Union, but I am now American. People who tried to kill you are probably Russian or Armenian. We will know when we identify all of them."

Tears streamed down Varner's face. "So, Parker was right all along."

"Right about what?" I asked.

"The conspiracy."

I took a deep breath to avoid appearing overanxious. "Look, Ms. Varner. We need to get you someplace safe, where no one else can get to you while we make sure that everyone involved in the operation to kill you has been apprehended."

She stared at the body on the floor. "Or killed?"

I nodded. "Yes, ma'am. Or killed. We need to go. Would you feel more comfortable coming with us, or would you prefer the police officers escort you?"

"Is it Bubba?"

I smiled. "Yes, ma'am, it is. He took out two of your would-be assailants with his car on your front lawn."

She let out a nervous chortle. "That sounds like Bubba. I'll come with you."

Before stepping back into the hallway, I called, "Clear! Three coming out."

Scarlett Varner walked between Anya and me as we left the room, and Singer and Gator offered respectful nods as we passed and descended the stairs.

At the front door, I yelled, "All clear, Bubba. I'm coming out with two more."

He called back. "Come on. We're good out here."

"I think I'm going to pass out," Varner said as we reached the last step leading from the front porch.

I caught her and set her on the grass. "Mongo, bring the med bag."

The big man appeared in seconds and took a knee beside the woman. "Hello, ma'am. My name is Marvin Malloy, and I'm a combat medic. May I have a look?"

She swallowed hard and nodded without a word. Mongo began his assessment, and I stepped away.

"CIC, Sierra One. Scene is secure, and primary is safe."

Skipper said, "Nice work. How is she?"

"Shaken, but she's going to be all right. Mongo's checking her out. I want to get her back to the ship if she'll come."

"What about Gasparyan?" she asked.

"Have Cardone roll him up. I want to have a little chat with him."

Skipper said, "Stand by. I'm going to patch Cardone into our comms."

A few seconds later, the SOG leader asked, "Are you there?"

"I'm here," I said. "We've got Scarlett Varner, and she's unharmed. I need you to chain Gasparyan to a lamppost for me."

He said, "You understand that I don't have any authority to officially arrest him, right? Even if I did, he's going to scream diplomatic immunity."

"So don't show him your ID. It's time for you to be one of those friends in low places we talked about. Let him scream all he wants. If he's running a team of assassins in *my* country, there's no immunity of any kind, diplomatic or otherwise, that can save him."

He said, "How fast can you be here? I'm not flushing my career down the toilet by kidnapping a diplomat and holding him hostage indefinitely."

I ran the scenario through my head and concluded that the only way to make the rest of the day work was to pick up Gasparyan in the same helicopter with Scarlett Varner.

"Can you get him to Andrews Air Force Base?" I asked.

Cardone laughed. "Yeah, right. I'm going to haul a foreign national with diplomatic immunity onto an Air Force base. Pick someplace else."

"Do you know what a Sea Knight is?"

He said, "Sure. It's a little Chinook."

"Exactly. Pick a spot big enough for me to put one down, and I'll meet you there in two and a half hours."

"You've got a Sea Knight?"

"Give me the coordinates, Cardone."

He said, "Head north. I'll call you when we've got your boy bagged and gagged."

"On my way."

I took a seat on the grass beside Mongo and his patient. "How are you feeling, Ms. Varner?"

She laid a palm against her chest. "My heart's finally stopped racing, and Marvin says I'm going to be fine. Listen, I don't know how to thank you for . . ."

I shook her off. "We don't do this for thanks, ma'am, but you're welcome. I want to take you back to our ship, where you'll be untouchable. Are you okay with that?"

"The Secret Service has a ship?"

"Well, it's not exactly a government asset, but it's extremely comfortable. Are you okay spending a day or two aboard until we can wrap all of this up?"

She glanced at Mongo, and he nodded slowly. "I guess so."

I hopped to my feet. "Good. Let's get you on board the chopper. We have one more stop to make along the way. There's another passenger we have to pick up."

* * *

Forty minutes into the northbound flight, Cardone called with the coordinates, and I passed them to Gun Bunny and Gordo in the drivers' seats.

The flight was shorter than I estimated, and two hours later, we touched down in a field at Mockley Point on the banks of the Potomac River. Kodiak lowered the ramp, and I walked off the chopper, flanked by Mongo, Shawn, and Anya.

Sitting alone on the hood of a nondescript pickup truck at the water's edge, Cardone had his hands folded behind his head as if he were simply enjoying a day in the sun.

"Where's our man?" I asked.

Cardone shrugged. "I wouldn't have any idea what you're talking about. I don't even know who you are."

Shawn and Anya took positions a few feet behind the truck with their rifles at the ready as I gripped the tailgate latch. At the curl of four fingers, the tailgate clicked open and lowered with a clang. Anya and Shawn raised their rifles, and Mongo grabbed a pair of bare feet inside the darkness of the covered truck bed. In an instant, our giant yanked a pale-skinned man with bound wrists and ankles from the truck and deposited him on the grass.

Through horror-filled eyes, the man looked above the strip of duct tape wound around his head and covering his mouth.

I took a knee beside the man and pulled at the lapel of his jacket. "That was a beautiful suit, Gasparyan. It's a shame someone tore it up like this. I wouldn't worry too much about that, though. It'll probably be covered with blood soon anyway."

He grunted and squirmed beneath his restraints, and the truck's engine roared to life. Before I could get to the cab, Cardone pulled the vehicle into gear and drove away.

I motioned with my chin and said, "Get him on the helo. Let's get out of here before we attract more attention than we can deal with."

Mongo hefted the man over his shoulder and let him slide down his back and onto the hard ground again. "Oh, I'm sorry. I've been so clumsy lately. I guess I should drag you instead of risking dropping you again, huh?"

Gasparyan moaned his protest, but Mongo didn't seem to care. What was left of his five-thousand-dollar suit didn't survive the trip across the field and up the cargo ramp of the Vertol.

Scarlett Varner watched in disbelief as Mongo dragged the bound man past her and lashed him to the forward bulkhead. She stared up at me from her seat. "Who . . . what . . . who is that?"

"That's the man who's going to lead us to the person behind your boss's murder, your attempted murder, and the assassinations of a bunch of innocent people."

She glared at Gasparyan, released her seat belt, and stormed to the man's side. After she delivered all the powerful kicks I thought appropriate for the moment, I nodded, and Anya encouraged Varner back to her seat.

She caught her breath. "What's going to happen to him?"

Anya smiled. "When I am finished with him, he will think kicks from you were soft and gentle."

Scarlett narrowed her eyes. "Let me kill him."

Anya sat beside her and buckled her belt. "Perhaps this will be possible, but first, we must get him back to ship and drag from him everything he knows."

Kodiak closed the ramp, and we lifted off with the nose of the Vertol pointed out over the North Atlantic. Gator passed out bottles of water and protein bars.

When everyone had theirs, Gator knelt beside Gasparyan. "Thirsty?"

He nodded, and Gator ripped the tape from his mouth, tearing away flesh and hair in the process. When the man whimpered in pain, Gator stuck a boot on his forehead and a bottle of water into his mouth. Gasparyan coughed, spat, and gagged until the bottle was empty.

"Ever heard of waterboarding?" Gator asked. "That was just an appetizer. The main course is much more satisfying."

The man cried, his body convulsing with every sob. "Please. Why are you doing—"

Gator shoved the empty bottle into his mouth hard enough to silence him. "I'm going to give you a little moment of reflection to consider the absurdity of the question you were about to ask."

Our young interrogator extended a hand, and Shawn tossed him a roll of tape. With the crushed water bottle still in Gasparyan's mouth, Gator made three passes around his head with the tape until not even a whimper could escape our prisoner's mouth.

* * *

We landed on the helipad aboard the RV *Lori Danielle*, twenty miles off the coast of Wilmington, North Carolina, where laws were difficult to enforce and diplomatic immunity meant absolutely nothing.

## Chapter 36
# *Even Beyond*

Four days later, I rang the bell at one of Yerevan's most exclusive addresses, and a jacketed attendant opened the opulent door. In courteous but firm Armenian, he said, "Yes, may I help you?"

Of course, I couldn't understand a word he was saying, but the former SVR assassin standing beside me answered in what I assumed was passable Armenian. "We are here to see Ashot Vardanyan."

After only minutes of encouragement aboard the *Lori Danielle* under Gator's tender mercies, Hayk Gasparyan made the immeasurably wise decision to tell us everything he knew about Ashot Vardanyan's irrevocable ties to the Kremlin and to President Vladimir Putin himself, as well as the decades-long veil that had been painstakingly woven to hide those ties from the Armenian people. Vardanyan's passion to become the next prime minister stemmed not only from his need for self-aggrandizement, but more critically in Putin's desire to control and even annex the sovereign country of Armenia back into the Motherland as he strove to rebuild the glorious Soviet Union that, in his mind, had never fallen, but only temporarily stumbled.

Gasparyan begged for his life and gave sworn testimony about the elaborate web of Putin and Vardanyan's political maneuvering to acquire the prime minister's seat, making the position little more than an extension of Putin's own office. That was only the beginning of Hayk Gasparyan's dissertation on Eastern Bloc misconduct. The story he told of Ashot Vardanyan's mistress, one Alexandra Debrovna, became the key that would open the door in front of us.

The attendant at Vardanyan's entryway said, "I'm sorry, but he is not available."

Anya smiled in anticipation of the denial and signaled Clark Johnson to bring the woman he held by the arm from the shadows.

Clark obeyed, and Anya said, "In that case, Ms. Debrovna and I will come inside to see Mrs. Vardanyan."

The jacketed man at the door flushed pale. "That is not possible. I'm afraid you will have to leave, or I will be forced to call the authorities."

Anya smiled again and motioned across the street to a pair of unmarked, yet clearly government-owned vehicles. "Do you mean those authorities? Officers of the Central Bureau of the Armenian National Police Force?"

The man stepped back and shoved the door forward, but he lacked the strength to damage either my boot or the prosthetic foot inside that boot.

I shouldered the door inward like a linebacker and drove the man to the floor and onto his back. "How's your English?"

His eyes said he understood fear, even if not the words leaving my mouth. "Some."

"Do you know the word *run*?"

He nodded, and I shook him violently enough to leave no doubt that I was a man of ultimate determination. "Good. Do it. Run fast and far. You do not want to be part of what's about to happen inside this house."

I hefted him to his feet, but he proved that his understanding of my native language was stronger than I expected. As he vanished into the darkness, Anya called to the officers across the street. "Please give us ten minutes, and you will never see us again."

One of the officers called back, "*Tol'ko ne ubivay yego. On zasluzhivayet gorazdo khudshego.*"

"What did he say?" I asked.

Anya laughed. "He wants me to promise we will not kill Vardanyan. The officer says he deserves far worse than death."

Clark growled. "I tend to agree. Now, let's go find the bastard who tried to assassinate my father."

The house was large, but not massive by American luxury standards. We encountered four armed security guards who proved to be far less loyal than Vardanyan would've expected. Fortunately, they would live to see another sunrise, but I couldn't speak to what Premier Putin would do to them when he learned of their cowardice.

Alexandra Debrovna came with us, though obviously against her will and better judgment.

We found Ashot and Mariam Vardanyan in front of an immense fireplace in an elaborate sitting room. Each of them held a glass of wine, and Ashot rose to his feet when Clark kicked the door from its hinges.

"What is the meaning of this?"

That's what his tone suggested he was saying, but his words could've been Klingon for all I knew.

"We speak English," Clark yelled. "And so do you."

Shaking with fear, Mariam curled into a ball at the end of the sofa, where she'd been sitting comfortably only seconds before.

Clark shoved Alexandra Debrovna onto the sofa beside her and ordered in Russian, "Tell her who and what you are."

Anya and I guarded the door while Clark did what he had done better than anyone else for decades. He yanked the wine glass from Ashot Vardanyan's hand, gripped it by the stem, and shattered the bowl against a statue, leaving only a jagged shank of crystal in his fist.

Giving Vardanyan the same boot he'd given the door, Clark knocked him onto an antique chair that was likely worth more than everything I owned. He pressed the broken stem of the wineglass to the man's throat and hissed. "Please lie to me. Please resist. Please give me any reason to turn you inside out."

Defiance burned in the politician's eyes. "You'll never get out of this house alive."

Clark put on a demented grin that was so unlike the crooked version that had unlocked doors all over the world—especially those of fair maidens unable to resist his charm. "That's the beauty of this. I don't care if I get out alive, as long as I inflict as much pain as possible on you before I go."

"Who are you? What do you want?"

Clark dragged the glass along the man's neck, drawing just enough blood to ruin his five-hundred-dollar bespoke shirt. "I'm the United States of America, you little communist bitch, and I want you to *un*-fire the bullet you shot into my father's chest."

Vardanyan flinched. "United States?" He shot a look at his wife, Mariam, who sat listening to Alexandra Debrovna speak in quiet Armenian.

Clark said, "It's over, Vardanyan. The gig is up, and your house of cards is going up in flames. We know absolutely everything. You see, we have Gasparyan, and he gave us"—he pointed at Debrovna—"her. But that's not all he gave us."

Vardanyan yelled, "He's a liar! A miserable sycophant and liar. Whatever he told you is an absolute and utter—"

Clark delivered an elbow strike that left stars dancing around the Armenian's head. "Thank you. I was hoping you'd say something like that. Now, if you wouldn't mind, please do something else stupid so I can give you another shot."

Vardanyan rubbed his jaw and moaned, no longer the confident man of power he'd been only moments before. "I can pay you. I am a wealthy man, and I have powerful friends."

"How much you got?" Clark asked.

"What?"

Clark leaned down. "I asked you how much money you have. The way I see it, you owe the families of everybody you had assassinated one billion dollars each. We'll start with Congressman Parker Kemper the Third. Then his grandfather. And of course, the four people your goons murdered on Jekyll Island. Let's not forget about David Bellingham. You didn't kill him—he took his own life—but you forced him to by blackmailing him into giving up our friend, Sidney Throckmorton. Do you have that much money?"

Vardanyan's expression seemed to dissolve as realization washed over him.

Clark said, "By the way, we rescued Bellingham's granddaughter. The kidnappers you hired were only slightly higher on the food chain than petty thieves. You should pick your muscle a little better. You see, we've got every detail, and you're going to hang for what you've done."

Mariam leapt from the sofa and threw her wine glass into her husband's face.

Anya translated the obvious string of obscenities that poured from Mariam's mouth, though I'm certain she cleaned it up a little. "She said he deserves whatever he gets and she will tell police everything she knows."

With his Colt nineteen-eleven drawn, Clark held it in front of Vardanyan's face. He dropped the magazine and thumbed six rounds from the stack before slapping the magazine back into the pistol and racking the slide. "One bullet for one coward. You can shoot me in the back with it as I walk out of this room, or you can eat it. It's up to you."

He dropped the pistol into the disgraced and destroyed man's lap and spun on a heel. Mariam left the room with Debrovna, and I watched Vardanyan as Clark marched toward the door. The man made no effort to lift the pistol as Clark walked past Anya and me, so we turned to follow and stepped between the six Armenian National Police Force officers waiting just outside the opening where a door once stood.

The hollow click of the hammer of Clark's nineteen-eleven falling on the dummy round in the chamber brought a smile to my face, and just like Lot's wife, I couldn't resist turning to watch Sodom burn behind me. Ashot Vardanyan sat, his eyes darting between the worthless pistol and the officers who were waiting to take him into custody.

* * *

We gathered as a family, not around the farmhouse table at Bonaventure, or the cannon beneath my beloved gazebo, but at a sprawling banquet table in a private dining room at the Jekyll Island Club Hotel. That was where my first steps into the world—the only world I now knew—were taken so many years before. Clark sat flanked by the two women he loved the most. On his left was my cousin, Maebelle Huntsinger Johnson, and on his right was his mother, Wanda Gene Johnson. Wanda's right hand was laced perfectly into the hand of the man she loved, Dominic Fontana, even through all of his misdeeds and misadventures. His wounds would never fully heal, but the time he had left would be spent with the woman he could never deserve—because a woman who refuses to stop loving a man never truly lets him go.

The remaining seats at the table were filled by every member of my team—my family—and I couldn't imagine what my life would be like without them. I loved each of them collectively and individually, and I would give my life for any of them without hesitation, knowing they would do the same for me. It was a moment I would never forget, and I hoped the same was true for everyone else at the table.

I slid my chair back, reached into my pocket, and dropped to one knee in front of Anastasia Robertovna Burinkovna. A unified gasp rose from the table, and Anya bit her lip.

My voice cracked, but the words still came. I hadn't rehearsed them, and I didn't know what they would ultimately be, but in the end, it didn't matter what I said. All that mattered was her one-word answer that I prayed would come.

I held up the antique diamond ring that had graced the hand of Empress Alexandra Feodorovna the night she was slaughtered by Bolshevik forces in July of 1918. "Anya, my love, together we've watched life taken by violence and given in mercy. Not only have we watched, but we've been the instruments of that violence and of that mercy when it was demanded of us."

I glanced at Pogonya. "We've even created the most beautiful life I could ever imagine possible. Now, I'm asking you to give me the life I could never earn, or deserve, and the treasure no mortal man would ever dare to claim for his own. Will you give your life, just as I'm offering mine, so that we may become one instead of two? I will love you as long as my body harbors my soul . . . and even beyond."

# *About the Author*

**Cap Daniels**

Cap Daniels is a former sailing charter captain, scuba and sailing instructor, pilot, Air Force combat veteran, and civil servant of the U.S. Department of Defense. Raised far from the ocean in rural East Tennessee, his early infatuation with salt water was sparked by the fascinating, and sometimes true, sea stories told by his father, a retired Navy Chief Petty Officer. Those stories of adventure on the high seas sent Cap in search of adventure of his own, which eventually landed him on Florida's Gulf Coast, where he spends as much time as possible on, in, and under the waters of the Emerald Coast.

With a headful of larger-than-life characters and their thrilling exploits, Cap pours his love of adventure and passion for the ocean onto the pages of the Chase Fulton Novels and the Avenging Angel — Seven Deadly Sins Series.

Visit www.CapDaniels.com to join the mailing list to receive newsletter and release updates.

Connect with Cap Daniels:

Facebook: www.Facebook.com/WriterCapDaniels
Instagram: https://www.instagram.com/authorcapdaniels/
BookBub: https://www.bookbub.com/profile/cap-daniels

## Also by Cap Daniels

**The Chase Fulton Novels Series**

Book One: *The Opening Chase*
Book Two: *The Broken Chase*
Book Three: *The Stronger Chase*
Book Four: *The Unending Chase*
Book Five: *The Distant Chase*
Book Six: *The Entangled Chase*
Book Seven: *The Devil's Chase*
Book Eight: *The Angel's Chase*
Book Nine: *The Forgotten Chase*
Book Ten: *The Emerald Chase*
Book Eleven: *The Polar Chase*
Book Twelve: *The Burning Chase*
Book Thirteen: *The Poison Chase*
Book Fourteen: *The Bitter Chase*
Book Fifteen: *The Blind Chase*
Book Sixteen: *The Smuggler's Chase*
Book Seventeen: *The Hollow Chase*
Book Eighteen: *The Sunken Chase*
Book Nineteen: *The Darker Chase*
Book Twenty: *The Abandoned Chase*
Book Twenty-One: *The Gambler's Chase*
Book Twenty-Two: *The Arctic Chase*
Book Twenty-Three: *The Diamond Chase*
Book Twenty-Four: *The Phantom Chase*
Book Twenty-Five: *The Crimson Chase*
Book Twenty-Six: *The Silent Chase*
Book Twenty-Seven: *The Shepherd's Chase*
Book Twenty-Eight: *The Scorpion's Chase*
Book Twenty-Nine: *The Creole Chase*
Book Thirty: *The Calling Chase*
Book Thirty-One: *The Capitol Chase*
Book Thirty-Two: *The Stolen Chase*

Book Thirty-Three: *The Widow's Chase*
Book Thirty-Four: *The Sacred Chase*
Book Thirty-Five: *The Assassin's Chase*
Book Thirty-Six: *The Reckoning Chase*

**The Avenging Angel – Seven Deadly Sins Series**
Book One: *The Russian's Pride*
Book Two: *The Russian's Greed*
Book Three: *The Russian's Gluttony*
Book Four: *The Russian's Lust*
Book Five: *The Russian's Sloth*
Book Six: *The Russian's Envy*
Book Seven: *The Russian's Wrath*

**Stand-Alone Novels**
*We Were Brave*
*Singer – Memoir of a Christian Sniper*

**Novellas**
*The Chase is On*
*I Am Gypsy*

www.ingramcontent.com/pod-product-compliance
Lightning Source LLC
LaVergne TN
LVHW091121080826
845145LV00008B/2004